DMITRY SHELEG

SON
OF THE MOROZOVS

Remember the heroes of yesteryear!

D. Sheleg

Living Ice

BOOK THREE

PUBLISHED BY MAGIC DOME BOOKS
IN COLLABORATION WITH 1C-PUBLISHING

Son of the Morozovs
Living Ice Book 3
Copyright © Dmitry Sheleg 2025
Cover Art © Darya Loktionova-Solovykh 2025
Art Designer © Vladimir Manyukhin 2025
English translation copyright © Clare Urbanski 2025
Published by Magic Dome Books in collaboration with
1C-Publishing, 2025
All Rights Reserved
ISBN: 978-80-7702-228-6

Living Ice

A Portal Progression Fantasy Series
by Dmitry Sheleg:

The Heir of an Ancient Bloodline
Demon Hunter
Son of the Morozovs
Cadet Morozov
Head of the Bloodline

Table of Contents:

Prologue

IT SEEMED LIKE TIME had come to a halt.

My mind was in something like a trance, and my body fluttered around on invisible waves of air like a weightless snowflake.

How long this lasted I couldn't say, but at some point it became clear to me that my body was starting to fill with spiritual energy, getting heavier and dropping lower and lower with each moment. This went on for quite some time, until eventually I realized I was lying on a hard, flat surface.

Opening my eyes resolutely, I understood that I was in my own internal world. Everything here was familiar to me — both the slab of ice with its ghostly blue flame glowing in the center and the darkness enveloping the surrounding space.

Stop. I froze, turned, and carefully examined the ice slab. Something was different about it, I noticed — and right away I saw that it had simply become several times bigger, and inside of it a burning globe was shining quite brightly.

Coming closer to the edge of it, I carefully examined the fireball and noticed that a lot of little tongues of flame were gliding around inside of it.

I had no understanding of how there could be flames inside of an ice slab, but it was all happening right before my eyes, so I decided to ponder that a little later. Right now, I just needed to try to leave this state of meditation and get my bearings. Because the memories that preceded my withdrawal into my internal world gave me cause for concern.

"How is he?" I heard a vaguely familiar voice with clear notes of a commanding tone.

"The patient is in stable condition — there's no cause for concern," said a quiet, confident voice in response.

"Then why is he still unconscious?" It seemed the second man's calm attitude only made the first man hotter under the collar. "Do you mean to try my patience?"

"Of course not! But you must understand, sir, that self-induced initiation like this is no joke!" said the second man with some fervor. "He managed to create a globe of ice just before being severely wounded! Surely you remember what an uproar it caused throughout the empire? Not only because the boy is the last of the Morozovs, but because this hasn't happened in such a long time! Self-induced initiation, I mean, of course."

A dissatisfied and extremely expressive cough interrupted the effusive monologue of this intellectual I didn't know, but after a few seconds of silence, he continued:

"In general, given the situation, it's surprising that the boy is just sleeping and not frightening everyone around him with wild screams — he should be in terrible pain from his lacerated magical channels."

I wished I could gulp.

Demons' sakes! What, so my magical channels had been torn open? I had no idea, of course, what kind of consequences that would have, but there was clearly something very bad about it.

When a phrase started with the word "lacerated," nothing good could come after it. And this "uproar," to boot! I figured it was no good being surprised that in whatever time had passed, people had fully been able to identify me as the last Morozov — or, to put it another way, as the boy who'd tragically died two years ago, Ivan Temnikov. That meant my father definitely knew about it.

I had a keen desire not to leave my state of meditation anymore. In the meantime, the two men in the room continued their conversation.

"But it's already been five days!" roared the first man, neither yielding nor becoming less concerned. "How much longer must I wait until he finally wakes up?"

Five days? That was too many! I needed to make sense of my surroundings right this second!

Learn what had ultimately happened to George, old man Taras, and Theophane back there! Figure out who this vaguely familiar voice belonged to, where I was, and how Father would react to my reappearance!

I accidentally came out of my meditation, and in the next moment I sensed that I was naked and lying on a soft mattress under a warm blanket. I could hear the sounds characteristic of various medical devices. After the long hours I'd spent in the cellar room with my now-deceased grandfather — a paralyzed old man, a great mage, and the head of the Morozov bloodline — it seemed I'd learned to identify that sound instantly. Grandfather had saved me — he'd brought me back from the other side, resurrected me with his magic. And my father had killed me... so Theophane had secretly taken me away from the estate. We'd hidden in Morshansk, on the border of the Wasteland. Ivan Temnikov, or Ivan Morozov, had been dead to everyone. But now it had all come to light...

To my immense relief, I felt just superb. No pain in the lacerated magical channels, generally no pain anywhere else either. My body was full of strength and energy, and my thoughts were moving through my head with simply supersonic speed.

Probably for that exact reason, I was able to determine that I was inside of a moving car — or, more likely, a big van, since a large bed and all this medical equipment was happily settled inside of it.

"Don't fake it," said the second man quietly.

"My equipment is showing that you're already awake."

Deciding not to put on a show for my mysterious attendants, I opened my eyes and immediately met the gaze of a short, fairly frail middle-aged man in a white robe.

A healer, I realized immediately.

Turning my gaze to the man standing behind him, I had to stop myself from cursing. Figuring I had nothing to lose, however, I said slowly:

"Well, hello there, Father!"

Chapter 1

REALIZING THAT HE WAS obviously unnecessary to this conversation, the healer hesitated briefly and then decided to tactfully leave this section of the vehicle.

As I could see through the half-open door, I was in fact being transported in a van. More precisely, in its rear section, where a bed and a bunch of medical equipment were comfortably situated.

Father and I stared at each other silently for a few minutes. I sat up in the lotus pose with the blanket thrown over me like a toga, and he sat comfortably in a chair next to the bed.

Father finally broke the silence. He crossed his arms, leaned back against his chair, looked me in the eyes, and spoke.

"You don't have anything to say to me?"

On second thought, starting something would

be pretty stupid in my position. I was under my father's thumb, so I couldn't entertain any grand delusions. He was a seasoned and fairly powerful mage — I had no chance against him. He'd crush me and think nothing of it.

Something in me didn't want to resign myself to that, though. I decided not to cut him any slack. Or to feign childishness either.

I'd had enough! Whatever happened happened! I'd already had enough of being scared! Enough and a half! Today might be the last day of my life!

"What do you want me to say to you?" I said coldly, not turning my gaze aside, then said in a squeaky voice: *"Papa dearest, please, don't kill me again?"*

It was probably just me, but I thought I saw Father look troubled for a moment. The next second, though, there was no trace of it on his face.

"How could I have killed you, if you're alive and sitting here right in front of me?" he asked after a bit.

"You're asking the wrong question," I answered. "You should have asked how I could be alive, if you personally left my lifeless corpse behind in the ritual hall."

"You're unhappy with me," said Father after a bit, shaking his head.

"Well, what did you expect?" It was my turn to be surprised. "That I'd fling myself into your embrace as soon as I saw you? That we'd hold hands and tell each other how we've been during these long years full of loneliness? That I'd start calling you 'Papa dearest?' After everything that happened? After you killed me because I was a Normal? Or maybe because of the Morozov money? After I had to spend two years living next to the Wasteland and hiding from you? Are you sure you haven't lost your mind again?"

Once I'd gotten all that out, I went quiet and waited for a response. I expected Father to blow a gasket, start yelling, try to act with force. But he just let out a short chuckle. I didn't like that chuckle.

It sent shivers down my spine.

Raising his hand, he made a few sweeps of the room, and the sounds of the road outside the window fell silent.

"I don't want anyone to overhear us," he explained. "You may not believe me, of course, but in the moment when your abilities became known, I wasn't entirely myself. I'd been drinking a lot and taking narcotics, and on top of that, someone slipped me some kind of mysterious poison that not only clouded my reasoning but also made me wildly emotional and aggressive. I could have flown off the handle at the slightest little thing! It was only because my body reacted that way to this reality... I'm not going to beg for forgiveness, fall at your feet and tell you what a terrible man I was not so long ago. Even now, don't you know," he said with another very unpleasant laugh, "I'm not a particularly agreeable person. But I do realize that I acted in error. It may have been in the heat of the moment, but I killed you — my own child! I think gratitude to my deeply esteemed father-in-law for your marvelous resurrection is in order."

Apparently, something flashed through my eyes — Father smiled with satisfaction.

"I knew it was all his work. Your grandfather was truly an amazing man."

"What's the point of this conversation?" I knit my brows. "These unnecessary excuses you're making... do you think I need to hear them?"

"What is it you do need?"

"For starters, I'd like to know what you're planning to do with me."

"Why, nothing." He shrugged. "You're returning to the estate, and you're going to live as the heir to a princely bloodline should."

"Liar!" I snapped. "I don't believe you! I have no desire for your hospitality. I'd be better off living on my own."

"You can't do that," he said. "One way or another, you're my son."

"I did it just fine for the past two years. What's different now?"

"Oh, just that everyone knows you're alive!" said Father, agitated. "We're living in the digital age. The attempt on George's life was caught on five different cameras, and your heroic little feats are visible in a few of them. The moment when you created that Globe of Ice is especially well documented! Yes, you showed everyone that someone from the Morozov bloodline is alive. Your appearance, along with the fact that you were riding in the same car as George, led others to suspect who your real family is. I had to dash off to that Morshansk place and spend the trip coming up with a spin for the press about what exactly was underlying your death, why we did all this, and what we're going to do now!"

"Oh, I'm so sorry for you!" I interrupted him. "You've made your bed, now lie in it! I didn't force you to snort drugs and then murder me!"

I almost got a light jab from a tendril of darkness and blocked it with a Spirit Shield.

"Stop speaking to your father with that tone," said Father, standing up slowly. "Or you'll regret it!"

His eyes filled with darkness. All of the surrounding space clouded over with dark fog that made it incredibly hard to breathe.

Concentrating, I expanded my Spirit Shield around my whole body, and with a mocking look at Father, I said:

"Okay, let's go! Show me what you're capable of! I wanna hear another round of your excuses! Apologize again and tell me how much I provoked you!"

As I'd imagined, those words sobered him up a bit. He immediately calmed down, got his dark aura under control, and sat back down. Mentally wiping sweat from my proverbial forehead, I relaxed a bit, but all the same I didn't take down my Spirit Shield.

"You're right," said Father after some time. "You don't believe me. That's your right. However, whether you want to or not, we'll have to live with this going forward and even cooperate."

"What was that? You actually want to cooperate?"

"Listen." Father laughed. "Your oldest brother said exactly the same thing. He didn't believe that proper cooperation was possible either. But after I came to Morshansk and had a nice little chat with him, he changed his mind and is now working for the good of the bloodline."

"Why you always lyin'?" The well-known catchphrase from Earth's internet came to mind. "Cooperation doesn't work after something like this."

"It works." Father shook his head. "When there's no other way out."

"You're saying I don't have one?"

"What did you think?" he said, surprised.

"I think that you, my dear father, are extremely disinterested in the promulgation of a story that explains the reason for my two-year disappearance in any other way. And you'd be all the more unhappy with my version of events and your role in them becoming public knowledge."

Father didn't say anything, so — encouraged by my first success — I continued:

"Without a doubt, *I'm* happy that my death would be a serious thorn in your side for the foreseeable future. Because if it happens, you really will have to explain why you allowed the last Morozov, so soon after his triumphant resurrection, to die. Actually, I don't know the situation in the empire as well as you do, but even so I think I'm right in assuming my sudden death would be a severe blow to you."

"You've really changed over the past two years," said Father, smirking ever so slightly and giving me a somehow peculiar look. "Your mentors taught you a lot."

Mentors, plural? Apparently he thought the second one was old man Taras. Whatever, no good dissuading him from that yet. Having two Heroes in my reserve was better than one.

"I even like you better this way," Father continued in the meantime. "I'm glad that I don't have to speak to you like a child. You need something from me. Enough empty words. Tell me what you want."

What? He was coming right at me with this? I wasn't ready yet! I thought I'd have to spend a while breaking him, but look at that. He valued his time. All right, well... out with it...

"Before we start settling this deal, I want to know what really happened to George."

"It's just as I said." Father smirked. "He stayed behind in Morshansk. The whole time we've been on the road, after we saw each other, he's been licking his wounds and preparing to finish the mission I gave him."

"He told me you barely won a magical duel with him and sent hitmen after him because of it."

"I had no reason to want to kill him." Father shook his head. "Whatever he might say, he is in fact my heir — the person who will become head of the family after I die. I only wanted to teach him, to show him, that it's too early for him to do that! I made sure of it personally."

"Right after he miraculously defended himself from a dozen murderers?"

"After he recovered," he corrected me.

"In that case," I said after a bit, "I'd like to return to Morshansk and live with him."

Father was silent for some time.

Then he smirked and shook his head.

"You really surprised me there," he said. "Although it really is an excellent idea, since you don't believe me…"

I didn't have time to get excited.

"However, I'll allow you to live with your brother in Morshansk only after you spend two months at your own home estate."

"I won't agree to that!" I said decisively. "That's the place where I was killed!"

"I couldn't care less what you agree to or not!" Father raised his voice. "If I wanted to kill you, I would already have done it long ago! So let me tell you exactly where you can shove your objections! You'll live at home for two or three months, and after that you'll return to Morshansk."

"No!"

"Yes! You have to do it to put the public at ease! Then you can run off and do what you want!"

"How am I supposed to put them at ease?" I said, surprised.

"I'll tell you how!" Father threw up his hands. "You'll host a ceremonial ball in honor of your return. Tell a few stories about how hard it was for you to hide from your killers. Spend some time with your brothers and sisters. Then you can run off to your oldest brother's house and stay there."

Father was speaking fully logically, so I had to agree, albeit with difficulty. I had still had to do more to guarantee my safety, though, and it seemed I'd come up with a way to do that.

Why not? It could definitely work.

"Give me a cell phone," I said after a few seconds of silence.

"What? A cell phone?" Father didn't understand right away.

"Yeah, give me a phone, I need to make a call."

Taking it as he offered one to me, I dialed a specially agreed-upon number for emergencies, and when I heard the sweet sound of it ringing on the other end, I breathed a sigh of relief. His phone was up and running, thank the Savior! I hoped he was all right.

"Finally!" I heard Theophane's voice, full of hope.

"I'm glad to hear your voice too," I said, and continued quickly: "Have you been doing everything according to protocol?"

"Yes." Theophane's voice perked up.

"I'm just calling you from my father's cell phone. He's sitting right in front of me."

"Oh, no! They took you!" said Theophane slowly. "And what about your father? He's not planning to kill you, is he?"

"It seems not." I glanced at him — my own father. "I just wanted to let you know that I came to an agreement with him on the following conditions…"

"Put it on speakerphone," said Theophane after I briefly told him about my discussion with Father. "Hey, Yegor, buddy." I saw Father's face change completely. "I'm sure you remember me. So, is what Ivan says true?"

"Yes, we came to an agreement."

"You believe him, Ivan?" Now it was my turn to answer.

"He has no reason to lie." I raised my eyes to look at Father. "You have a recording of this conversation, after all, and if something happens to me, you can easily inform the public about what really happened."

"Don't doubt it!" said Theophane, and he played the recording of the conversation we'd just had.

Good thing I made sure he was doing everything according to protocol! Otherwise he might not have had a recording.

"So you were standing by," said Father with satisfaction. "All the better. Now you have an additional safety guarantee, and you won't meet every suggestion I make with hostility. I promise that within a few months, you'll return to Morshansk and start living the life of a noble heir."

"I have to go," said Theophane in a satisfied voice. "Till next time, kid, we'll meet again!"

I gave Father back his phone and said:

"Now that we've settled the question of my safety, tell me — why do I have to host some ball, and what will I have to do there?”

* * *

Home, sweet home! was my knee-jerk thought as I looked at the majestic four-story mansion. Its walls were made of beautiful light yellow brick, and the roof was covered in red shingles.

Father got out of the car and headed straight for the entryway. Several people were already waiting for him there.

Trying not to pay attention to the people scurrying around here and there, I continued glancing around. In this place, everything seemed both very familiar and completely foreign to me at the same time.

For Ivan Temnikov, who’d been killed, who’d lived at this estate for as long as he could remember, it was his dear and beloved home. For Ivan Morozov, who’d risen from the dead and spent a long time in hiding as the heir to a bloodline, it was an unpleasant place associated with terrible memories. And for me, a guy from Earth who’d woken up in the body of the risen boy, it was unknown and strange territory that I was setting foot on for the first time.

“Young Master, your room is ready,” said a portly, black-haired woman in a dark blue maid’s outfit, breaking the flow of my thoughts.

“Lead the way,” I said robotically, and I saw the intense curiosity on her face give way to slight surprise for a moment.

Actually, on second thought, her face seemed vaguely familiar. Obviously, she'd worked here before I had to flee.

"Follow me, please." She nodded and headed for the doors to the manor.

As I followed her, I sensed someone's hostile gaze. I raised my head and saw a young, fairly attractive woman watching me from a second-floor window.

Belov! As she moved away from the window not quite quickly enough, I was reminded of my stepmother and how much she wanted me dead, if I'd sensed that right! Meanwhile, on the outside, she seemed like a completely harmless young woman. On the outside, she even seemed lovely!

Ah well, I should thank her for this peculiar and timely reminder of what she was really like. Now I'd try to keep a close eye out for her! And I wasn't falling for any cute faces.

My room was exactly the same as it had been two years ago. As if I'd left it only yesterday. The same bed, the same table with a framed photo of my late mother on it.

Now, isn't this unnecessary! I thought, shifting my gaze to the left and seeing my own photo there in a big black frame. *I'm not going to my eternal rest yet.*

Picking up the photo, I headed to one of the two doors leading to other rooms in the suite. Finding myself in a bathroom that was not of cheap quality, I quickly found the trash can and tossed my find into it.

Then I decided that it wouldn't be a bad idea to clean up, so I started filling up the huge hydromassage bathtub. After that, I headed for the second door that was part of my suite, which led to a pretty big walk-in closet.

I took a big, soft white towel from the shelf, looked around, and decided to do a brief inspection. The result: I found a large collection of clothes in my size.

Not bad. If Father had gone to the trouble of arranging that, he definitely didn't plan to let me croak just yet.

I took off the clothes that had been bought for me at one of the shopping centers we'd passed on the road, threw them into the laundry basket, and gladly undertook my watery proceedings.

As it turned to evening, the maid I was already familiar with knocked at the door and courteously invited me to family dinner.

"Just fifteen more minutes?" I muttered sleepily, emerging from a blissful slumber. "Just a minute, take me there."

Quickly putting on the outfit I'd set out in advance, I followed the prompt maid and fairly quickly reached one of the lesser dining halls, where — as far as I could tell from Ivan's memories — the whole family used to gather fairly often.

"This is a family dinner?" I said, raising an eyebrow at Father, who was sitting at the head of the table. Ignoring my stepmother Galina at the foot, I took the place that was indicated to me on the left side. "Seems like not a lot of people."

"The others aren't home," answered Father, who was skillfully using his silverware and devouring a delicious-smelling fillet.

He explained as he chewed another piece of meat.

"George stayed in Morshansk. Theodore and Ignatius are still in the capital at their universities. And Ruslan and the girls are on a trip — they should be back tomorrow."

How many brothers and sisters do I have again? I thought in puzzlement, straining my memory and trying to remember what they looked like. So George was the oldest — he was about twenty-six years old now. After him was Theodore, who was twenty-four, and after him the twenty-year-old Ignatius. Ruslan was around fifteen now, and as for the girls, Maria was fourteen and Anna was thirteen. I was twelve. If you left out my two brothers who had died, the whole family would have taken up most of this twelve-person table.

Galina scraped her fork against her plate, supposedly by accident. Father threw her a glance and continued:

"Your stepbrothers are still a bit too little, so they don't come to family dinners."

Stepbrothers? I was surprised as I looked at Galina carefully. If I had step-siblings, and step-brothers at that, there was one more person likely to have ordered the hit on George. Galina, after all, would lose more than anyone else if he came out on top.

"Is there something wrong?" Galina asked me

kindly with a sweet smile.

The picture of innocence! I snorted internally. All right, two could play at this game.

"You're just so beautiful!" I said to her, lowering my head and winking.

Was it just me or did Father just choke?

"How sweet of you!" said Galina, sounding touched, although I caught some bewilderment in her eyes.

After devoting several minutes to meaningless dialogue, I finally turned to Father.

"Am I allowed to leave my room and find things to do as I please?"

"It depends on what you want to do," he replied. "You're allowed to do anything the other children are allowed to do around the estate."

"Great, then I'd like to visit the training hall and the library sometimes. I think that'll be enough for the first few weeks."

"I have no objections, but plan your activities around the event we discussed."

"I will," I said, getting up from the table and setting off for my room.

* * *

"What's this event you're planning to hold?" Galina asked her husband. "Is there something I don't know about?"

"Yes." Yegor nodded. "But you could have guessed that after Ivan's miraculous return from the other side, a lot of people want to become acquainted with the new hope of the Morozov blood-line. I'm already being run ragged by daily letters and phone calls."

Galina pursed her lips. After Yegor had discovered the reason for the family's recent tragic events, he'd become quite cold to her.

All the better that I was the first to stumble upon the Morozov prince's notes about human sacrifice, or this would all be much worse! she thought. No matter, though! She'd find a way to regain her husband's favor and figure out how to start directing the family's affairs again.

"Are you planning to hold a ceremonial ball in his honor?" Galina nodded towards the doors that Ivan had just exited through. "You don't think that he's still too young for such an event?"

"He is," Yegor agreed. "If only he were at least fifteen! But it's no good forgetting that the Morozov magic has accepted him. I'd advise you to watch the video with the shot of him fighting and taking initiative. It already has a few million views."

* * *

The next morning, I had breakfast alone. After spending a few hours in the training hall and spooking a few of the house's warriors who were in there using it, I got myself up and running and headed to the lesser hall, hoping to find something there for myself. However, it turned out no one was there.

I took this as a good sign — it meant no one

would spoil my appetite — and attacked my food, all while replaying the details of last night's dinner in my head. They hadn't left my head for a long time last night, and now I finally understood why.

It was all about Galina. The utter hatred in the glance she'd thrown at me, the likelihood that she was the one behind the attempt on George's life, the fact that after she'd joined the family two of my brothers had died completely by accident and (according to him) Father had come under the influence of some kind of unknown poison. Apparently, the same poison that had later been found in Ruslan's blood. And, last but not least, the fact that she wasn't curious about where I'd been in the past two years, who'd been buried instead of me, and who exactly had been providing for my safety.

Incidentally, it was worth remembering what Theophane had told me — it was her people who'd showed up in the cellar looking for my corpse. They'd known that Father might have killed me. That meant Galina was the one at fault for the death of Ivan Temnikov — the former host of my body — and that I had to watch out for her more than anyone.

It was in that same lesser hall that one of the stewards found me and introduced me to an elderly, incredibly stern-looking woman in an old-fashioned business suit.

Thanks a lot for nothing, Father! I thought in disappointment, sitting at the table in front of the woman, who clearly knew her job and how to do it very well.

"To start off, I would like to find out what your knowledge level is," she said. "So if you could answer a few questions for me..."

What could I say? I was totally right. This demon in the shape of an old woman picked on poor little me until lunchtime.

As it turned out, she was the specialist who was supposed to not only help organize the ceremonial ball in observance of all traditions, but also provide necessary information to the one who was to blame for these festivities.

I'd take a couple of extra workouts with Theophane over having to learn such extensive layers of knowledge in the shortest time possible! All the better that I'd never let myself slip, and I'd been responsible about my studies!

That was what had allowed me to train my memory, and what now prevented me from getting dragged through the mud as Elvira — that was the woman's name — interrogated me about my schooling.

"Well, then, I believe you'll do all right," she said, and she took her leave of me.

I didn't get a chance to relax after lunch, because the younger siblings started getting home.

"Ivan!" I heard the joyful voice of one of my sisters and turned around. "It's really him!" cried the thirteen-year-old Anna, and she and the fourteen-year-old Maria — who almost seemed to have appeared out of nowhere — rushed over to me.

They were both wearing Imperial Academy

uniforms, which made them look almost identical — Anna was just a head shorter — so it was no wonder I couldn't tell them apart.

"We thought you were dead!"

"But then Father said he was just hiding you from the killers!"

"Yes, Father said that you spent two years in hiding!"

"Uh-huh! We saw the video online, too!"

"Yeah!"

The girls competed with each other to talk and wouldn't stop giving me hugs, shaking me, and smoothing out the wrinkles in my clothes.

"C'mon, leave him alone!"

I heard an amused voice and saw Ruslan.

"Hi!" he said, and tried to give me a little smack on the ear, but I reacted in time and ducked quickly. "He still remembers!" Ruslan laughed. "Although I used to get you pretty often."

The girls laughed, and I felt some kind of strange heaviness in my chest.

They were so sincerely happy that I was alive — it was visible in their eyes, which were gleaming from happiness — and my conscience started tormenting me. It wasn't me they'd been waiting for, it wasn't me they were happy about. Ivan Temnikov really had died, and now I'd taken his place...

Enough moping! I cast those thoughts off resolutely — they'd been harmful in similar situations. What happened happened! I needed to keep living, not give myself over to needless suffering!

Anna and Maria kept bombarding me with

questions, not seeming all that preoccupied with whether I answered or not.

"Okay! Stop!" I said, raising my hands. "I propose that we go sit comfortably in the garden somewhere, grab some quality snacks, and chat there. Sound good?"

"Sounds good!" said the two of them in chorus.

"Ten minutes, at the door to the garden," said Ruslan, and we all scattered to our rooms.

Hmm... pretty soon, I'd have to get some practice in speaking formally.

Chapter 2

HIT! HIT! HIT AGAIN! Battering Ram! Spirit Shield! Reinforced forward rush and another Battering Ram with both hands! Dodge an imaginary spell and counterattack quick as lightning. Spirit Shield behind me and back to attacking! Power Whirlwind...

Great, I thought with satisfaction as I finished my morning workout and felt the little drops of sweat rolling down my back.

I remembered when I'd first come to this world and had to work myself to the bone on Theophane's varied and extremely tough workouts, and I'd thought that as soon as I escaped from his company I'd stop working on strength exercises right away. Because only masochists and people who simply had nothing better to do with their energy were so cruel to themselves, and I clearly wasn't either of those.

But I'd spent two years ceaselessly working on myself, Theophane was now somewhere far away, and here I was continuing to work out strenuously as soon as I woke up. I felt that if I slacked off, I'd get weaker, stagnate, and stop perfecting my skills, and I'd never get back to how I was now.

It would be the end... I wouldn't be myself anymore...

Theophane really had managed to accomplish a lot in such a short time. And his biggest achievement was by no means the fact that I'd become a very strong and skilled warrior for my age, even approaching Militant rank. No. He was an excellent mentor precisely because he'd managed to make a real fighter out of me. Someone with a hardened will, who'd passed through all kinds of trials and only become stronger for it.

Now, when I reflected on what I might do in the future, I had a question before me — run and hide so I could live an ordinary person's life, or rush into the fight, constantly risking getting my neck snapped with every new obstacle I overcame.

I'd learned how to fight for myself and my future, I'd gotten a taste of strength, and now I wanted to take my rightful place in this cruel world. That last thought seemed to have come from the most hidden depths of my soul. After all, no one was a stranger to healthy ambitions, and of course, neither was I.

Besides, I — an adult from Earth — had been lucky enough not to be brought back in the body of some ordinary citizen, but rather in the growing form of a young princely heir! Who, by the way, had excellent genes!

Yes! Now I was Ivan Morozov, of the princely Morozov house, until the bitter end! And I would overcome every obstacle in my path! As soon as I finished repeating that sentence in my mind, I felt my body fill with some kind of unusual energy.

Hmm... interesting.

I closed my eyes immediately and tried to concentrate on the unfamiliar feelings.

After standing there for a bit, I tried to push that strength into every part of my body, concentrating it partially in my limbs and partially in my stomach. It was surprisingly easy — clearly, my long hours of practice in controlling Shiki-Cho were manifesting themselves.

I decided to try an experiment and put the energy into my fists.

I opened my eyes and saw two long Ice Spears growing out of my hands. Cutting off the flow of energy, I got a more comfortable grip on the "spears," which turned out to be surprisingly heavy.

How did I manage this? I thought, puzzled as I examined the ice.

Deciding not to do dangerous experiments in a room that wasn't intended for it, I put the Ice Spears on the ground and noticed that the training hall's wooden surfaces within a three-foot radius of me were covered with a thin layer of frost.

At that moment the door to the training hall

opened, and on the threshold appeared a skinny, short, middle-aged man who looked like he was East Asian.

He was wearing a ragged dark blue kimono and giving me a puzzled look, as if he was trying to understand what I was doing here.

He looked like a guy straight out of Japanese history, I thought in surprise. I had yet to meet anyone of this heritage or tradition in this world before now. He could've been a lost Tokugawa.

The man noticed the Ice Spear lying on the ground and did a double take.

"Good morning, young sir Ivan," he said. He had no accent.

"Morning," I answered robotically, unable to stop myself from examining his colorful appearance.

"My name is Isamu Yamashita," he said, walking into the room and covering the door. He gave me a shallow bow and then added after a short pause: "So, it looks like you're the one who's been scaring my people away!"

Oh, and his name sounded Japanese too.

"Scared them away?" I asked — it was my turn not to understand. "Who are these people you're talking about?"

"The people I'm supposed to be leading morning training for."

"Oh yeah, now I remember," I said, nodding. "I thought I saw the doors open a few times while I was in here. So are you our local warriors' mentor?"

"Yes and no. I'm the leader of the estate guards."

"What gives, the guards don't want to work out with anyone but their boss?" I asked with a smirk.

He gave me a weird look, but he answered anyway.

"I consider it my obligation to be constantly up to speed on what my subordinates can do."

"Commendable," I said in response.

That got me another weird look from him.

"And you're practicing your family magic?" he asked, gesturing with a nod to the Ice Spears, which had started to melt a little.

"You could say that," I answered somewhat absentmindedly.

No good admitting I'd created them by accident and didn't know where to put them now.

"In that case, may I recommend the splendid training hall intended specifically for the study of martial magic? Otherwise, I fear that my people will have nowhere to train."

"Okay, yeah, I think that's a great idea," I said — and I finally got a glimpse of the ring on Yamashita's finger with his warrior rank.

Veteran? Not bad at all. He was still young — maybe in a few years he'd be a Knight.

"What would you think of doing some sparring?" I asked him, not expecting it myself.

Why not? If there was a strong warrior within arm's reach, it would be a sin not to train with him. Somehow I didn't feel like explaining to Theophane, when we met again, why I hadn't managed to stay in shape.

"Hmm..." Yamashita clearly wasn't overjoyed at this proposal.

I could see clearly, despite his unbreakable poker face, that he'd been extremely curious to meet the prince's son who'd risen from the dead.

He'd gotten his wish, but he'd immediately stumbled into a proposal that would mean having to waste time to no end, since a twelve-year-old boy clearly wouldn't be a worthy opponent. Or rather, he wouldn't be an opponent at all. Even with the use of magic.

However, despite his lack of desire to fight, Yamashita said:

"I think some friendly sparring would be... hmm... highly educational. Besides, as the one who answers for the safety of all the house's inhabitants, it's very important for me to know your skill level."

Was he talking to me or was he talking himself into it? I smirked.

"Then can we start?" I asked, grinning.

"Well... hmm... not here. This isn't the best room for using magic, after all."

"I don't intend to use magic. I just want to limber up and do some sparring."

Yamashita's face didn't lose its indifference, but I got the feeling he was even more vexed now. I didn't even intend to use magic!

Moving away from the Ice Spears, he beckoned to me.

I rushed at him as he stood there with his

guard down, not taking me seriously. Stopping two yards short of him, I increased my speed spasmodically a few times over, then immediately dealt him a fairly powerful blow to the chest with my knee.

The surprise worked! It was no accident I'd started running towards him slowly but finished the move much faster!

Yamashita clearly hadn't gotten his Veteran rank by looking pretty, because in the next moment he managed to put up a Spirit Shield and even tried to block me with his arms, but that didn't save him.

After being thrown back a few yards, he somehow cleverly spun around in midair and landed on his feet. Now he wasn't letting his guard down anymore — he took a fighting stance.

Not giving him a chance to get his wits about him, I pummeled him with blows — many of which got past his shield — but he pulled himself together fairly quickly.

After retaliating "courteously" with a few less strong punches, he calculated my strength, sped up gradually, and started doling out punches and occasionally working me over with combos I'd never seen before.

A few of his punches were really annoying to dodge, but I tried not to fall behind and made diverse use of my small arsenal of spiritual energy techs...

"Militant?" said Yamashita, a bit more respectfully than before, when we'd finished our match and he'd sized up my frail figure once again.

"Second-level Soldier," I said, wiping off the sweat that had accumulated on my forehead.

"I've never seen a Soldier with such a skillful grasp of spiritual energy." He shook his head. "At such a young age, to boot."

"Thanks," I said, grateful for his fair assessment of my abilities, but he kept going.

"Though it seems to me that you're missing something — some kind of weapon." He paused for a bit. "Most likely a short or mid-length sword."

"I'm used to fighting with a saber," I corrected him, and realized with mild surprise that I really did miss my bladed weapon.

With it, I was much more deadly and could keep a healthy distance while fighting stronger and more powerful enemies.

After chatting with Yamashita for a bit longer, I arranged to participate in the morning workouts, and we parted ways feeling pleased with each other. Only after I got to my room did I remember, with some vexation, that he hadn't even shown me to the training hall for magic.

Ah well, the hall wasn't going anywhere.

* * *

According to preestablished tradition, I re-familiarized myself with the members of our large family that I didn't know so well that night over dinner.

In the hour before this momentous occasion, Anna and Maria categorically forced me to talk with them in the garden.

I had pretty much nothing important planned during that time, since I hadn't had time to come up with a consistent daily routine yet. So I met their suggestion with some amount of enthusiasm.

The Temnikov estate's main garden was behind the house. There were a few doors that led to it, but the girls took me through the main hall.

This was on the first floor and was intended for holding receptions and other ceremonial events. After a cursory glance around the place where I'd have to meet guests all too soon, I followed the girls through the tall fretted doors and found myself on a forking path that led to different parts of the estate complex.

The main garden was fairly big, so my sisters decided we'd just walk along the "main roads," which were tile-paved paths about six feet wide that allowed four people to walk along it side by side freely.

After we'd sat on a bench by the manmade pond for a while, we returned to the house, where one of the maids met us and informed us of the upcoming family dinner.

"I hate those!" Anna puffed out her lips.

"What's wrong?" I decided to ask, curious about why she'd had such a strong reaction.

"Oh, everything's wrong," said Anna. "Now we'll have to hurry to our bathrooms and get cleaned up. Then we'll have to sit at the dining room table with posture good enough to look like we swallowed mops, and eat our food all delicately! All while observing those boring rules of etiquette!"

Maria listened to her whole monologue and started laughing.

"Pay her no attention," she said. "It's just that not too long ago she let herself behave a little too freely at the dinner table in Father's presence, and her punishment was seven lessons with Elvira. You know the one, right?"

"Ohhhh!" I said, giving Anna a sympathetic look. "I've had occasion to become acquainted with her recently. I was impressed by her work. What an astounding woman."

"Yeah, astounding is right!" I heard Ruslan's voice approaching us from behind. He paused for a bit and turned to the girls. "You already know about the family dinner? Isn't it time to get moving? Or else you might be late."

"Lecture us more, why don't you!" snorted Maria.

Nonetheless, the girls remembered what time it was and hurried off quickly to go clean up.

"Did you hear?" said Ruslan in a conversational tone, coming closer.

"Depends on what you mean," I replied just as quietly, deciding not to make it obvious that I had no idea what he was talking about.

"The older kids are here," he explained. "That's why Father decided we should have dinner together. I think he'll also probably invite some others."

"I know about the older brothers," I said cunningly. "But this is the first time I'm hearing about other guests. Who is it that Father could be inviting?"

Among Ivan's memories, there were no dinners with outsiders. Only with the family and a few particularly close family friends.

"We're not expecting any guests, but don't be surprised if someone shows up," said Ruslan with the look of someone exposing a terrible secret. "Although I think Professor Petius will be there with his family and his deputies, and Diachenko and that warrior guy from security."

I thought about that.

According to Ivan's memories, Professor Petius had been the family's head mage even before I'd become a fugitive. Petius's family and deputies, on the other hand, were unknown to Ivan and didn't evoke any sort of associations, so I figured I'd have to devote some attention to them during dinner. "That warrior guy," as Ruslan had called him, most likely referred to Isamu Yamashita, whom I already knew. Who Diachenko was, however, I had positively no idea.

I asked my loquacious older brother about the latter personage.

"Yeah, he's the head of security." Ruslan gave me a puzzled look. "He's been here for a while already. I thought he was the one who organized your disappearance — it was after that that he got his position."

"I see," I said thoughtfully, making a mental note to tactfully ask these dear folks about what happened at the estate after that ill-fated night. I also decided to ask Ruslan: "And what guests were you talking about? I don't remember other people coming to family dinners in the past."

"That's because at that time, Father barely got out of the house and didn't pay much attention to his duties. But not too long ago, everything completely changed. Now we've had a chance to meet people he knows pretty frequently — some business partners or other, or just nobles from smaller houses coming for an audience. There have started to be a lot of them, surprisingly."

At that moment, the girls returned all dolled up, and our friendly quartet headed for the lesser hall I was now so familiar with.

So the guests' arrival hadn't been planned in advance after all — otherwise, we would've been invited into a somewhat bigger room.

Those already seated at the table were my older brothers, Professor Petius with his wife and daughter, and Yamashita with a fairly young man I didn't know.

"So, here's the one we got dragged all the way back here for!" said one of my older brothers with displeasure.

I didn't like his dandyish clothes or his overly familiar behavior, which radiated his feelings of his own superiority and his inordinate ego. I didn't like the first-level Master's ring he was wearing on his finger either.

Ignatius, I determined based on his age. He really looked like a spoiled rich kid. As a mage, though, he was strong for his age. It would be interesting to see what he could do.

"Don't go at Ivan," said another one of my brothers. "You know he had absolutely nothing to do with this."

The twenty-four-year-old Theodore, second in line by age, was much bigger and stronger than Ignatius, who was sitting next to him. It seemed to me that the difference couldn't be their age, since George was a pretty svelte guy.

Theodore's bruised knuckles told me that my guesses were fully justified.

"Then who did?" said Ignatius, raising an eyebrow. "I did have plans tonight, and the up-and-coming Morozov has simply ruined them!"

Morozov? Why exactly was he calling me that? He wasn't jealous of my position as an heir, was he? Or of the fact that his youngest brother, born so long after him, was going to become the head of a family, while he'd be stuck as nothing but one of the ordinary members of his? I'd have to think about this long and hard.

"Hmm!" Professor Petius coughed very expressively, and Ignatius shut right up.

Aha, so Petius was the one I should turn to if I needed to tame this impudent fellow, I thought as I looked at my brother. Well, and I should turn to him when it came to mastering my magical talent too.

I gave the professor a grateful nod and turned my attention to his family.

His wife, who was sitting next to him, was pretty good-looking and was clearly a mage herself, as was her daughter sitting next to her.

Eighteen years old, I figured, memorizing her face and the faces of two men dressed in traditional mages' clothing.

Those were clearly the professor's deputies. They'd be hard to mistake for anyone else.

The other two attendees were Yamashita, whom I already knew (incidentally, I was extremely curious to find out this world's name for his nationality), and the man I'd noticed earlier.

That had to be the famed head of security. I wondered how he'd managed to get such a high position at such a young age.

Father and Galina arrived to dinner last.

As soon as they'd greeted everyone and taken their places, maids came into the room and served us plates of hot, delicious-smelling food.

I'd been apprehensive, but they didn't serve us anything unusual. Putting Ivan's memories, the etiquette courses I'd taken, and my own experience from Imperial Academy lunches into action, I remained dignified through three courses. I also heard a couple of snide remarks from Ignatius, who was very demonstratively surprised that I hadn't lost my skills after living who-knew-where for two years. Just before that, Father had been telling the curious guests about the reasons for my absence and notifying everyone of the ball coming up in the near future.

The conversation turned to a discussion of the upcoming festivities. Who needed to be invited, how to organize the evening, which food and drinks to prepare. The mages were charged with checking on the security alarms, and the security service with fortifying the guard posts and doing other security checks.

"So we're stuck here for a few more weeks?" Ignatius asked Theodore when dinner was finally over. Receiving an affirmative response, he threw an irritated glance in my direction. "It would be better if you were still in that backwoods town! Everything I was doing, down the drain!"

Well, thank the Savior! At least one person wasn't ecstatic about my resurrection! I smirked. Outside of that, everything seemed to be going too well. Everyone here was being so nice that I couldn't badmouth anyone... and that kind of thing just didn't happen!

"Ivan." I heard Theodore's voice. "I know a nice little spot around here. Let's grab some chips and some other junk food and go hide out there, and you can tell me your amazing story! There were a couple of things that I didn't understand at all, and Father said that if I was curious about the details I could ask you personally."

Father, you scoundrel! Dumping all the dirty work onto me! I thought, annoyed. I gave Theodore a thoughtful look. Should I push him away just because Father was a swine? On the contrary, I needed to secure the rest of my family's support if I wanted to play it safe and put a stop in advance to some of the undesirable things Father might do.

"Let's go," I answered decisively. "Show me this awesome spot."

* * *

Elvira sat across from me in a comfortable arm-chair in front of the fireplace, taking small sips of dry red wine with clear satisfaction and listening attentively as I answered her question.

"A few centuries ago, ball season started at the end of fall. Because that was when nobles with a lot of arable land finished the harvest and were able to dedicate their free time to amusements as they pleased. The season lasted all winter and ended in the middle of spring."

"Good." Elvira nodded. "So why are balls held with no seasonal constraints nowadays?"

"Because modern-day nobility doesn't have the same dependence on the harvest. They get their funds from investing in industry and services. It's been a long time now since their income depended on the produce grown in the summer."

"Good. We'll end the digression into the history for now," said Elvira with another small sip of wine. "Now tell me the procedure for inviting guests to a ceremonial ball."

I paused, collected my thoughts, and got started on my answer.

"To invite guests to a ball, I have to send letters with invitations four weeks before the upcoming event. So that they get to the addressees no later than twenty-one days before the start of the event, and they have time to respond as to whether they'll be there or not."

Elvira stared at me silently, waiting for me to continue. Realizing that she hadn't accepted my answer, I kept going.

"It's essential to remember that the invitations being sent must be simple and laconic, with no superfluous verbiage. The guests know the conventions of balls, after all."

"How interesting," said Elvira. "And what kind of wording do you consider simple and laconic? Without superfluous verbiage?"

Well, that was an easy one — my etiquette textbooks had a standard template prepared, I thought, and said:

"Well, for example, something like this: *The heir to the princely line of Morozov welcomes you to and requests that you do him the honor of attending a ceremonial ball, on the something-th of the month of this year, at the Temnikov estate, at six o'clock in the evening.* And that's all."

"Excellent!" Elvira took another sip. "For the time being, I'm pleased with what you know — unlike with your sister Anna."

She was silent for a bit, then asked me:

"What do you know about ballroom dances?"

I knew a lot about ballroom dances, if only because Ivan had been taught about them ever since he was little, and he'd subsequently passed his memories on to me.

"Every ball opens with a ceremonial polonaise," I replied. "Everyone in attendance must participate regardless of their interests. I think it's because that's a very simple dance that doesn't require much stamina from the participants. After the polonaise comes a series of waltzes, polkas, quadrilles, and mazurkas. The mazurka is one of the most important dances. Because after the mazurka, a gentleman can lead a lady to the table for dinner, where he can talk to her and try to make an impression."

"And how do the gentlemen know that there's going to be a mazurka? They have to invite ladies to dance with them in time, before the competition gets there first."

I thought about it and was forced to admit that I had no answer to this question.

Elvira smiled.

"It's plain to see that you've gleaned all of your information from reading — otherwise, you would've had an answer to that question right away."

She took a sip of wine and continued:

"There's a fixed order to the ballroom dances. They can swap places arbitrarily, but the attendees know that after the fourth quadrille comes the mazurka. After that, as we already discussed, is dinner."

Elvira took another sip from her wine glass and continued:

"From my experience in hosting festivities at this estate, I know that the Temnikovs traditionally hold dinner in the side sitting rooms, where groups can gather around small tables as they please. In addition to that, there's also an open buffet nearby with all different kinds of food, as well as both hot and cold drinks."

After checking that I'd mastered the new information, Elvira went on.

"A gentleman's most important duty at dinner is to entertain his lady and hold sociable conversations, seeing to it that she has everything she wants."

She stared at me attentively, putting emphasis on that last part. I nodded, showing that I'd memorized her words, and she continued speaking.

"At dinner, it's appropriate to talk about music, theater, the latest news from the gossip columns, who's marrying whom, and so on..."

After my lesson with Elvira, I left the room with my head spinning.

Five of these lessons in one week... it was really tough.

Chapter 3

"PRINCE PAVLOV, WITH HIS WIFE and his daughter Svetlana," the well-placed voice of the herald reached my ears as I greeted guests with Father and Galina.

Measuring out one welcoming bow, I — not for the first time — imperceptibly glanced at the big, beautiful clock hanging in the hall.

Half past eight. Another half hour of standing here, and then I could relax a little, I thought with hope — because when the ball started, the hosts were no longer obligated to greet guests who arrived late. Although I hadn't previously suspected that hosting ceremonial balls would be such a tiresome thing to do. If only the dancing would start sooner!

I was stupefied at that thought.

I never would've imagined myself waiting so

hopefully for ballroom dancing, especially not while I'd been running around in the Wasteland...

My gaze fell once again on Father as he spoke to Galina, and I clenched my fists tightly. My recent attempt to test the limits of what I was allowed to do had shown me that I wouldn't be able to leave the estate unimpeded. I'd be stopped by not only the cameras all over the grounds, which were placed so as to avoid "blind spots," but also by a special group of guards on duty who had to follow me around.

"Marquis Ogneyer, with his wife and his son Godimir," the herald's voice sounded in the earpiece hidden in my right ear.

This man, specially prepared in advance by Elvira, was feeding me the names of the guests as they arrived. This kind of aid was not infrequently provided to young nobility if they had to host various events. It was, of course, not very warmly welcomed, but little toys like this were treated with understanding.

It all came down to the fact that at celebrations of this scale, a very large number of people were usually invited. Something around a thousand. And it was impossible for someone unprepared to memorize even half of the guests' names in a short time. So noble children making their debut in society were often supplied with such "accessories." After all, no one wants their kid to screw up and — for example — call Marquis Kuznetsov "Viscount Rodnikov." That was no good. Both the marquis and the viscount would be offended. A scandal would be guaranteed.

Elvira, who had me in a proverbial death grip, had admitted to me that this practice wasn't to her liking either. She preferred to rely on training one's memory. She'd suggested that I should only host an event after I was ready, but Father had rejected her suggestion. This event had a political character and could do a lot of good for the family.

Despite the fact that I'd studied at the Imperial Academy and devoted a lot of time to training my memory, as much as that allowed me to memorize a lot of information quickly in a short time, I had not in fact been able to fulfill Elvira's wishes.

You'd think I could've, though! I'd memorized seemingly everything and could even answer her questions without mistakes! But now I had to remember in time whom I was seeing in front of me — Marquis Vorontsov? Or Vorontsov-Gorozin?

That moment of hesitation was a death sentence at a ceremonial event. So I got my earpiece in the end.

"Good evening, Marquis Ogneyer! I'm pleased to welcome you and your family to our festivities!" said Father to the commandant of Morshansk.

As I'd learned, the two of them had had time to become acquainted after the second attempt on George's life, when I'd been unconscious and Father had been taking me home.

"Oh, come now!" replied Ogneyer. "The honor is all ours, to be present at an event of this degree, especially since we know the one behind the celebration personally."

He bowed his head politely, turned, and spoke to me. "I'm pleased to see you, Ivan, in your proper place."

While the house heads had been exchanging their brief pleasantries, I'd managed to inconspicuously wink at Godimir and get a look at his mom, a pretty and young-looking woman whom I hadn't seen before.

"I thank you," I answered Ogneyer curtly.

"Ah, yes! Where are my manners?" Father said to him, smiling. "Allow me to introduce my wife Galina…"

The men talked for a few minutes, and then I got an announcement about the arrival of other guests. It wasn't especially customary for them to stand around and chat like this during the guest-greeting ceremony, so I concluded that quite possibly, I'd soon hear about the Temnikovs gaining a new ally.

When Ogneyer finally left, I noticed my friend Godimir — who'd seemed tense to an extreme point — starting to relax a little. Clearly, on the way to this reception, he'd been afraid that after regaining my status as a princely heir I'd start to look down on my former companions, and on him as well.

He'd better not count on it! I wasn't like that at all. Although, when I thought about it, there was *someone* from my branch of the Imperial Academy who could do with being taught a good lesson!

The time left until the dances flew by imperceptibly. A fairly large number of guests arrived during that time. A few times, my earpiece started to malfunction when certain guests showed up. I was almost always warned about them in advance. A couple of pranksters were somehow managing to mess with the transmitter's signal, which in a few cases threatened trouble for their cordial host, who was no longer able to figure out what was going on.

Not inviting those people to the ball would've been entirely problematic — that would've led to a scandal in and of itself — so said pranksters were here, and I was expecting dirty tricks from them. In their view, after all, I was still just a child...

When we were done greeting guests, Father and Galina headed to the main entrance to the grand hall. I quickly climbed upstairs, went through a couple of rooms, and found myself on the little second-floor balcony.

I got there just in time. The guests were already standing in pairs not far from the entrance and chatting quietly. The first notes of ceremonial music played, and the voices fell silent as if a spell had been cast. The doors to the grand hall parted slowly, and Father and Galina began the slow dance procession.

After a few moments, the barely audible sounds of clicking cameras started to add themselves to the music.

The press has been activated, I thought, counting the people with cameras. And how. There were about thirteen of them. I hadn't thought that so many of these newshawks had the credentials to get past our Yamashita!

Before Father and Galina could get too far away, two separate columns of couples took shape behind them, wanting to participate in the ceremonial dance.

Men in one column and women in the other, standing side by side and raising their hands in front of themselves, they moved smoothly to the sound of the ceremonial music.

The polonaise really was a pretty undemanding dance, I realized as I watched their slow movement. Holding this dance first here was the right way to do it after all. If memory served me, on my Earth, events like this used to open with a waltz.

From my spot, it was very easy to observe the dancing couples. That was just what I did, paying particular attention to their unusual attire.

After some time, I was able to come to some conclusions.

For example, it became clear to me that dinner jackets were considered fashionable among the modern nobility. The majority of this world's noblemen had come to the ball wearing one. However, a number of the older men had decided to pay tribute to traditions and show up in old-fashioned (but no less interesting) tailcoats.

I also noticed that regardless of their social status or means, absolutely every one of the men was wearing a snow-white undershirt and white gloves. Although, as far as I remembered, etiquette dictated that the undershirt could be any color.

I'd had the pleasure of hearing Elvira's lecture ten times about how important it was to wear gloves to a ball, and I'd come to understand firmly that at an event like this, a lady could refuse to dance with a gentleman who wasn't wearing gloves. As it turned out, it was better to show up to a ball in black gloves than without any at all.

Among the men invited, there were several high warrior ranks. It was easy to count them from their ceremonial full dress, covered in all sorts of regalia, and their fairly muscular figures.

The scrawnier noblemen, most likely every single one a mage, looked washed-out next to them.

A few representatives of the Mage League were here in professional regalia. I didn't know why, but many of them didn't want to part with their own clothes even during a ceremonial event. Good thing they hadn't brought their magic staffs with them too — that would've been real weird.

I finished surveying the men and focused on the "weaker sex" — although, magic was a standard higher than all others in this world when it came to personal strength, so a lot of women were regarded as pretty strong individuals.

The ladies lit up the hall in their beautiful evening gowns of all colors and styles, and many of them wore small hats or berets. Sure as anything, most of them were holding fans, which could be used to easily hide a smile from a gentleman.

As I'd managed to notice, most of the women present were wearing dresses in shades of white, sky-blue, or pink — or, especially, of ivory, the highly sought-after color of elephant tusks. That very clearly spoke to the fact that a lot of the young noblewomen at this event were unmarried.

As it should be, I guess — Father had five unmarried sons, so it wasn't surprising half the empire had raced to get here.

Since it wasn't just the men's hands that got sweaty during the dances, all the ladies were wearing gloves too, but unlike the gentlemen they were allowed to choose theirs based on the color and style of their dresses.

"What are you hiding out up here for? You picking out your future bride?" I heard Godimir saying quietly and laughing.

"Hi!" I said to him, turning and offering him my hand. "C'mere. It's more interesting to watch this from up here — you get a really great view."

Godimir stood next to me and looked down.

"So, you remember how the first day we met, I asked you what bloodline you were from?" he asked me unexpectedly after a short pause.

"Yeah, something like that." I remembered my first trip to the Morshansk amusement park.

"And you said you were just a normal guy," Godimir reminded me, narrowing his eyes shrewdly. "But I had a sense something was up."

"You didn't keep getting that sense when we hung out together, though," I laughed.

"That's not true," he said. "I just thought you were a bastard child of some noble family, so I kept my mouth shut. And now look how things turned out. One might even say you're a princely heir."

"I guess so." I brushed it off. "I'm still the same Ivan you knew — only I'm not 'Ivan Frost' anymore, I'm Ivan Morozov."

"Exactly. Morozov! More precisely, Prince Morozov." Godimir raised his finger. "Incidentally, why not Temnikov? You're not even sixteen years old yet! Or did the esteemed Prince Morozov manage to officially take you into his bloodline just before he died?"

"You could say that." I remembered the moment of my own death on Earth. That was exactly what had happened — I'd been taken into the bloodline. "My passport might still say 'Temnikov,' but my family magic recognizes me as a Morozov, and Father is preparing the necessary documents."

"Cool!" Godimir shook his head in astonishment. "Can you already do rituals? For now I still have to do a lot more sitting in. Father doesn't let me do any serious magic."

"I've had to learn a few things," I said. "We had to set the record straight about which bloodline I belong to."

Remembering that ritual — or, rather, remembering what had preceded it — sent real shivers down my spine.

First of all, because Father had been completely unwilling to accept my refusal to participate in the ritual. That wasn't even getting into the fact that the last time we'd gone into the ritual hall together, nothing good had come of it.

Second, because after I'd tried to show resistance and stand up for myself, I'd been very easily tied up and delivered to the spot where the ritual was going to take place.

I'd struggled with all my might, tried to use the spiritual energy I had at my disposal or some intuitive magical defense, but it had all been in vain. Laughing softly the whole way, Father had dragged me to the ritual hall, and there he'd lovingly held me to the floor a few times.

"You know I don't intend to kill you!" he'd bellowed, infuriated by my resistance. "What, don't you understand that your death would be truly disadvantageous to me? So many terrible things could happen because of you! The bloodline's reputation would suffer! And you must remember that your Theophane has a recording that's very unhelpful to me! So calm down and prepare for the ritual..."

"Ivan! Ivaaan!" I heard Godimir's voice. "Who are you looking at so hard you left the planet?"

"Just a little lost in thought," I explained, trying to hide how agitated I was at my powerlessness in my struggle against my father.

He'd gotten tired of my shenanigans real fast! But I was surprised that he hadn't taken precautions anyway. He hadn't even punished me for trying to leave the estate right after that ritual. He'd just had a few more stern chats with me.

Although, frankly, I'd suspected this might happen if we became enemies. An experienced mage couldn't lose to some hack who'd spent two years learning how to kill. To Father, I was just a little boy. He knew my attempts to run away were hopeless. So I was going to behave almost unobtrusively, keep my ears open, and try to turn the situation in my favor. Actually, the situation had already turned. At the very least, I'd been legally declared a Morozov and was going to get the perks that came with being the heir.

"Why don't you tell me instead what's new back in Morshansk?" I said, knowing that I'd drawn out that pause a little too long, which would make me look bad in front of my friend. "How are things? How's school going? How are the guys doing?"

"Hmm, how could things be going for us?" said Godimir. "What could possibly be new with us? Everything's just the way it was. Wait, no!" He went still, looked at me, and said in a serious tone: "This one commoner in Class B suddenly turned out to be the heir to the dead Morozov bloodline. He faked his own death and hid from hitmen."

"Oh, shut up!" I said as Godimir laughed cheerfully. "Your report is outdated, that's old news already."

"Sure, maybe it's really outdated. But it was the pebble that brought an avalanche of interesting incidents down with it."

"And what were these interesting incidents, may I ask?"

"Oooh!" Godimir smiled with satisfaction. "All kinds of stuff happened! For instance, it'd take me more than a week to describe how much the students, teachers, and school leadership all freaked out when they found out your real name and status. It got a couple times worse when that video popped up online of you and your adventures! That was really something! Cinematic gold! The guys and I rewatched it a few times! I especially liked how you blew up a couple warriors with techs I've never seen before, then burned a mage with some weird fire, and then shot at him with those crazy little fireballs! What the heck was that?"

"It's a homebrew tech," I answered somberly. "You should tell me about school instead."

"Homebrew? Okay, fine, but I wanted to ask you to teach me how to do it." Godimir got a little sad, and after a bit, he added: "As for school... I just remembered that a lot of people were wringing their hands and moaning because they treated you badly. Girls were whining that they missed their chance, that they felt your hidden aura, but they were too shy to admit it. Now you're the most popular guy at the school. More popular than me, even!" Godimir smirked. "A couple of people, like that Rodnikov guy, have absolutely no idea what to do now. They know you have a good memory and you could come back and get even for how discourteously they treated you."

"I do have a pretty good memory, but I really don't want to do anything bad to people because of my status. Although a couple of them could use a lesson so they don't do it again. I've shaken them off, of course, but someone else could wind up in my place."

"Oh, yeah," Godimir remembered just then. "Your class has a new lead teacher."

"That was poorly timed," I said. "I would've liked to see her flip out when I come back to school."

"You're planning to come back?" said Godimir, surprised and overjoyed. "I thought you were staying here!"

"No way." I shook my head. "I somehow managed to get used to Morshansk in the time I was there. Father said that he'll let me go to school there if that's what I want."

"Cool!" said Godimir happily. "Are you going to move to Class A with me?"

"No," I said. "Why don't you move to my class instead? I don't want to look like a snob. My class suits me. Or, let's go back to our first lead teacher, just in general. Why did they replace her?"

"I don't know — all I heard was that on one lovely day she showed up to school and handed in her resignation of her own volition. But the principal managed to convince her. I know other teachers wanted to do the same thing, but the principal intimidated them by saying that if they left, they'd never get a job at another branch of the Imperial Academy. And they pay good salaries. Nowhere else higher."

"So *they* remember how badly they tried to beat me down!" I coughed with satisfaction. "Well, then, I'll let them stew over that and wonder what my reaction will be."

"Yeah," said Godimir. "Incidentally, after you

left, it set off the rivalry between the classes. Your classmates are saying that since there was a prince in their class, it means Class B is much better, 'cause all Class A has is the commandant's son."

"Oh, come on!" I started to laugh. "Only that!"

I heard someone approaching us and turned. Theodore was standing on the threshold.

"And what are we doing here?" he asked, chuckling. "Hiding from the guests?"

"Theodore," I said, "Allow me to introduce my friend Godimir Ogneyer."

Theodore extended his hand, shook Godimir's, and said:

"So you'd be from Morshansk, I take it?"

"Yes," said Godimir.

"I've heard of you." Theodore smiled and turned to me. "A new polonaise will be starting soon, and most of the guests will start to look for things to do based on their interests, so you should come downstairs and get to work."

I nodded.

"Aw, c'mon, let's talk for at least a little longer!" said Godimir.

"I can't," I said. "Let's get out of here. The hall of Préférence-players awaits us."

* * *

Godimir, understanding that I couldn't devote much time to him because I had to pay attention to the other guests, went back to his family, getting a promise from me beforehand that I wouldn't forget about him and that I'd come over to him and chat.

When I got to the hall where people were playing cards, men of all different ages were already gathered there.

They were sitting around special tables and starting their games with pleasure.

Wandering along the hall from one table to another, I made sure none of the guests were bored and even talked to a few of them for a bit. By and large, none of them really cared about me. They were all interested in the idea itself that they could talk to the Morozov heir — it was the kind of thing they could tell their friends about. To my surprise, there were quite a few women in the hall. Some of them were curiously following the men's games; others were sitting at the tables.

After watching a few interesting rounds of Préférence and poker, I went with a clean conscience to the next room, where I was already expected.

I found a lot of children of varying ages there. More specifically, the ones who belonged to a certain age category — that is, boys and girls thirteen and under. The older kids were already trying to prove themselves in the dancers' world.

The kids here were divided into small groups based on their interests. They were all sitting here and there, chatting merrily. Both the boys and the girls were having lively conversations.

Fastening a polite smile onto my face, I headed first towards the closest group of girls, who seemed embarrassed at my approach. "Good evening, ladies," I said quietly. "How are you enjoying the party?"

I went from one group of kids to another and managed to get acquainted with everyone. I figured that would come in handy in the future. I talked with my sisters, who were in here, for a bit, then headed back to the grand hall — I had to make an appearance there too.

No dice, as it turned out — in the main hall, I was caught by an already-inebriated Ignatius and the members of his small friend group.

"Oh! Here he is!" said Ignatius, gesturing in my direction. I was quickly surrounded on all sides.

Everyone approaching me was holding a champagne glass.

Was it really possible to get wasted on just champagne? Or was it not just that?

"He's so tiny, Iggy," said one of the guys, narrowing his eyes. "Are you sure that's the guy from the video? Something doesn't add up."

Iggy? I was surprised. Very few could allow themselves that kind of familiarity. Especially in front of others. Who was this, his best friend? My brother may have been human garbage, but he had great self-esteem. Just look at how he was pursing his lips.

"Whom do I have the honor of meeting?" I asked politely, trying to remember the names of everyone present. As it turned out, I was seeing most of them for the first time. But not all of them. Now I understood why my earpiece had stopped working.

"What a stuck-up brother you have!" said one of the young ladies, grinning and winking at me. "We're just friends of Ignatius."

That's not what I'm seeing, I hemmed internally. Ignatius, realizing the conversation could go the wrong direction, quickly introduced everyone around him.

"We need your help answering something," said Stephen Krilitza, the guy who'd called me "tiny" and turned out to be the prankster who loved disconnecting microphones.

"I'm all ears." I made it obvious how ready I was.

I was curious what scheme they'd cooked up.

"We were arguing about whether that was really you in that video. Because what the video showed is really improbable. I don't know anyone who could use spiritual energy like that at your age. So I think those shots were staged. Why don't you dispel our doubt?"

I glanced around at my brother's friends, who were expecting an answer, and said coldly:

"So do you think the head of the Temnikov family is a liar? I'll tell him you said that, Marquis."

"What? No, don't!" said Stephen in surprise. "I just wanted to know if you could repeat the move you showed off in the video online."

"So you're accusing the Temnikov family of being liars? Did I understand that right?" I wasn't going to let myself fall into this trap. Nothing doing, putting on a show for them and who knew who else.

"No," Stephen replied, and with a prideful tone he said, "Answer us like a man! What are you always hiding behind your father for? You won't be able to do that forever! You understand?"

What, do they not have any other source of entertainment? I thought in irritation, but I answered him calmly.

"I don't understand what you're talking about at all."

"The kid knows how to get out of answering a question," said Stephen with a smirk, looking at his friends. "Then, perhaps, as the host of today's festivities, you'll demonstrate a bit of your knowledge for us?"

"I'm certainly not burning with the desire to show it off to just anyone," I answered him, and when dissatisfaction appeared on all their faces, I added: "But, as a hospitable host, I can show you a little something."

All their faces immediately took on good-natured expressions.

"Such as?" asked one of the young women right away, coming closer to me.

"A Power Whirlwind, for instance," I said, raising my hand palm-up and doing the tech.

"What the hell is that?" One of the guys expressed his doubts after a bit. "It could just be an ordinary light or something from the Morozov magic, but that's no spiritual energy. Let's go out to the courtyard instead and test your shield's durability."

Nah, no thanks, I thought, and grabbed his glass out of his hands with what I liked to call my *Star Wars* villain tech.

It still sapped up a lot of energy, but it allowed me to demonstrate my capabilities without wreaking much havoc.

After returning the glasses, I formed a small "flame-thrower" fireball in my hand, and after a few moments I stopped feeding it energy.

"That's still nothing to write home about," said Stephen with a shrewd smirk. "Maybe the courtyard and shield thing is better."

"No thank you, I have many other guests to speak to besides you."

I didn't manage to end the conversation diplomatically.

My instincts were trying to throw my body to the side, but there were people standing there, so I had nothing left to do but put up a Spirit Shield. A very weak wind-element spell smashed into it.

"Is this an attack on a member of the Temnikov family?" I said coldly, looking Stephen in the eyes.

"It was just a joke!" he brushed me off. "A test."

"It was disrespect that was just shown to you personally," I snapped at Ignatius. I nodded at Yamashita, who'd appeared nearby, giving him the go-ahead to escort a particularly rowdy guest out.

I was in for a rough night. All this before dinner!

Chapter 4

I WAS IN THE SPECIAL HALL for magic training, meditating and once again trying to feel magical energy within myself. To my great disappointment, I hadn't been able to do it since that one time in the warriors' hall. What really frustrated me was that I couldn't understand the essential source of the problem either.

After weeks of fruitless exercises, I'd been forced to turn to Professor Petius, so that he could give me one of his famous explanations as to where I was making a mistake. It turned out that the old and deeply revered mage didn't want to bother himself with teaching a neophyte, even if said neophyte was the prince's son, so he'd proposed an alternative to me.

"It wouldn't be entirely too rational to work with you personally in the beginning stages," he'd explained, taking an unhurried sip of his green tea as his servant walked up to him to tell him something.

Yeah, so the rational thing to do was inhale tea all day! He was busy beyond belief! Running to and fro and doing this and that, I grumbled internally, although I understood why Professor Petius didn't want to deal with such trivialities.

With a cautious knock on the door, a young man with a small, clean staff in his hand came into Petius's study.

"Here, Ivan, this is your teacher for the beginning stages," said Petius, gesturing to the mage. "His name is Simmeron. Master-rank."

Was that so! I started to recall the mage hierarchy. Like warriors, they had seven ranks. First Acolyte, then Bachelor, then Master, then Doctor, then Scholar, and the final levels of mastery were Professor and Archmage. If this Simmeron guy was only a Master, did that mean I was being pawned off on someone fresh out of college? What could he possibly teach me?

Professor Petius clearly didn't like my knitted brows and screwed-up face. Either that or he wasn't convinced that a preteen princeling could work independently.

"He's the best graduate the regional academy has had in the past several years," explained Professor Petius. "Simmeron has an excellent knowledge of everything that a young mage needs as a foundation, and in this situation I believe that his youth will be an indisputable advantage. It wasn't so long ago, compared to me, that he himself was taking his first steps in the mastery of magic, so he can help you better than anyone. In addition, when one of the more experienced mages' availability opens up, we'll swap him in."

"All right," I decided after a bit, noticing some dissatisfaction flashing across Simmeron's face for a moment. "I trust your decision."

"In that case, go now into the mages' hall," said Petius. "Simmeron and I will discuss the curriculum for your education."

Seemed like Simmeron was about to get it real bad for that grimace, I thought. Too bad Ruslan had refused to help me. His excuse for refusing was that he was busy, and that the first thing I had to do was meditate on my own and try to feel my magical core.

Though Simmeron really did turn out to be fairly knowledgeable and constantly gave me short, interesting lectures during the breaks between meditation sessions, I didn't have any breakthroughs in my magic.

Maybe it was because I couldn't fully relax with him in the room. At certain moments I started to feel as if he was watching me with superiority, which often turned into something visibly hostile.

It annoyed me that despite my complete lack of results, my teacher seemed fully pleased with life, and after his visit to Professor Petius's study he'd come out even more encouraged.

Either I was doing something wrong or Simmeron didn't want to help me. I didn't believe for the life of me that mages had no quicker way to sense their magical cores. Being ordered to "meditate and try to feel your magic" wasn't getting me anywhere.

"First things first, before studying magical arts, you have to learn how to sense magical energy." Simmeron repeated the platitude for the umpteenth time, and his eyes once again glittered with superiority.

"That's what I did for a few days straight," I answered, irritated. "Until I discovered that nothing was working. Then I went to Professor Petius, who said that I had to do the same thing! But why should I keep doing it if it's not getting me results?"

"A few days?" Simmeron smirked and gave me a highly skeptical look. "My classmates and I spent anywhere between six months and two years on this, kid, and you've decided you can get it done that quickly?"

At first I wanted to make Simmeron stop being so cavalier in how he addressed me, but my Earthly self rebelled, begging Ivan not to be a barbarian and let an elder talk to me how he pleased. Back there, after all, I'd been no sort of nobility — in my own world, I'd been an ordinary person. Simmeron, however, had come to the conclusion that he could do whatever he wanted, so he'd stopped holding his tongue.

Well, then! That was a great life lesson, I thought gloomily.

"First off, I did that self-induced initiation." I

frowned in response to Simmeron's disdainful tone. "And second, I'm a hereditary mage with strong blood. Based on what I've studied in the books in the library, my magical talent should be more clearly expressed than in others."

My words seemed to strike a nerve. A dark, not very nice one. He looked at me with hatred, then tried to calm down, but he didn't manage it.

"You just got lucky with the initiation," he said articulately, his face turning red. "Ordinary mages aren't any worse than hereditary mages. The only thing that really makes hereditary mages different is their will, which lets them cast spells without staffs. But that's only in the beginning stage! After that, many ordinary mages don't need staffs either!"

Hoo boy, he was seeing red! I was surprised at how stormy his reaction had been. He wasn't even shy about looking at me with those eyes!

After a short pause, Simmeron started lecturing me again on a topic I was familiar with. I knew a bunch of stuff in it already, and I'd heard a bunch of it multiple times, but I didn't break my focus — maybe I'd catch wind of some brilliant idea.

According to Simmeron, magic was everywhere. It was in nature, in animals, in people, in the earth, and even in the air. Truly, in every atom! The other thing was that different elements could carry different amounts of energy. So, for instance, there was very little magic in the air, but there was a lot more magic in stones. To the point, that energy also existed in people, and they'd learned to use it in two ways.

The first was the path of the warrior. The way fighters learned how to transform the magical energy of their bodies into Shiki-Cho and then impact the world around them by using techs. Roughly speaking, the magical energy inside of human bodies was Shiki-Cho.

The second was the path of the mage. This was when people learned how to sense magical energy first inside themselves, then in the world around them. Once they could sense outside energy, they could start letting it pass through their bodies. After that, it changed — it adapted to the person and accumulated in the body, shortly thereafter turning into a magical core.

It was believed that because of their gifted ancestors, hereditary mages had great quantities of magical energy in their prospects, but this was only true if they had a good work ethic and diligence.

"If everyone has magic in them to begin with, why can some people become mages but others can't?" I wanted to understand that. "And just in general, how can anyone determine whether someone's fit for the study of magic or not?"

"It's all about the amount of magic in the body, and the body's ability to accumulate it without the mage's conscious desire. If enough energy accumulates, and it increases on its own, that person is a mage. That's what the special ritual determines. The amount of magical energy and its accumulation process.”

“I see.” I nodded. “Then I have another question. If Shiki-Cho and magical energy are primordially the same thing, does that mean the spiritual energy core is in the same place as the magical core?”

Simmeron rolled his eyes.

“Demons’ asses!” he cursed. “I just explained all this to you like you were five! Magical energy exists in the human body! It exists in every element! And there’s magical energy that we take from the surrounding world. When it’s inside us, it changes and becomes something else, so that it can turn into a source!”

To say that the tone Simmeron was using with me was ticking me off would be an understatement.

What did I do to him? How had I offended him? Why was he talking to me like this? How dare he?

With incredible strength, I kept it together and stopped myself from putting the young mage in his place. I didn’t start unraveling. In any case, Simmeron had explained to me what I hadn’t been able to understand for so long. And somehow, my self-respect wouldn’t let me put him in his place with a reminder that I was from a princely bloodline and he wasn’t. What good was it to boast of my ancestors when I myself hadn’t had any success yet? No, that just wasn’t for me. If I decided to put him in his place, I’d do it with my own strength. I could do it.

“So that means during that attempt on

George's life, when I made the ice globe, my body accumulated enough energy and my magical core formed?" I asked as calmly as possible. "Or are all mages capable of such powerful spells at their initiation? How did I manage the ice globe in general? I didn't intend to do anything like that."

"It was most likely your self-preservation instincts at work," replied Simmeron, a little more calmly but still enunciating every word. "For young mages who've undergone their initiation, things like that happen fairly often. It's believed that in times of mortal danger, they want to survive, and their magic responds to that earnest and well-understood desire. I think that at that moment, you didn't have much spiritual energy in your body, but your magical reserve was filled to the brim, since your body had been consistently accumulating it inside itself. So then your self-induced initiation happened."

"In that case, there must be a lot of magical energy inside me now! Because the core formed, and it's bound to be accumulating energy."

"Of course it must be! And there must also be a magical core! That's what you're supposed to be searching for inside yourself while you're meditating! To be sensing! What, have you never done this before? A hereditary mage, demons' sakes!"

"Yeah, that's what I've been trying to do this whole time! What difference does it make to me if I'm trying to feel my magical core or just magical energy?" I said, feeling my muscles twitch. "I needed all this information to be organized at least somehow and given to me in the first lesson! Not now! If you're a teacher, then teach! What's actually happening is I'm somehow expected to extrapolate information from who knows where!"

Simmeron's ears turned red, and he leapt to his feet.

"Because you need to get there yourself, that's why! To show your potential! Not to expect someone to hand it to you on a silver platter with a gold lining! So you can announce, 'Oh, I'm a hereditary mage, so everything comes to me easier than to others! I induced my own initiation, I was able to sense my energy right away! I'm not like those unlucky peasants!'"

So that was it. That was what was offending him, I realized. That he had a noble kid in front of him. A hereditary mage of the nth generation — it must mean I considered myself stronger than him and my future brighter by birthright. Was he crazy? Serving any of the important bloodlines with this kind of attitude? *I despise you, but I'm getting paid for it?* Something about his words differed from the generally accepted norms. Who'd hired a guy like this, anyway? Why was security unbothered? Why didn't they see a damn thing?

"My friend, you aren't purposely trying to get in the way of my education, are you?" I asked out of the blue. "I did manage the self-induced initiation, after all! That means I should be able to sense my core faster!"

"How dare you!" Simmeron exploded.

"Oh, I dare!" I replied. "What can you give me,

besides instructions to sit in the lotus pose and try to sense magical energy inside myself?"

"That's something you have to spend a long time learning!" He got even redder and glared at me with obvious anger. "Not any upstart can just swoop in and have the skill! You need to be taught a good lesson for accusations like that!"

When he said the last sentence, Simmeron's face lit up a little.

"Oh, that's right, Professor Petius said that I'd have to set you straight if necessary! You're unruly and undisciplined. I have the right!"

"Is that so?" I said, getting out of my lotus pose and standing up. "And how, may I ask, are you supposed to set me straight?"

Simmeron lit a small fireball on the pommel of his staff and gave me a condescending look.

"My rank is Master, and I know a lot of offensive magic spells for teaching lessons to little milksops."

"My rank is Soldier," I replied in the same tone. "I know nothing but offensive techs. And I deeply regret the death of my good relationship to you — you don't deserve it."

Simmeron laughed.

"Only weaklings and failures take the path of the warrior! Their bodies can't even store up energy! They're nothing against the strength of a mage!"

"Nothing at all, against a strong mage," I said, and a whirlwind of Shiki-Cho began to shine in my hand. "But you can't do anything without your staff."

I was extremely annoyed at my lack of success in the field of magical arts, and Simmeron was openly provoking me, so I decided not to hit the brakes on another fight. I'd give him a good dressing-down and hand him off to Father. Otherwise this revenge-minded man might decide to show these hereditary mages what was what and attack Anna or Maria. The two of them wouldn't dare to say a word against an adult mage.

Simmeron didn't wait — he struck the first blow. Dodging his fireball, I filled my body with spiritual energy and rushed forward.

My Power Whirlwind shattered his magical shield, and I threw him back a few yards and planted him right against the wall.

Weakling! I cursed internally, running up to my groaning, confused "teacher." What, had he really not expected anything serious from a warrior? He'd seen that video of my initiation! Was there an ounce of logic in his brain?

Simmeron looked at me with dazed eyes, and suddenly some kind of spell ripped out of his staff.

Oh, you S.O.B.! I thought, jumping to the side and putting up my Spirit Shield, which tanked the second spell. He'd come to his senses!

For the next minute, all I did was dodge spells, studying Simmeron's magical battling technique and determining the maximum speed at which he could cast spells.

If I could tear his staff right out of his hands, I wouldn't be running around in circles through the hall like a hamster on its wheel!

I let him come to his senses a bit and get a firm sense of his superiority, then sped up abruptly and hit him with a powerful Battering Ram, breaking through his newly erected shield.

A kick to the right arm, and the staff flew to the side. Another kick, and Simmeron was on the ground.

After he'd gotten a few weak clips to the ear, he stopped trying to get up and covered his head with his arms.

I gave him a couple dozen more cuffs to let off some steam.

"Listen to me, you snake!" I hissed in his ear. "If you dare to speak to me with that tone again, I'll mutilate you!"

He went silent — didn't move and didn't try to raise his head.

"I don't hear an answer!" I roared, kicking him a couple more times.

"Understood, understood!" he cried.

"Great!" I said to him. "Stand up!" I commanded.

After he'd gotten up and lowered his head, I spoke quietly.

"Now do you realize that even as a Master of magic, you can't do anything against an ordinary warrior?" I paused briefly, then bellowed again out of some strange inspiration: "Now tell me what I need to do to sense my magical core! What are you hiding from me?"

"Nothing," replied Simmeron, shielding himself with his arms — he'd stood up without his staff and was completely defenseless.

A kick to the chest hurled him to the ground, stopping his attempt to make a break for the door.

Grabbing Simmeron by his long hair, I shook him real good a few times and decided to use Theophane's method — accuse the person I was interrogating of something so awful that he'd swear his innocence and possibly tell me something in an attempt to preserve his life and his health.

"Who ordered you to sabotage me instead of teaching me?" I yelled in his ear, playing the psycho. "WHO?"

Beaten to the depths of his soul, Simmeron looked at my bloodshot eyes and wild gaze. Clearly remembering the video of the people I'd killed, he blanched.

"*WHO?*" I screamed in his ear, shaking him and forming a very visible Power Whirlwind at the same time. "*WHO?*"

"Petius," mumbled Simmeron, looking at me with glassy eyes. "Professor Petius."

What in the Dwarf Saws? I thought in surprise. I didn't stop shaking Simmeron. I really hadn't expected something like this! I'd just wanted to know if this guy, who was harboring this resentment towards hereditary mages, was really the one getting in the way of my progress. And if there was another way to sense my magical core. As it turned out, we had some breaking news here!

"*WHO?*" I growled, looking him in the eyes. "Do you take me for a fool? The professor could never do something like that!"

I threw Simmeron a couple yards and reappeared right next to him.

"You're lying!" I said to him threateningly.

"No! Not at all!" he babbled. "It was Petius, sir! All of this is his fault, sir! He said that I shouldn't give you straight answers! And that I should interfere with your ability to sense your core! But that was hardly necessary — it's impossible to sense magical energy so early on!"

He'd started calling me "sir" — that was progress, I thought, and shook him up good again.

"What were your instructions?"

"To observe! Only to observe and report!" he answered, shielding himself with his hands. "That was all. And not to help! Not to sabotage you, but not to help you either!"

"Why did he do that?" I asked, looking him in the eyes.

Simmeron went silent.

"If you don't tell me why he needed to do that right now, I'll stick your staff where the sun don't shine, and you can cast your spells from there! You understand me?"

Simmeron kept silent for a bit longer, then said quietly:

"I lied."

"What?" I didn't understand.

"I lied about the professor making me do it," said Simmeron, wiping up the blood coming out of his nose. "I was just trying to hide my hatred for hereditary mages. Everything comes to you just like that."

Well, well. I smirked. Clearly, he was more afraid of Petius than he was of me — he was trying to cover for him now.

"You lied... that means..." I said quietly, grabbing him by the throat and starting to choke him.

An hour of this heart-to-heart communication yielded nothing. Simmeron kept repeating that everything that had happened was purely of his initiative. That he'd hated hereditary mages ever since he was a child and wanted to do them a bad turn. To show that they weren't as powerful and skilled as they tried to act.

What kind of madhouse are we running here? I thought, irritated. Who hired someone like this, and to what end would the much-respected Petius have appointed him specifically as my teacher?

"Tell me, who hired you?"

"Princess Galina," replied Simmeron. "The head of the family's wife."

Who would've doubted it? I spat. Although I also wanted to understand what role Professor Petius played in all this.

I had no intention of putting the brakes on this situation with the teacher who'd been thrust upon me. So I went to Father right away, dragging Simmeron along behind me.

Bursting into his study, I said a few choice words to my negligent progenitor and created a nice little scandal. Everyone was there — the head of security, Petius, and Father. I didn't say a word about suspecting the professor in this sabotage. I stressed the fact that some psycho who hated the nobility had been pawned off on me. After that, I managed to get myself a new teacher and a sooner departure date for Morshansk.

Father agreed to everything, but he said that he'd only let me leave the estate after I'd attended the next upcoming ball, since according to the etiquette I was obligated to accept a few invitations in return from the guests who'd come to ours.

I agreed.

Despite the positive outcome of our conversation and the shortened wait for my return to Morshansk, I left the study with a very discontented face.

Someone was clearly playing some kind of strange, unintelligible game with me, and I didn't know the rules. If someone needed me not to make progress in the magical arts for a while, then it would be a real pain, but I needed to take this leap with my studies and throw a wrench in those plans. Otherwise everything could end very badly.

As to who would need that and why, however, I had absolutely no idea. So I decided not to stew about it too much yet and resolve my problems as they came up. The first thing I needed to do was sense my magical core.

Returning to the training hall and brushing aside my unwanted thoughts, I switched over to my internal world and stared at the slab of ice glimmering in midair.

After standing there for a bit, I got closer, touched the ice slab, closed my eyes, and once again tried to call forth the same state I'd been in during the attack on George.

I'd felt pain and weakness, which had changed after a little while into fear, anger, and decisiveness. Then they'd yielded to excitement and satisfaction. Then had come the pain...

I'd felt it pulsating in my wounds when a few simultaneous spells had shattered my Spirit Shield. Terrible exhaustion had been steadily accumulating in my body. I'd had almost no Shiki-Cho left.

At that moment, I'd felt a great desire to live! I'd wanted to defend myself from all the deadly spells...

That was it! I realized that my guess would most likely turn out to be right. I'd only managed to make my magical energy work after I'd almost completely run out of Shiki-Cho! My body had simply had no other choice, and it had stretched its limits to that energy I had inside me. I'd been told about this — it would be easier for me to feel my core if there wasn't any spiritual energy left to get in the way of my magical circulation.

Leaving my meditation, I turned my face towards the self-healing dummy standing at a distance from me, and I used both hands to hit it with my "flamethrower" tech...

I finished emptying my reserve of spiritual energy and, with satisfaction, got to work...

Fortune smiled on me on the second day of my urgent search.

Once again free of Shiki-Cho, I was sitting in

my meditation pose and trying to bring back the feelings from the attack on George.

To my surprise, it worked almost immediately. After that, it seemed like I felt something vaguely familiar in my solar plexus.

Thump, thump, thump. My magical core pulsed in time with my heart. *Thump, thump, thump.*

There it is! That's how to do it! I thought, over-joyed — and I lost the feeling. Now it would be eas-ier! Now I knew where the source was, and that I could tune into it with the help of my heartbeat!

I spent a few minutes getting used to the unu-sual feeling, trying to remember it as best I could, then slowly opened my eyes.

The second step of mastering the core was done, I thought, deciding not to get too excited yet. Now I could sense it with my eyes open too. I could move on to the third step.

My attempt to stand up led to me losing con-centration at a certain point, and the feeling of my core went away again. I had to sit down on the ground in annoyance.

Well, then! Time to start over!

My independent training gave me better re-sults each time. I'd started off being able to sense my magical energy after only a few minutes of meditation, and by the end of the day I'd learned how to do it standing up with my eyes open. I didn't have much success trying to sense my mag-ical core while moving, and when I had a lot of spiritual energy in my body — even sitting down — I couldn't feel anything. But giving up was against my nature. Because I knew that diligence and hard work weathered all obstacles.

I got sent a new teacher, Doctor-rank, pretty efficiently. After only a day.

How quickly Petius was settling all my problems, I thought skeptically as I looked at the new guy. I wondered — if this one turned out to have issues, would he send me a Scholar?

The Doctor, noticing the characteristic magical "noise" coming from me, was clearly surprised by my successes. After giving me a little test, he said that he'd be gone for a short while and quickly left the room.

I couldn't resist following him, and I discovered that he was reporting my successes to Professor Petius. That meant there really was some sort of conspiracy against me.

I managed to get back to the training hall faster than the nervous Doctor, so he knew nothing of my unplanned leave of absence. He had a determined look on his face, and he immediately started dumping loads of interesting theory on me.

What had they decided — that if I started wasting time on theory, I'd stop paying attention to my magical senses? Fools! I could do it constantly! While I was eating, while I was showering, while I was out in the garden with the girls, and... while I was supposed to be sleeping. It wasn't for nothing that Theophane had taught me to make use of meditation in place of sleep. A few hours and I was good as new!

However, the lessons turned out to be extremely educational and interesting.

"A mage needs four things to cast a spell. Strength, desire, will, and control," said the Doctor drily, watching carefully to see if I was listening or not. "Strength refers to magical talent, which makes you what you are, and energy, which we expend when casting spells. Desire is what defines our needs — what we want to do with our strength. Will allows us to use our strength to accomplish our desires."

He stopped talking, so I had to prompt him.

"And control? What's that needed for?"

"Control is what mages create their spells with."

"How's that?" I didn't understand.

"Let me explain. For instance, high-rank mages can cast fireball spells with their strength, desire, and will. Those are, of course, primitive and weak spells, but still. Whereas if the same mage wants to give the fireball fixed parameters — speed, temperature, and all that — then control must be used."

"I see," I answered after a bit. "So ritual pentagrams and things like that — those are mages' tools, so that means they're 'control?'"

"Exactly." He nodded. "Astute observation."

"You could've just called it a tool," I muttered.

"That's a little too peasant-like," said the Doctor. "'Control' sounds better."

I rolled my eyes and said:

"What about spells? How are they formed? With what tools?"

"With runes," replied the Doctor. "More precisely, different sequences of runes, but that's if you're talking about simple spells. Complex spells are inaccessible to you for now."

After digesting that information, I asked my next question.

"Why was I able to create that ice globe while George was being attacked? I didn't know about control then, and I didn't direct my will towards using magical energy. How did that happen?"

"Your self-preservation instinct." The Doctor repeated Simmeron's words. "When your body found itself in front of a fatal threat, it took your desire to survive at any cost and reached all the way to the strength inside you. That's all."

"And why did the spell take on that particular form? Not a defensive wall, not something like a magical shield, but specifically a globe of ice?"

The Doctor smiled.

"Because you're a Morozov."

"Great answer!" I gave him a thumbs-up and made a sour face. "That's like saying it's raining because it's autumn. I don't need the obvious stuff, I need the nitty-gritty! Of course it's logical that since I'm a Morozov, my spells will be linked to ice and the cold and so on and so forth. But I'd like to know why I, a Morozov, created a spell like that!"

"I understand. In your situation, something called your 'family gift' was in play. I'll put it like this, it's a predisposition that any member of a family of hereditary mages has to a particular field of magic. So for spells like that, hereditary mages don't need control — desire and will are enough for them. In this case, very little energy from the source is consumed.

"Ordinary ages needs special staffs to cast any spell. And they have to use control, too."

"That is, they need staffs to amplify their will?" I confirmed.

"It's more likely that staffs help them focus their will in using their control. Well, and it's a bonus that you can suspend a few spells within a staff, so you can use them later once you've used up all your strength."

After absorbing what he'd said, I clarified:

"So does that mean my success with my family magic is completely tied to my will? And that I don't need control to use it?"

"That's right," said the Doctor, very cautiously for some reason. "But in order to use your inherited magic, you have to practice general magic. And before that, you absolutely need to learn how to absorb energy from the world around you and turn it into more complex things."

Uh-huh, of course, I thought skeptically. As my teacher's reservations showed, the first thing I needed to do was just to learn how to use my family magic. Even something simple would be enough for starters. After all, my core could still handle the energy absorption without my doing anything. If it seemed like my paranoia was running away with me now, then good. I'd learn how to use my family magic and get a grasp of accumulating energy later.

"Thank you for the fascinating lesson," I said to the Doctor, getting up. "It was extremely educational, but now I want to get some rest. I only just realized that all these magic lessons are really tiring me out somehow. There was that Simmeron guy, too..."

"Yes, of course." The Doctor nodded with obvious relief. "You need to give yourself some breaks so you don't burn out. That's an important principle for any smart mage."

"Nothing but rest for now," I said cunningly, looking him in the eyes. "I'll be a very smart mage."

Chapter 5

AT THE FATED HOUR, our family — more precisely, the younger half of it and two adults I didn't trust in the slightest — got into a comfortable private helicopter and headed off to a ceremonial ball at the estate of Prince Beregov.

Up till then I'd never flown in one of those — I had worked near the North Pole, but I'd never had to encounter helicopters like this one.

The first thing that caught my eye was the vehicle's sort of unobtrusive luxury. It looked pretty up-to-date technologically, roomy, immaculately clean, and expensive.

After I went inside the coach, this impression grew stronger. I was delighted by the comfortable leather armchairs, their heated massage features, and the helicopter's fairly large capacity, which let me not feel like I was sitting in a tin can. One surprising discovery that made me practically fall in love with this mode of transportation was the unnatural silence prevailing throughout the coach.

In my attempt to solve this fascinating riddle, I made dozens of different guesses that could dispel my bewilderment as to how such noise resistance had been achieved in the coach. Only after a few minutes of reflection did I think to look around the helicopter with my Eyes of the Wolf tech.

The bright symbols that jumped out at me from the helicopter's paneling burned my eyes. The helicopter was glowing like a Christmas tree!

Well, of course! Elementary, my dear Ivan! It was all magic! Put silence amulets in the coach, and nothing would bother the passengers. They could fly in comfort.

Now I found the purpose of the other amulets and runes interesting too. They were most likely a defensive thing, since both the Temnikov prince and the two fighter helicopters accompanying us throughout the flight were fully capable of substituting for heavy weaponry.

The escort helicopters looked something like a cross between Soviet Mi-24s (the main bodies looked very similar, by quite a lot!) and American Apache helicopters, if the latter were to increase their ammunition capacity no less than twofold.

It was a very comfortable flight. I read an electronic etiquette handbook that the vigilant Elvira had dumped on me on my phone. I felt no need to relieve myself either, thanks to Ruslan's advance warning that we'd need to fly for about two hours and weren't planning to make any stops.

We were in the air for a pretty long time, about an hour and a half. The family that had invited us to this party didn't live that far away — in the neighboring region.

After we landed safely, I opened the GPS on my phone so I could find out how far we'd flown, and I felt incomparable surprise. It turned out that during our flight, we'd gone something in the order of three hundred miles! Not bad if you considered it almost hadn't felt like we were going so fast.

I couldn't even remember if helicopters on my Earth could achieve such feats. Not yet, it seemed.

"Don't be glued to your phone, they're waiting for us already," said Ruslan, walking past me. I hurried to hide it in my jacket pocket and went on ahead so I could catch up with the rest of the family as they headed forward quickly.

It also turned out that Father was putting up a special shield that was supposed to protect the ladies of the family's hairdos from gusts of wind created by the helicopter's propellers, as well as protecting our suits from any dust that got stirred up. So my fairly expensive tuxedo could have paid dearly for my tardiness.

All the better that Theodore and Ignatius had left for the capital after the ball at our estate, I thought for the dozenth time, glad that Ignatius wouldn't be spoiling my evening by being pretentious and demanding I demonstrate my family magic.

A servant personally escorted us through a beautiful garden to the main entrance to the estate, which was just as imposing and historic as ours.

Our hosts — a fairly elderly couple, both somewhere around seventy — were already waiting to greet us in the hall.

The husband was a tall, gray-haired man with his long hair in a combover, dressed in an austere black tailcoat. The wife was a short, plump woman in a beautiful dark green dress. She looked pretty good for her age and had a truly lovely smile.

Their healer and their dentist were clearly doing good work, I thought for the second time as I looked at the Beregovs — I remembered them well from the Temnikov ball. Possibly because they'd been among the first to arrive.

"It is an honor," said Prince Beregov very drily, pursing his lips and proudly raising his triangular chin.

"Oh, come now," Father answered, lowering his head in a polite bow. "We're the ones who are happy to be here in your hospitable home..."

While he cooed like a nightingale, I paid attention to how our hostess was looking at us. Her smiling eyes seemed very warm, kind, and welcoming, but all she had to do was look at Galina and her smile slowly faded.

How interesting, I thought, rubbing my hands in satisfaction. So Galina wasn't entirely in the good graces of some noble houses. I didn't know how yet, but I figured I could use that. Now I had to pay attention to how other important nobles would treat her.

The exchange of courtesies finally came to a close, and we headed for the great hall, which was a little smaller than ours. I had to admit, I was a little tired after trailing behind the older generation for about half an hour. Father once again headed towards someone he knew, next to whom we lingered for a little while.

I realized it wasn't a coincidence when I saw a fairly pretty fifteen-year-old girl whose dress went really smartly with Ruslan's suit.

Ruslan, it seemed, also noticed this. He even got all serious and started shooting condescending looks at me — I was supposed to go to the children's sitting room soon. He was older, after all, and could amuse himself on the same footing as the adults!

I get it! I thought as I glanced from one teenager to the other.

So they wanted to set Ruslan up with this charming lady. Hmm... they really didn't look bad together. Just had to give them time to dance a bit and get to know each other better. Then it would be clear.

I immediately remembered the ball at the Temnikov estate, where I'd had to open the final round of dances after dinner. My dancing partner had been a nice little girl from a marquis family who'd danced just splendidly.

I'd known what was waiting for me, of course, so I'd spent a very long time preparing for it.

Thanks to Elvira's vigilant tutelage, I'd perfected the skills I had, and I'd managed not to make a single mistake under hundreds of watchful eyes.

While the adults talked and Ruslan exchanged furtive glances with his mysterious dame, my sisters and I were invited to go to the sitting room prepared specially for us.

Father allowed it, and after just a few minutes we found ourselves in a room filled with a lot of children of different ages. Looking around at everyone with an attentive gaze, I noted with satisfaction that I'd been able to get acquainted with most of the people here at our ball.

That meant today wouldn't be as rough as I might've thought.

Despite not feeling particularly inspired to talk with the children, I tried to be an attentive, interesting, and pleasant conversationalist. I knew full well that the young nobles here wouldn't be children forever. In ten years, I might have to settle some kind of business affairs with many of them. And you remember the people you know as a child well into old age.

From what I could gather, the children at today's event were left to their own devices. There was an extensive buffet in this room with all kinds of desserts, a few tables were set up with some board games, and all kinds of cushiony couches lined the walls beautifully.

While chatting with the other kids, I continued training with my magic and my core. Over the past couple of days, I'd started being able to sense my core in any stationary position. True, it took me about ten seconds of full concentration to do it, but it was worth it. I also knew full well that in my particular situation, it was all about the training. I could gain skill pretty quickly — I just had to avoid slacking off.

To my great disappointment, I was having a very rough time getting acquainted with other facets of the magical arts. My proficiency at absorbing magical energy from the outside was stuck because of one thing. No matter how hard I tried, no matter which methods and analogies I came up with, the amount of energy in my core wasn't increasing.

The second problem keeping me up at night was my practice with the family magic. According to the mages who'd been teaching me, someone with hereditary gifts only needed desire, strength, and will to create spells. However, I couldn't cast any at all.

Sensibly judging that since I was a Morozov, spells related to my family gift should come to me more easily, I'd tried to create something ice-related, and I hadn't been wrong. I'd actually managed a few decent Ice Daggers, but I hadn't been able to create anything like the spears or the globe I'd seen before.

After that, I'd been as tired as if I'd done an intense workout with Theophane when he was angry at me.

After these lessons, I'd started to have greater respect for George's power, and for that of my so-called father. It was truly impressive how easily they used their family magic!

That kind of power forced me to ponder something seriously, though. Why wasn't Father trying to use force, despite my behavior? Why was he talking to me and acting through intermediaries? What was holding him back? And what would happen if this invisible barrier between us went away?

Demons curse them all! I needed to get out of that estate fast. Maybe right after the ball, I'd...

"Hey, we have a new guy!" a thunderous shout interrupted me in the middle of thinking and not interfering with the lively conversation starting around me, and three new participants joined our company of six boys on two of the small couches.

Raising my head, I saw some boys of about thirteen I didn't know, who were sizing me up. Or rather, one of them was doing that — the others were clearly his entourage.

Not waiting to see what they did next, I went back to the conversation they'd interrupted.

"Long story short, if you don't have the Eyes of the Wolf or an analogous spell, it's better not to mess with Night Hunters. Crazy demons! They cast illusions, and then you can't do anything."

I hope I won't get into any fights with anyone today, I thought optimistically. Otherwise, I was already so sick of being so courteous to everyone that I'd... was that why so many kids in this world loved to show off their strength and superiority? Or almost children — puberty hadn't hit yet. Was that why they all came at me with their beef? Was

I cursed? Or could something in them sense the enemy from another planet in me? The intruder from another world? I didn't know. But every time I went to a new place, some jerk showed up and totally killed the mood!

"Yeah, it's the fabled Ivan Morozov." The boy started talking again, already openly alluding to me. "The heir of an almost forgotten bloodline!"

"Yep, that's me," I answered calmly, not showing any signs of agitation. I really didn't want to start a fight!

"My name's Oleg Glinov," said the boy, raising his chin haughtily, then introduced his toadies, who for their part didn't say a word to me.

"Nice to meet you," I said, not changing my expression in the slightest.

"Is it true what they say, that the video of you from the attack in Morshansk was staged?" asked Oleg, giving me a look as if to challenge me. "How much did your father shell out for that video to be made? Huh?"

All the chatter in the room died down. I felt the attentive stares of the children listening in on the conversation.

So? Why shouldn't they listen? It'd be something to tell their parents about at home. So they wouldn't think they took them to the ball for nothing!

My sisters, noticing something was wrong, hurried to get closer. I noticed an obvious dislike for my opponent in Maria's face.

Seemed like she was ready to tear this Glinov

guy a new one! Did she know him or something? Hmm...

"Who's saying that?" I asked perfectly calmly after the silence became awkward.

Glinov was obviously expecting me to blow up and start cursing or stop playing innocent, but I was completely calm. And that pissed him off.

"Everyone," he answered, not confidently.

"Who's everyone?" I asked just as calmly.

"Everyone around us!" Glinov started to fly off the handle, but then he got a hold of himself and kept talking. "Ask anyone — everyone's talking about it!"

I turned to the boy sitting to my right.

"You talking about it?"

"No!" he laughed. Turning to face Glinov, he added: "That's the first I've heard of it."

"I'm not either," the boy to my left piped up right away.

"Me either," someone else chimed in.

"Or me..."

Look how that worked out, I thought, surprised at the other boys' unexpected support. Show some ordinary politeness, take an interest in what they were doing, gain a reputation as pleasant guy, have a couple of heartfelt conversations, and here they all were standing by me. Or was it just that they'd been sick of this Glinov guy for a while?

"Well, I'm talking about it," said one of Glinov's toadies abruptly, trying to get the conversation back on track.

"Me too," the second boy in Glinov's entourage added quickly.

"C'mon, that's far from everyone," I said, coughing. Glancing at Glinov, I added: "Actually, it's almost no one."

"I'm talking about it too." Glinov took the bait instantly and stared at me defiantly.

"Cool." I nodded at the three of them. "You can go on repeating your ignorant gossip, but you should know that I'll tell the head of the Temnikov family that he was insulted and his business reputation was threatened."

"What?" said one of Glinov's toadies in surprise. "How did we insult him?"

"What do you mean?" I said, perplexed. "You just confirmed in front of everyone here that you think the Temnikov family is full of liars and schemers. I don't think my father will have much patience for insults like that, and I think he'll demand public apologies from the adults in your families."

"You don't have to hide behind your father!" fumed Glinov, trying to stop the situation from getting out of his control. "You should be answering for your own actions!"

"That's exactly what you should be doing," I said with a thin smile. "Your actions have already dishonored your family — publicly insulting the Temnikov house in my presence. So I have no choice but to take this information to the head of the family."

"We didn't mean it like that," said Glinov after

a few seconds, still not stopping his attempts to turn the situation around. "We just wanted to know — is it true that everything happened just like in the video, or was it some kind of edit?"

"But instead of asking that question like a civilized person, you decided to insult the Temnikov family." I didn't follow his lead. "On top of that, I gave you a chance to salvage the situation and make it into an unfortunate joke, but you refused."

I saw the boys' faces growing gloomier with each word I said. They'd expected, of course, that I'd fall for their provocation, and they'd be able to amuse themselves at my expense, but everything had been turned on its head.

I sensed that the other children here were watching with curiosity and obvious approval as the three quarrelsome boys got dragged through the mud.

"You could also admit to your own mistakes and apologize to someone in his family," said Maria abruptly and clearly, watching with obvious pleasure as I tormented the boys, which simply shook them to the core.

Glinov's eyes burned with hatred as he rolled them at her.

"We didn't do anything, Temnikov!" he said to her sharply.

"You insulted my family," said Maria coldly. "And you did it in polite society."

Glinov was about to say something, but he turned and left quickly. His toadies withdrew right behind him.

"You sure showed him!" said the boy on my right. "I'm so sick of that Glinov. He thinks just because he's from a princely bloodline he can get away with anything."

"It's not that." A pleased-looking Maria approached us. "It's just that at the last ball, Ivan danced with Milania, and Glinov is secretly in love with her."

I decided not to ask how he could be "secretly" in love if our Maria knew about it already, but I did ask:

"Just because of that? Was it just me or do you have some beef with him?"

"He goes to our branch of the Imperial Academy," said Maria, and added with a satisfied smile: "At the last tournament, I tore him to pieces!"

"You had a tough time beating him," Anna corrected her, walking up to us.

"Either way, I won!" said Maria stubbornly. "That means I'm stronger than him."

"That's not all the reasons either," said one of the boys standing nearby abruptly.

"You know another one?" Maria asked right away, as a bunch of people curiously turned their heads towards the boy who'd spoken.

He seemed embarrassed for a moment, but then he continued.

"A lot of people are aware that after the dancing, we're going to be asked to demonstrate our magical knowledge."

The guys nodded, and my sisters and I gave them puzzled looks.

"Yeah, it's because there's an envoy of the emperor at the ball."

The next moment, the sitting room was like an upside-down beehive. Even the girls started chattering and tugging at their dresses anxiously.

"Did I miss something? What's the connection?" I asked one of my neighbors.

"What, you don't know?" He looked at me with surprise, then nodded to himself and continued, "Six months ago they announced that they're planning to start recruiting talented young nobles for classes with Vitovt the Second — the heir to the imperial throne.

"So it's obvious why the imperial envoy is here. He's going to select an up-and-coming youth of our age. Glinov has been dreaming of being the first to make it to the imperial heir's team, but I think you'll eclipse his swampy stuff with your Globe of Ice!"

So that was what was going on! I understood the goal of Father's machinations. He didn't want me to learn magic alongside the heir to the throne, otherwise I could run my mouth where I shouldn't and slip out from under his guardianship.

While the children chattered excitedly, Maria came up to me and said quietly:

"You handled Glinov beautifully — now a lot of people want to be friends with you."

I nodded.

"If he approaches you apologizing, send him to me, got it?"

Staring into Maria's burning eyes, I nodded —

refusing a request like that could seriously offend her, but I really didn't like this situation...

* * *

I spun my young, smiling dancing partner around and watched with surprise yet again at how gracefully the girls here danced even at our age.

The dances for the children weren't very long at all and took up about twenty minutes after dinner. During that time, the children had a chance to feel almost grown up. After that, our host introduced the imperial envoy to the guests — a short, balding man in an imperial minister's uniform.

Asking everyone to spare him some attention, he babbled like a brook for a good half hour, first praising our host, then the emperor, then the guests and their children. Then he moved on to the growing role of the Nosiriansky Empire in the world, to how difficult it was to fight enemies from the outside, to the need to unite, consolidate the people, and strive forward.

In conclusion, he listed the names of several young nobles, one of which was me.

Should I show him what I was capable of or not? Should I try to gain guardianship from the emperor? Or should I remain under the thumb of my father, who could spring a trap on me at any moment?

Lately, I'd gotten tired of anticipating a dirty trick around every corner. Despite being calm and friendly on the outside, I hadn't forgotten for a minute who I was, where I was, and what could have happened to me if Theophane weren't so prompt. So I couldn't call the time I'd spent at the Temnikov estate peaceful. Father was starting to get up to something again, too...

As it turned out, there were only five contenders for the class. We stood in single file at a few yards' distance from each other and waited for our orders.

Yes or no? I looked at Father's imperturbable face and Galina's condescending smirk.

No. It didn't seem so. She really believed that I wouldn't be able to manage anything. For people like her, everything was written on their faces.

Maybe she was the one who'd strong-armed Petius, I thought, getting angry. I cleared my mind and started meditating.

"Please demonstrate your magical talents." The host of the ball's voice reached me, and at that moment, a thin but long and very sturdy icicle started to grow between my hands.

I judged sensibly that they wouldn't require me to create a couple of Ice Knives at once. So it was better to make one, but slightly bigger. Once I'd started the process of forming the blade, I decided not to dream up anything too complicated and stick with my thin icicle — which, incidentally, turned out just fabulously.

Sensing that my strength was on its way out, I used up my magic supply, opened my eyes, and heard applause from the nobles present in the hall as a reward for my efforts.

I'd managed to create a thin, three-foot spear that was shimmering beautifully. Glinov had created a small marsh, something like three feet by three feet, and the other three had basically just made a mess of things. I could only get that from their angry faces, though. I'd been standing there with my eyes closed this whole time, after all, so I hadn't seen their attempts at magic.

Before accepting my congratulations from the envoy, I shot a glance at Father and noticed that his eyes were burning with dark, furious flame.

He was clearly unhappy, I thought with relief. That meant everything was as it should be!

Chapter 6

THIS TIME, THE TRIP TO MORSHANSK seemed much more pleasant and comfortable to me than the last one. And that was no surprise! Because now there were no chases in store, no one fixing to beat me up at a cafe in the village of Rudnia-Anton, and not a single corrupt clerk at the hotels along the way who'd risk setting a band of lowlife criminals on a child. All because on this journey I was accompanied not by one defenseless- and sick-looking old man who was dead on his feet, but a whole eight warriors and one mage. A full battle squad, can you imagine!

Leading this subdivision of warriors was Isamu Yamashita, whom I already knew.

I had to admit, this move on Father's part really surprised me. I understood, of course, that Yamashita was training with me every morning for a reason, trying to earn my trust at a leisurely pace. But I couldn't assume, either, that someone with such a high position in the house's hierarchy could be sent out on a long trip with the head of the house's youngest son.

When I'd learned this news, I'd gotten a little tense.

Could Father have decided to get rid of me anyway after what happened at the ball? I'd thought at that moment, but I'd remembered in time: if he really needed to get rid of me, he would've thought of something simpler. For that matter, if something happened, he'd have to justify himself in front of the public, who would undoubtedly wonder where that youngest son of his got off to again — not only a self-initiated mage, but the heir to the Morozov bloodline?

Our small band confidently covered mile after mile of our journey in two armored cars. Five of the warriors were in the car in front, and only four people in the car in back. The people in our car were the driver, the mage in the passenger seat, and me and Yamashita settled comfortably in the back.

The mage keeping us company was very gloomy and quiet — probably because his seniority in the group was playing second fiddle to some warrior, and he was accompanying us as supplementary offensive support.

It was no skin off my nose. I felt fully comfortable in Yamashita's company, and I wasn't bored for a moment the whole trip. Although, I had to admit, I didn't trust this personable man. He'd wormed his way into a place of trust too professionally. If not for his slip of the tongue on the first day we'd met, from which it followed that he hadn't known the level of my training, I wouldn't suspect him of anything. However, I had no intention of sharing my thoughts with anyone, especially not Yamashita — I couldn't let him suspect anything. Furthermore, I was able to chat with him about various interesting topics and get some good training in, which was something I needed.

"I didn't think that Father would add you to my escort group," I said in the middle of one of our conversations, and added curiously: "Doesn't the head of the guards have other things to do besides escorting the prince's youngest son?"

"I do," Yamashita replied after a bit. "However, the scope of my job includes not only organizing security for the family's estate proper, but also for every other part of it. Including all the family's businesses, various offices, and other homes. The house that George lives in at the moment too."

"That is, this trip is also a kind of inspection at the same time? I thought he got a group together just to bring me safely to Morshansk."

They'd come up with a good cover story for Yamashita, I realized instantly. He was coming along for the inspection, you see. Those were his duties, you understand. I figured, however, that his main goal was keeping tabs on me. To make sure I didn't, for instance, run off somewhere along the road to Morshansk... because, in fact, aside from him and a few of the high-ranked members of my family, no one could beat me in a fight. True, I wasn't counting the three Militants I'd trained with a few times. In my fights with them, I hadn't even been showing off half of my capabilities. I was pretty sure my Globe of Fire would have really surprised them... to death... so Yamashita, of course, seemed like the best candidate. Moreover, by his reckoning, I trusted him.

"That's the main reason," said Yamashita in response to my question. "But Prince Yegor needs to know how George's security is being provided for."

All right...

Since nothing delayed us on the road, we got to Morshansk fairly quickly. Once we got stopped at a section of the road cordoned off by the Hunter League. There was a pair of demons somewhere in the woods. However, as soon as the hunters saw the signs that our car belonged to a prince's family, they let us through right away.

I wondered how many real demon worshipers used their position in society to vanish from the scene of the crime with impunity in this type of situation. I made a mental note to investigate this question or ask it to Theophane. I figured it would be interesting to think over.

They were already expecting us in Morshansk. Our car was let into the city without an inspection, and after a little while we were driving through the hospitably open gates onto the property. On the wide porch I saw the tall, lean figure of the man who was greeting us, who was joined by one other woman after the cars stopped.

While I looked over the house, I was approached by the elderly, gray-haired butler with shrewd eyes, prim manners, a balding head, and an unusual goatee.

"Good evening, sir," said the butler with no emotion in his voice. "My name is Evstrasty — I manage the house. You may address any non-urgent matter directly to me."

Seeing a tall man with a shaved head, a sword, a holster on his belt, and a machine gun on his shoulder report something to Yamashita, I said:

"I'd like to see my room, have a little something to eat, and talk to George. Is he home now, by the way? Or is he in the Wasteland?"

Evstrasty turned his eyes to the side for a second, but he answered nonetheless:

"He's here, in his study... he's working."

He said "working" somehow unconfidently. And for some reason George had decided not to greet me today. What, had he gotten a big head? He'd been very worried about me the last time we'd seen each other! Or was it that after I'd fallen into Father's hands, I'd stopped being his trump card? I'd have to see...

"Then let's do this," I said after a short pause. "Someone can lead me to my room, and then I'll go see George. I don't want to waste time on unnecessary searching."

Finding myself in a fairly spacious and tidy room with a big double bed, I collapsed on it for a few minutes, then got my thoughts in order and went to go find my brother.

After knocking at the door to his study, I didn't wait for him to invite me in — I stood there for a bit and then grabbed the door handle decisively.

The strong, hearty smell of alcohol immediately struck my nostrils. Frowning, I went over to open the window.

That was when I saw George. He was sleeping, his head collapsed on his desk, and holding an open bottle of some kind of swill.

Seemed very expensive, based on the label, I thought. Why did it reek like that?

My presence didn't remain undetected — George started to get up and said angrily:

"I told you, don't let anyone come in!"

Coughing, he drank a little from his bottle and focused on me.

"Oh... it's you?" he said more calmly. He opened his eyes all the way, sat down more comfortably in his chair, took another swig, and added somewhat angrily: "Well, c'mere, then!"

For some reason he wasn't very happy to see me, I thought. As if he already didn't want to know what I had to say.

I unhurriedly took the guest chair and gave my brother a long hard look. His eyes bored into me with hostility.

George didn't say anything, and neither did I. The silence dragged on. It seemed like he wasn't in a rush to get anywhere, so I decided to take the first step and started with a tried-and-true method.

"Ruslan and the girls told me to say hi to you."

"That's great," said George caustically, and immediately continued angrily: "So *how did he buy you?*"

Oh, boy! Here came the emotions! I was actually surprised by how angry he was. What had I done wrong? What was all this about? Who bought me? Father? As if I'd had a choice!

"Express yourself more clearly," I said coldly. "No one bought me, or tried to, so I don't understand what exactly you want from me."

"How can I express myself more clearly?" George tried to yell, his words slurred. "How did he buy you? How?"

"Judging by how angry you are, I believe that by *he*—" I put emphasis on that last word, "—you mean Father?"

"Yes! Nocers' asses!" shouted George. "Of course I mean him! Don't try to play dumb!"

"I'm not playing anything." I kept my response in check by speaking just as coldly. "No one bought me, so I don't understand what you're on about!"

"Oh, sure!" George nodded and, already calmer, continued: "Of course no one bought you! So you sold yourself out!"

Taking another swig, George continued:

"I already talked to Theophane! I know exactly what happened at the estate two years ago and how you managed to survive! He killed you, Ivan! He killed you! And you did what? All he had to do was want it real bad, and you went back home! Under his roof! And you didn't even dare to make a move these whole two years! After that, what are you but a damn sellout?"

"Did you accidentally hit your head?" I asked, trying to stay calm, though everything inside me was resounding with anger. "I didn't wake up until a few days after I saved your sorry hide! I couldn't influence the situation or refuse to surrender my-self to captivity! You were supposed to do that! I came to hoping to see my brother! Instead I saw my father, who I'd spent so long hiding from! What do you think I should've done? Run? How, exactly? He's a Professor-rank mage! And that's at mini-mum! He also has an excellent command of his in-herited gifts! Which he demonstrated to me! Do you really think I would've had any chance at all? You're the total idiot here!"

"Well, you could've run away afterwards!" George bellowed.

"I couldn't even go from the house to the gar-den without being watched! There were several people watching me at all times! And you're saying I should've run away! How?"

"But you could've at least not agreed to host that ball!" George sprang to his feet, staggering. "Or told everyone the truth at that ball! That would've solved all our problems!"

"Yeah, okay!" I looked at him like he was an idiot. "Did you accidentally drink away the last of your brains? How was I supposed to do that? Re-fuse to host the ball? You think Father couldn't have forced me to do everything the way he needed me to? If you do, you really are an idiot! I'm weak! I'm only twelve, and he's a full-fledged mage! One lesson from Father showing me my weakness was enough for me! So whether I wanted to or not, one way or another he would've used me for his ends. One way or another! And if he'd suspected I was going to start telling everyone the truth, I wouldn't have lived to make it to the estate! He would've just taken me out of the picture! You absolute blockhead! And no one would've done anything to him!"

I fell silent, took a breath, and kept talking, already calmer.

"That's why I decided to take advantage of the situation and turn it into something I could use. I agreed to Father's plan, and I got some options for myself from it! I managed to escape the estate and come here. I'm legally a Morozov. I met a lot of influential people, so I could attract even more of the public's attention to me! Because at the moment, that's exactly the best guarantee of my safety — acting like a hotheaded teenager and trying to run headfirst into dangerous spells certainly aren't."

"So you're saying you were a coward, is that it?" George looked at me sullenly, and a dark cloud formed behind his back. "I spilled blood for you!"

"Oh, yeah?" I said caustically, looking him in the eyes. "Then why aren't you the head of the family, in that case? Why should I provide for my own safety exactly the way you're telling me? Didn't you promise to beat Father? Didn't you promise to protect me?"

That last sentence simply enraged George, and a powerful Air Fist took out the chair I'd just been sitting on and broke through the wall.

If something happened, I was going to jump out the window and make a break for it. I couldn't fight him, I thought, getting into an advantageous position. In the meantime, I'd try to make my brother come to his senses. What if I could resolve all this peacefully?

"Okay, let's go!" I yelled in George's face. "Hit your littlest brother again! Show me you're the real heir to the bloodline! Be like our dearest father and finish what he started! Kill me!"

"I'll never do something like that!" George bellowed, his face red with anger, and he hit the table with all his might a few times, busting his hands up and covering them in blood.

The pain sobered him up a little, and his fury started to subside.

But just then the door burst open, and Yamashita flew into the room with three warriors.

"Get out of here!" George roared. A wave of dark energy knocked the newcomers back out of the study, and the door slammed shut with a thunderous crash.

No one else dared to burst in on us. Either because they were afraid of punishment or because I'd had time to signal to Yamashita that I had everything under control.

Seemed like losing to Father was consuming George very badly. Or was it his excessive alcohol consumption? I noticed a heap of empty bottles behind his desk. Good thing comparing him to Father had calmed him down a little.

"I'll never become like him," said George again, collapsing into his chair.

After thinking for a bit, I followed his lead; dragging my comfy armchair closer to his desk, I said:

"So how did you fall into this way of life?"

George spilled the information like a cornucopia.

As it turned out, after his would-be killers had left, he'd gotten away from that place with the help of old man Taras and given me to the care of a healer who'd showed up. He hadn't intended to tell anyone who I was, but right after the assassination attempt, the video had popped up and put an end to those intentions, and he'd barely had time to blink before Father had turned up in Morshansk.

By then, George had already managed to recover and was incredibly angry that he'd only recently avoided dying at the hands of murderers. So he'd been happy to dispute Father's claim to being head of the family, and he hadn't doubted for a moment that he'd win. Because at the time, with all the trips he'd taken to the Wastelands, George had become much stronger and more experienced. On top of that, Father, as a head of a family far away from the estate where the family altar was, had clearly been weaker. Their ritual duel had been brutal, but despite his increased mastery George hadn't managed to break through Father's powerful shield.

At a certain point, Father had managed to suppress George's magical aura with sheer power and force him to submit. Now George had to spend a year fulfilling a mission from Father without returning, or else he'd lose his family magic.

"How's that?" I was surprised. "Is that really possible? How can you feel that you're obligated to obey?"

"I don't feel it!" George snapped. "I know it! Not so long ago the family magic was driving me forward, telling me to protect my brothers and sisters, and now it's gone over to his side. It's like it's saying that I have to listen to him, like back when we had our first fight at the estate!"

What's this, withdrawal hallucinations? I thought, puzzled. *Or does he really feel something like what he's describing?*

"And what made you decide the family magic is on his side?" I decided to ask him anyway. "Is it possible you just lost a ritual duel and now you have to meet the head of the family's demands according to the codex?"

"Sure, it's just that when my aura came into contact with Father's," said George, choosing his words with difficulty, "I sensed Death herself in front of me... I felt sharp steel piercing my heart, felt it being torn to pieces, felt my life leaving my body... I saw all that like it was happening before my eyes," he finished, seeming lost.

I didn't understand this family magic business at all. Some authors had written about the whole thing being a fabrication. Others had written that family magic really did exist. Something like it existed, of course. Even in me, it was there, there was something... unintelligible... making me do stupid things and fly off the handle when I wasn't treated right, like what had happened with Simmeron. I'd have to unravel this whole thing.

Neither of us said anything for a while. I gave George time to collect himself and asked him my next question.

"Listen, if you fully disagree with Father's politics to this extent, if you're calling on me to stand by you till the end and oppose him with all the resources I can get, then why have you been here for more than a year already yourself?"

When he'd been sent into the Wasteland, he'd just needed to check in and kill a couple of demons, and that was it. He'd stayed here for almost a year, though.

"I'm here in exile," answered George with a melancholy tone after a few minutes of silence. "At first, I just wanted to get some fighting experience in the Wasteland. But now I'm carrying out a specific, defined mission... that loss cost me dearly."

"All you did was take a beating," I said indignantly. "Do you really have to kill yourself over it like this? Is your mission really all that horrible?"

"Took a beating?" It was George's turn to be indignant. "I only took a stance against Father because he didn't want to take care of the family's affairs, and he'd stopped raising his children in a way befitting his status. We buried two of our brothers, and then you were killed! Then Ruslan was poisoned! What did I have left? On top of that, the family magic was clearly making me much stronger!"

"You did everything the way you should've," I said to him. "Maybe that's exactly why Father is actively interested in the family's affairs now. So much so that he took away Galina's control over a large part of the industrial enterprises."

"Oh, come on." George was genuinely surprised. "That can't be right! Although..." Going quiet for a second, he grabbed some kind of leaflet, then kept talking in astonishment. "Now I understand... because something like that would change anyone..."

After a few more minutes had passed in silence, I watched George resolutely set his bottle to the side, and he said:

"Go — I need to think this all over for a while."

* * *

The street I knew so well met me with silence. Telling my driver to stay in the car, I hopped the fence and found myself in the front yard of the house that had become a home to me. Walking up to the front door, I lifted the welcome mat and used the key I found there to enter.

A quiet, clean, and neglected house greeted me.

Right... Theophane wasn't here, Father's people had probably turned the place over, and the poor landlady Marissa had had to clean it up.

Finding no signs left for me by my thoughtful mentor, I rummaged around in my room, took my saber and a few other useful things, and headed back outside.

I definitely needed to talk to old man Taras and Marissa. I hoped they were all right, I thought as I put my things in the trunk.

My favorite Avtiukians weren't home either, but a neighbor who was peering out at me timidly reassured me.

"They went to the marketplace, they'll be home soon."

In the end, she threw a glance at the Temnikov coat of arms on my clothing and hurried to get away from me.

This knowledgeable woman turned out to be right. I waited a short while, and after only half an hour I ran into Taras and Marissa coming back from their errand and embraced a deeply emotional Marissa.

"Oh, how you've grown! How you've grown!" She was amazed. "You've shot right up! In only two months! Taras, look at how handsome he is!"

"I see it." Taras gave me a fervent wink, extending his hand to me for a handshake. "But Marissa, why are we standing out here in the street with Ivan? Let's all go in and have a bite!"

"Thank you for saving my life," I said to old man Taras while Marissa set the table beautifully. Taras nodded, and I admitted honestly: "I would never have known you were a warrior! Let alone a

Hero!"

Taras chuckled and waved me off.

"And no one *will* know. That's my style," he said. "A few people around the city know, of course, but only my students."

"Your students?" I was truly surprised at that. "What, you really teach people that drunken style? Would you take me on?"

I remembered how Taras had evaded his opponents' attacks as if completely by accident, how he'd broken shields and shattered bones with his clumsy strikes and flailing arms.

"You're still too little for the drunken style," said Marissa, frowning with displeasure as she set dishes of delicious-smelling chicken soup on the table. "Better you study what Theophane taught you."

My stomach immediately growled, and I set upon the food with great pleasure.

"Don't listen to her," said Taras quietly. "My style is the best. And on top of that, I can drink all the time!"

"Don't teach the boy bad habits," said Marissa sternly, then added in a kind voice: "You were just starving! Homesick for home-cooked food, I dare say! Eat up, dearie, eat up — you won't find such delicious food in any noble house!"

"And have a cibulka." Old man Taras handed me a plate with little green onions on it.

"A cibulka?" I repeated.

"An onion," he translated. "And here, take some lard too."

Glancing at the thin, aromatic slices, which had a lot more layers of meat on them than the lard itself, I swallowed again as my mouth watered.

"You're just spoiling me today," I said as I chewed the homemade delicacies.

"Taste my magic with sour cream and butter, and you'll already be telling me what a good hostess Marissa is," said Marissa, who was frying something at the stove.

Her "magic" turned out to be potato pancakes browned on both sides and stuffed with mincemeat.

"When did you have time to grate up the potatoes?" I was astonished.

"It's a secret." Marissa grinned, putting some potato pancakes on my plate. "Eat up!"

When I finished my food, I leaned back in my chair.

"That's enough! I can't eat any more! There's no room."

"Weakling," said old man Taras, knocking over the stack of potato pancakes and eating one with an onion.

I talked with them for a bit about some idle topics, learned what they'd been up to, and then returned to our main questions.

"Old man Taras, why did you stay in Morshansk?" I asked cautiously. "It seems the powers that be should've been curious about the drunken master who defended me and George from those killers, and they'd have come to you for answers."

"Oh, they were curious." Taras looked at me shrewdly. "But then they abruptly stopped being curious. The authorities forbade them."

"Just like that?" I asked.

"Yep." Taras nodded.

If the authorities had forbidden the top brass from exploiting a Hero, and just like that, then in all likelihood one of the drunken master's students was the commandant himself! It was the best protection for someone who was tired of fighting and wanted to have some peaceful time to himself in his old age, if nothing else...

"So you and Marissa didn't go through anything unpleasant because of what happened?" I said with heartfelt relief.

"No, we didn't," Taras confirmed.

"Thank the Savior," I said, though I noticed Taras and Marissa sharing a glance. "Or else I would've started to worry. 'Cause Theophane is a lone wolf without a family, but you and Marissa..."

"Thank you for your concern." Marissa smiled warmly. "But don't speak ill of your mentor. You're wrong about Theophane."

"Yes." Old man Taras nodded and started to laugh. "He's actually a very productive guy."

"Not in front of the kid!" Marissa smacked him with a towel.

"Stop! Stop! I surrender!" Taras raised his hands to protect himself from the towel and fought not to laugh at the same time.

"He has a family?" I was stunned. "But how? Wasn't he my grandfather's only servant for a long time? When did he have time? I've never heard even once of Theophane having a family!"

"It's better if you ask him that yourself," Taras laughed. "I can't vouch for any of this."

"I'll ask him when I see him," I said, and added cautiously, "Incidentally, you don't know how to get in touch with him?"

"No." Old man Taras shook his head. "Not at the moment. He told us to tell you that he'll get in touch with you himself. Right now he's busy with those rats who are playing around with demonic magic. He happened on some kind of lead out of almost nowhere."

"Does that mean I shouldn't expect to see him in the near future?"

"Most likely." Taras nodded.

"Then he can avoid seeing his student for even longer," I said, and started telling them about what happened at Prince Beregov's ball.

Chapter 7

"HELLO?" SAID GODIMIR'S GROGGY, not-fully-awake voice over the phone.

"What, are you still asleep?" I said indignantly. "It's two in the afternoon, for heaven's sake! It was time to get up a long time ago!"

"Oh, hi, Ivan!" Godimir recognized my voice. "We didn't get home until early morning, so I'm still totally out of it."

"And where were you hanging out last night?" I asked, curious. "Am I right? You spent the whole evening with some girl?"

"Oh, you can shove it!" said Godimir, and yawned sweetly. "We were at Commandant Mozyria's ball. That's all. And what about you? When are you coming over? The new school year's starting soon, after all."

"Well, I've actually been here for a few days already," I replied in an innocent tone.

"You're kidding!" said Godimir cheerfully, then added sleepily after a short pause: "Although... I'd be happy to see you, of course, but later. Right now what I want more than anything is sleep. And having pizza with you too."

"Great, it's decided. Today at seven at our favorite snack bar, then," I said. "You get some good sleep in the meantime and regain some strength."

"Should I call the guys?" Godimir asked.

"I'll do it myself," I answered. "Incidentally, you can write down this number — it's my new one."

"Done," said Godimir, and hung up.

My conversation with Godimir over, I found Constantine Machin's number written in my special notebook.

Now to talk to him...

After talking for a bit on the phone with Constantine and inviting him to the mini-party, I made Ilya Viyukhin's day with the same news, then stared at Sergei Kolzov's number pensively.

Although he and I were in the same friend group, I hadn't developed as warm of a relationship with him as I had with the others.

It was all because Sergei, despite my achievements in mastering Shiki-Cho, didn't consider me his equal. Yes, he'd acknowledged my successes in the field of mastering martial arts, but he thought that in a few years he'd become a full-fledged mage and easily beat up a commoner warrior.

It irritated him that some outsider kid had inserted himself into the friend group and was on equal footing with the heir to an entire bloodline. Something similar had happened at first when I'd met Simon Rodnikov, a member of a newer viscount family, who'd been annoyed that a commoner would be in his class.

To call or not to call? That was the question... I stared at the phone as I mused philosophically.

Although, on the other hand, why not? Yes, I'd had some little spats with Sergei — I knew he didn't like me. The only thing about me that he'd truly been dissatisfied with, however, was my ancestry, and that was all good now. If that was where everything he was offended by and displeased with had come from, then I shouldn't have any more issues with him.

On top of that, if I suddenly stopped talking to him or somehow showed that I hadn't forgotten the rare but caustic things he'd said to me, that would be quite unseemly. It'd scream that I'd become conceited as soon as I'd been declared the heir to a princely bloodline. We'd become enemies just like that! Sometimes childhood offenses infested one's entire life. I'd create problems for myself out of the blue. I didn't need that. I already had Oleg Glinov, who'd hardly forget how he'd paid for what he said in front of Maria. It didn't matter that it was his own fault — I was the one who "got" him. Generally, as practical experience had shown, good relationships with the young nobility were an excellent investment. Anything could happen, and in a few years the one I might have to turn to with some problem wouldn't be a little boy, but a full-fledged noble heir.

Some of my chaotic thoughts finally subsided, and I tapped the call button decisively.

In the evening that same day, our merry band gathered at our favorite snack bar for the first time in a long while. Several aromatic pizzas were already waiting on the table for our arrival. I hadn't wanted to wait too long for them to be prepared. So after mutual hellos and claps on the back, we quickly sat down and attacked our food.

"Well, you sure surprised us!" said Constantine while we ate. "An ordinary commoner, you said! Oh, and the way you scattered those killers! I watched that video about fifty times!"

"No, you're not completely right." Ilya shook his head. "Remember, we discussed why he was making such impressive progress with his warrior studies more than once. Then we decided that Ivan was most likely some noble family's bastard."

"Yeah," Sergei chimed in. "Then Godimir suggested that that was why you were living in Morshansk with your mentor. That, like, someone was paying for your expensive education from the Imperial Academy and from Theophane."

"You're such detectives." I coughed and took a big gulp of juice. "You almost guessed it."

It was no good telling them the real reason Theophane and I had settled here and where exactly we'd gotten the money. At first I wanted to say that we were self-sufficient because we were doing special ops, but that was clearly a weak story. If we'd been doing something like that, no one would've forgotten about money for sure. Even more so because princely houses had more than enough.

"Incidentally, are you in Morshansk for long?" asked Constantine after a bit. "Or what?"

I gave the smiling Godimir a questioning look.

"What, you didn't tell them?" I said to him.

"Didn't tell us what?" Ilya repeated immediately, narrowing his eyes.

"That Ivan is continuing his future studies in Morshansk," Godimir announced.

"Really?" Constantine and Ilya shouted in chorus.

"Shhh!" I shushed them. "You'll scare everyone here."

"We're not scaring anyone," Constantine brushed me off. "So can we expect you to move to Class 7A with us?"

"Why would I do that?" I was surprised. "I'm going to keep studying with my own class."

"Class B?" Sergei asked me in a skeptical tone. "Aren't you from a princely bloodline? You need to be in our class, it's better!"

"How is it better?" I said, surprised. "The curriculum is the same."

"Yeah," Sergei agreed, "but in your class there's no us."

"A considerable downside," I agreed. "But my class is also full of good people. And besides, it wouldn't be very nice to be in that class for two years and then switch to yours after having my identity revealed. I may not be participating in the war between the classes, but I think my class is good too."

"Yeah, lay off him." Constantine stood up for me. "He's totally right. Better for him to study with his class. We can meet up and chat after classes too. We're at school to learn, after all, not sit around."

"Study," Ilya coughed. "I remember how you studied last year. You just passed notes back and forth with someone."

"But I'm one of the top ten performers among our peers," Constantine retorted. "So I can do that!"

Passing notes? That was interesting.

"And what does that get you?" said Ilya, surprised. "Your position among the top ten?"

"Well, first off, the ability to tell you why school is useful." Constantine raised his pointer finger. "And second, I'm planning to try out for the academic tournament in math."

"Oh?" All of us were surprised. "Are you sure? Last year a lot of people didn't even make it to the second round. It was such a stinker."

"I'll manage," Constantine brushed us off. "I spent the whole summer studying!"

"Why did you do that?" Ilya was surprised for the second time. "Summer's for relaxing."

"Just so I can participate in some tournament or another, like Godimir, and be a star on the day of the ceremony. It's no secret that Godimir will be participating in the tournament again, after all. I'd like not to drag my own name through the mud."

"Hmm, okay," said Ilya pensively. "And now Ivan will participate too. Right?"

I thought about it for a minute, then nodded.

"I didn't spend all of last year working my butt off for no reason. Besides, now I don't have to hide under another name!"

"Man! This isn't fair!" Ilya said, agitated. "Sergei and I never would've thought to do something like that! It's three against two!"

"Four against one!" Sergei coughed. He'd been quieter than usual today. He was surely trying to take stock of my status. "I did some work over the summer too."

"Nerds!" Ilya growled, and we started laughing. "That means now I have to study for something too. I don't want to be the odd one out."

"Then let's drink to our future success!" Godimir proposed.

"To our future success!" I seconded him, and we clinked our juice glasses.

Incidentally, this was a great incentive for me to grow as a warrior. The whole year wouldn't be wasted, either! Now I'd have to do some more intense training with Boemir's soldiers and resume my trips to the Wasteland. I hoped that George wouldn't refuse me this small favor and that he'd accompany me.

* * *

I didn't stop independently teaching myself magic for even one day. So my workouts got me unsurprising results. Now, in Morshansk, I could get to my magical core at any moment and even did so at the same time as when my body was filled with Shiki-Cho.

I kept training and trying to sense my magical energy in tandem, past my body's limits, so that I could then learn to let it flow through me and accumulate it in my core. However, I still didn't have any success with that.

The mage that George appointed to look after me explained that this was a prevalent problem, not only for neophytes but also for more experienced mages. This step of mastering my strength was just as difficult as the first one, but there was no need to despair. Since I'd learned to sense my core, I could consider myself a full-fledged mage.

So as not to stagnate, but rather to make progress in the magical field, I decided to train with my family magic and fully give my all at casting the simplest ice spells. Because my desire, strength, and will were always with me.

In addition to that, replenishing magical energy in my core after I'd spent it was a natural and independent process. After all, Shiki-Cho accumulated in my body without me meditating — meditating only reduced the time it took to accumulate. I figured magical energy would do the same thing.

It also wasn't an accident that my temporary mentor had said I could now officially consider myself a mage, and that many never succeeded in channeling much energy through their cores — they just used what their cores accumulated by themselves.

If that was the case, then once I'd emptied my core of energy, I could train it up at least a little bit. I had no doubt that if I constantly emptied it right out, I'd increase the amount of energy it could accumulate.

I usually did this training in the morning, right after my practice sparring with Yamashita. But today I did neither the former nor the latter. The thing was, George answered my prayer and agreed to go to the Wasteland with me.

After our conversation, he'd pulled himself together, come out of his intoxicated state, and earnestly taken up the family's affairs.

"I haven't gone there in a long time," he said to me after thinking for a bit. "Well, all right, I'll put together a little excursion for you. Let's go get ready."

*　*　*

Our group wasn't big — only seven people. Its members were me, George, Yamashita, a mage, two warriors, and the guide George had hired.

In theory, after going to the Wasteland with Theophane, I could have been the guide myself for the first circle of the Wasteland, but I decided not to show off my knowledge, because George wouldn't want to listen to a little boy who'd never been to the Wasteland even once as far as he knew.

How exactly does my family's recon work? I thought in surprise. Or was it just that after losing to Father, George wasn't interested in learning the details about my life in Morshansk?

It didn't take me much time to gather my things. Thankfully, I'd prepared in advance and not only brought the necessary things from my and Theophane's house, but also bought some equipment from one good store. I only needed five minutes to pack up. Looking at myself critically in the mirror, I paid attention to how alien my thread-bare saber sheath — which had been in more than one battle — my knife, and my washed-out back-pack looked against my new camo. Putting on my fingerless leather gloves, which I needed so the handle of my weapon wouldn't slip out of my sweaty palms, I headed resolutely for the exit to the house, feeling the familiar weight of my saber on my belt.

I was one of the last people outside, but neither Yamashita nor George was there yet.

A light chuckle from the direction of the cars prepared to head out forced me to stop contemplating the beautiful scenery and see what was so funny.

Turned out it was me — or, rather, my equipment.

The warrior who'd chuckled got elbowed by his older companion and immediately lowered his head.

Do I really look that comical? I thought with dissatisfaction.

I didn't feel like putting the warrior in his place, although I remembered how that kind of thing had gone with Simmeron.

No matter — when we started our first demon fight, I'd see how he handled things. Everyone would fall into their places right away. If memory served me, after all, this very same warrior had arrived in Morshansk at the same time as me, so that meant he had no experience fighting in the Wastelands.

Yamashita, who came out of the house next, didn't make any comments whatsoever on my appearance — his face rarely expressed anything in general. My brother, on the other hand, didn't hold back.

"You're fitted out like you're going to war," he said to me. Looking at my scabbard, he added: "What do you need a sword for?"

"Sharpening pencils," I answered him in a serious tone.

"Pencils? What?" He didn't get it.

"You know, wooden ones," I said just as seriously.

"Are you making fun of me or something?" he guessed.

"What were *you* doing?" I said. "You don't know why people take weapons to the Wasteland?"

"No, I'm totally serious. I really don't understand why you need to bring a sword. I'll be right next to you, and nothing will touch you."

"Seems to me someone's forgetting that scuffle where we fought side by side," I reminded him. "I didn't do all that bad, did I?"

"No." George shook his head. "You did great. That's exactly why I decided to take your suggestion. But even so, in the Wastelands we'll have to fight real demons, not humans."

I got in the back seat of the second car wordlessly and said:

"Let's go."

"Why are you so wound up?" George asked me in a displeased tone as we drove through the city. "Don't think I'm underestimating you — it's just that believe me, I was a little scared myself my first time in the Wastelands. I'd only seen live demons one time before that, and that was during a practical lesson."

I stared at him silently and decided not to answer him.

How was this possible? He really did have no idea what I'd been up to this whole time after all! Well then, in that case, it'd be a surprise for him. I'd teach my older brother a little lesson — I'd show him that having information was essential.

The cars parked in the lot outside the customs building I was already well acquainted with. This was where I'd first gone out into the Wasteland.

The waiting room hadn't changed at all in that time, so I strode forward confidently. I didn't need to show my documents — the customs officer took some kind of paperwork from George and bowed to him, and after a few minutes our group was called to proceed to the exit.

Turned out going to the Wasteland with my brother was very convenient, I thought, happy that we wouldn't have to wait in line for a long time.

Incidentally, our guide was a sturdy, middle-aged man with a Militant's ring on his finger and a defensive amulet earring in his ear, wearing tattered old camo and a nearly identical copy of my backpack on his chest. Overall, he inspired confidence.

When we found ourselves in the Wasteland, the guide immediately sniffed the air, looked around on all sides with Eyes of the Wolf, and then moved forward decisively.

Yamashita, the two warriors, George and I, and the mage followed him. At this point, as George walked next to me, he bombarded me with a large quantity of unnecessary information about Wastelands.

I wanted to see the look on his face when he realized I wasn't a newbie here!

I preferred turning on my Eyes of the Wolf tech and studying my surroundings over idle chatter. As it turned out, it wasn't for nothing, because we ran into our first demons after only ten minutes, and apparently the guide walking in front couldn't see them yet.

Using my extensive experience, I managed to determine that there were about ten demons — not a small group.

Such a big gang? Is it because there are so

many of us? I thought, perplexed. I noticed that the guide had finally seen something, and I said:

"There will be demons here in a few minutes."

"What?" George looked at me in surprise. "There's no one out there!"

"But I'm not looking with ordinary eyes," I replied, looking at him askance.

"Your brother is right," the guide confirmed. "They're getting closer."

"Warriors in the front! Mages, guard them! Ivan next to me!" George immediately collected his thoughts and appointed the order of things.

Realizing that they'd been spotted, the demons rushed forward with wild screeches. George didn't take long to think — he immediately flung a powerful lightning bolt at an approaching enemy. The lightning clashed with the shield the demon put up. This mage demon with a long, ornate staff that turned out to be among the group immediately drew George into a duel.

Rolling to the side away from George, I shot a streak of fire and — not listening to George's command to stay next to him — rushed a Nocer, which almost playfully tossed one of the warriors to the side. I took my saber from its scabbard with a light movement and took the nearest demon's head off with one beautiful stroke. Using the inertia, I did a somersault and instantly threw two Anthroi to the side with a Battering Ram. The fortified wave of energy tore their bodies open midair. In the next second, the fight was over — George had finished off his opponent and decided to come to the aid of the others.

I looked around again, searching for any creatures that had hidden themselves; I didn't see any, so I turned to the warrior with the ugly gash across his whole face as he got to his feet.

"Give him some kind of healing potion — he certainly didn't think to bring his own," I said to the group's mage, paying no attention to the surprised stares from everyone around me — instead, I did a quick spot check with the guide.

Glancing around at the corpses, I took a deep breath, grabbed my trusty knife, and got to gutting them.

Yes, I had to admit, I had no great need for the income right now. The Temnikovs' treasurer had provided me with a special card that had an allowance of a few thousand thalers put on it monthly.

I decided, however, that I didn't want to lose my qualifications in such a lucrative skill just yet — what if I was thrown out of the house tomorrow with nothing to live on? How would I earn my living then?

The warrior who'd just taken his healing potion threw up when he saw what was happening, and the mage turned green.

Yeah, just like I thought. This new guy really had come to the Wasteland for the first time.

"Where did you learn that?" asked George after watching me for a bit.

"Where exactly did you think I could've gotten such good training over the past two years?" I answered his question with a question.

"So are you old Theophane's student?" the guide guessed. "You know, I knew the face of the prince's brother was really familiar, I'd seen it somewhere before…"

Over the next half hour we ran into a few even bigger groups of demons.

"There are a lot of them today for some reason," I said while I gutted yet another round of fourth- and fifth-circle demons. "And they're somehow too strong for this circle."

"When I go to the Wasteland, huge groups of demons always gang up on me," said George, continuing to watch what I was doing attentively.

"Don't you remember that there are four demons sneaking up on us with a Curtain of Invisibility spell?" I said. "Aren't you getting distracted?"

"I'm not," replied George. "I have a spell ready and waiting for the best moment to break away from my staff."

He wasn't lying — when the demons appeared, they ran into a cloud of darkness and immediately turned to withered corpses.

Holy crap! I jumped back, away from the black cloud. "What's that thing, for crying out loud? I hope not all mages can do that!"

"No, of course not," said George. "It's just one of my new, effective, and entirely wasteful things I can do with my family magic."

"No kidding!" I whistled, going back to what I was doing. "I didn't know there was anything like that in the Temnikov library."

"There isn't," George replied. "Consider it my

long-running experiment."

"If you can manage to make that spell less energy-consuming, you'll have something deadly on your hands," I said, wondering how one might defend oneself from an abomination like that.

"In that case, I'll have to make it simpler. I had to waste a couple hours just putting the spell into my staff."

In the fourth circle, to our surprise, we stumbled upon a fairly large section of woods covered in spiderwebs. We could hear the sounds of fighting coming from it.

"W-we need to go," I heard the anxious voice of the younger warrior. "Those are spiders. If we get into a fight with them, we're goners."

George narrowed his eyes at the warrior, who instantly went silent. However, that didn't save him from getting elbowed by his older companion.

"What could one of those abominations be doing here?" I asked the guide, puzzled, as I turned around. "Cross-Spiders live in the sixth through eighth circles, don't they? Or am I wrong?"

"You're right." The guide nodded, examining the web. "I don't know what they're doing here, but this is clearly a Queen and its minions. I've only encountered Cross-Spiders with webs like this once, and that was in the ninth circle. They're very dangerous."

"What do you suggest we do?" asked George thoughtfully.

"Despite the fact that I've seen you in action, I'd suggest we leave," said the guide. "There could be other demons here with the Cross-Spiders."

"Too late!" I said, flinging a few Globes of Fire forward.

Not expecting anything like that, a spider demon the size of a calf lost a few legs and became a convenient target.

"The Queen is primed!" shouted the mage with relief. "The minions will be easier."

"I'm not sure that's the Queen," I answered him, and yelled: "We've got company!"

The spiders that jumped out of the web were thrown back by a wave of air from George. Then we scattered, trying to escape the ramming attack of a Betlor — an enormous demon that looked like a rhino beetle.

Letting out a nasty screech, the beetle demon rushed past us. Getting a powerful Battering Ram from me to the back of its chitin shell, it ran forward a little further.

As I led the dangerous enemy away from the group, I was glad the Betlor hadn't let off poison gas as it had run by us — apparently, it had already given its all fighting the group before us. I hit it with a Globe of Fire.

To my great disappointment, the globe only singed the armored monster, which went even wilder and let off poisonous green gas at me anyway.

Oh no! So it hadn't run out! Holding my breath, I used my "flamethrower" tech to wipe out the green hues of death.

After that, I dodged to the side away from its oncoming ram attack and struck its feet with a couple of Power Whirlwinds.

Falling to the ground, the Betlor thrust out a wing in front of itself. My Battering Ram knocked it off, and it died instantly.

Because my saber had gone into the soft chitin under its wing, let a "flamethrower" tech pass through it, and destroyed the demon's insides.

Rushing to the aid of my group, I saw that they didn't need help anymore.

"Thank the Savior you're all right." George sighed in relief as the others, under Yamashita's guidance, extracted some unconscious people from three enormous cocoons. "Now let's see what's going on with these lucky fellows and turn back! I sense that something nasty is happening here, and the commandant absolutely needs to know about it!"

Chapter 8

ON THE FIRST DAY of the new school year, Class 7B met me with dead silence. Everyone's faces were in utter shock, although the class prefect Xenia Ognev was looking at me like she'd been waiting for my arrival for a long time.

"Good morning," I greeted my classmates. Not embarrassed at all by the intent attention they were paying to me, I headed to my desk, which — despite the fact that several new faces had appeared in the class — wasn't taken.

Must be new kids, I thought.

"Morning," a few people greeted me in response.

Paying no attention to those around me, I started taking my pen and notebook out of my textbook-overloaded bag.

I hadn't paid a visit to the Book Garden for

nothing, after all.

"Hi, Ivan." One of my old lunchtime companions — Nadezhda Zorin — greeted me with a smile. "So you've decided to continue your studies in Morshansk after all?"

"Hi." I smiled in return. "At the least, I'll finish middle school here, and after that we'll see. I don't want to transfer to another branch of the Imperial Academy, and my brother lives here too. He invited me to stay with him."

If nothing changed this year, then in high school I'd be studying alongside the heir to the throne, I thought.

"So you're not going to transfer to Class A?" said Vladimir Ischezov, another one of my classmates I used to have a decent relationship with. "'Cause Ogneyer asked you over all the time!"

"He did, but I'm good here," I replied, and everyone around me sighed in relief.

Right, there was that rivalry between the two classes — which one was cooler and more aristocratic.

"Well, that's great," said a contented Vladimir. "Incidentally, congratulations on returning to your family."

"Thanks." I nodded.

"So are you a Temnikov now or a Morozov?" asked Xenia. "You returned to your family, but as we've seen, your magic is different from theirs."

"I'm a Morozov born of the Temnikov family." I coughed as I remembered taking in that fact from Father.

"How strange," said someone thoughtfully. "He's part of one bloodline, but he has a different last name. That's not normal, right?"

"It's nothing too strange," a woman's loud and yet simultaneously soft voice rang out, surprising everyone. "Precedents for this kind of thing aren't such a rarity in our history. The teacher who's going over the Velvet Book with you should have called attention to them."

Whoa! I hadn't even noticed that someone had walked into the classroom! Who was this?

"Good morning!" the many-voiced chorus of children sounded immediately as everyone went to their desks.

The beautiful woman who'd just walked up to the teacher's desk was dressed in a striking pantsuit.

Is that really our new lead teacher? I thought curiously, watching my classmates' behavior.

"For the second time — hello!" said the woman, smiling warmly, when silence had fallen. "For those who don't know me yet, my name is Maria Theophanovna Dashkevich. I'm your new lead teacher."

After a short pause, she continued:

"I want to warn you all right away that this year will be fairly difficult for you. It will end with exams, after which you'll conclude your studies in middle school and begin high school. So I'd like everyone to take to their studies seriously from day one..."

After fifteen minutes of pedagogical indoctrination, Ms. Dashkevich finally got to the second question of the introductory lesson.

"And now, it seems the time has come to introduce the new students in our friendly class."

As it was revealed, this year our numbers had increased by five all at once, and judging by the glances being thrown at me, my presence here hadn't played an insignificant role in their choice of class.

There's something about this I don't like! I thought, looking at the new kids. I didn't understand — what advantage were they trying to get from knowing me?

After the first class session was over, Ms. Dashkevich asked me to stay behind and gave me all the materials from the sections of sixth grade that I'd missed.

"After familiarizing myself with your progress last year, I have no doubt that you'll be able to master these lessons in a very short time," she said after I'd stashed the pages in my bag. "And if you have any questions whatsoever about these materials, don't be afraid to bring them to any of your teachers. I've already spoken to them — they'll be glad to help you."

Well, of course they'd be glad to, I thought. Especially if they remembered last year and how much they owed me overall.

I thanked her and headed to another classroom, trying to remember along the way where I might have met this Maria Theophanovna Dashkevich before. I didn't know why, but she seemed familiar to me.

Hmm... her patronymic... Theophanovna? I actually stopped short for a moment. Meaning "daughter of Theophane?" No! That couldn't be it! Holy crap! The crazy things that popped into my head!

Chuckling at my own absurd ideas, I went to my next class.

After lunch, which I had with my usual group, I headed to Mr. Viktorov's office. He was glad when I showed up.

"Finally! I knew my favorite student would come in for a workout on the first day of school!" he said in an incredibly pleased voice. He waited for me to greet him, then added, "I hope the high-society life hasn't weakened you too much?"

"I hope not," I chuckled, gratefully thinking of Yamashita, who to my delight hadn't yet hurried to return to the estate.

"Then get to the locker room and change! And be ready to fight in ten minutes!" said Mr. Viktorov, grinning. "We'll test your worth."

Finding an unoccupied locker with some difficulty, I quickly changed, at a loss for who needed this perpetually empty fighters' locker room, then headed to the gym. Which, as it turned out, was simply packed with students.

"What in the..." I said in surprise, looking around at the students working out.

"Oh, don't you know, these are the consequences of someone setting a bad example," said Vladimir Ischezov gloomily, unexpectedly appearing next to me.

"Who was that?" I asked him, unfazed by his sudden appearance.

Vladimir got a somewhat insulted look on his face. He'd already tried to scare me like this a couple of times, but he'd never once managed it.

"You, of course," he said. "When everyone saw how awesomely you showed off in that fight and crushed a couple of hitmen with your techs, a lot of students decided to train up too. Not all of them, of course, but a lot of them. And since Mr. Viktorov is the warriors' trainer here, the honor of being called your mentor fell on him. So that's what happened. Now this place is booked solid — you can't even get a proper workout."

"Dwarf Saws' sakes!" I cursed gloomily. "What am I supposed to do? Are they all gonna stare at me while I train? How will I spar? This sucks!"

"Think of it as its own kind of training," Vladimir suggested, clapping me on the shoulder. "Everyone who constantly works out in here had to go through that in the third school trimester. So don't get upset — you'll get used to it pretty quickly. I know it from my own experience."

"Seems like there are a lot of girls," I said, looking around. "It used to be almost all guys."

"Yeah, there are even more girls than three months ago." Vladimir winked at me. "I wonder where that came from?"

He looked at my sour expression and started laughing. Meanwhile, I pondered the fact that Vladimir hadn't paid so much attention to my humble personage last year. It forced me to think of the worst-case scenario, although he'd been friendly to me even when everyone thought I was a commoner.

"Look at that!" I heard Godimir's quiet voice. "You see how many girls are here? "The place wasn't packed to the gills like this before."

"Let's go say hi," I suggested to Vladimir, nodding to Godimir. Vladimir agreed.

Godimir was standing with Ilya, Sergei, and Constantine and excitedly telling them something.

"Now I have an incentive to work out real good."

"Heya, suckers, you ready to suffer defeat in an honest fight?" I asked, sneaking up on them from behind.

"You're the sucker!" The boys turned and lit small fireballs in their hands in sync.

"All you can do is flail your arms and legs!"

"I'm ready to show off the magical skill of a real man."

"Not bad!" I appraised their attempt and clapped my hands. "You spend a long time working on that?"

"Not all that long!" Constantine coughed. "Now don't try to beat us by getting into our heads. Show us your own magical skills!"

"This involves you too, Ischezov," said Sergei, grinning.

Vladimir cleared his throat, vanished into thin air, and a moment later appeared behind the guys' backs with a fireball in his hand.

"Not bad," said Godimir. "Your family magic is interesting."

"My last name speaks for itself," said Vladimir — *ischezat*, to disappear.

"But we're still curious what our star of the show here can show us," Constantine coughed.

"I found your star," I chuckled in response, and after a bit I formed a small icicle in my hand. "I can't do fireballs yet. I just don't know how."

"Oh-ho!" said the guys, putting out their fireballs and clustering around me.

"I thought it would take you a while yet after your initiation before you'd be able to do that!" said Godimir, sounding insulted. "How did you learn to channel energy through yourself so quickly?"

"I still don't know how to do it," I admitted quietly. "The icicle is from what I managed to collect in my core at this stage. I'm casting on pure will."

"Ah," said Godimir. "I did magic like that too for the first six months, but it took a really long time to recover afterwards."

"Same," said Constantine.

"Me too," Sergei chimed in.

"Morozov." I heard Mr. Viktorov's loud voice. "Warm up, you're going in the ring soon. You need to show these kiddos what a real fight is."

After Mr. Viktorov had a chance to make the usual environmental manipulations with special amulets and set up protections against accidental techs, he said:

"At our branch, you have no worthy opponents yet besides me — the others are too weak. So starting today, you'll spar only with me. And yes, today we'll follow the usual agenda."

As always, we started our fight at medium speed. At first, we hit each other without using Shiki-Cho — I only practiced my technique. After that, Mr. Viktorov started increasing the tempo a bit, and then started filling his body with spiritual energy.

I tried not to fall behind him and precisely monitored all the changes in the pattern of the fight. However, after he let his Shiki-Cho circulate, it got really hard to fight him, and that was despite me doing the same.

Once he'd ensured that my sweat was flowing thick and fast, he closed the distance and said:

"Now let's see how reliable your techs are!"

I blocked his Battering Ram with a Spirit Shield, then hit him with a retaliatory Power Whirlwind and plunged headlong into the heat of the battle.

After a few minutes of exhausting fighting, I started to notice that my strength was on its way out, and I used my "flamethrower."

Dodging the unexpected strike with difficulty, Mr. Viktorov closed the distance and used a tech known as a Spirit-Step.

The essence of the tech was that it allowed the fighter to move a limited distance in a space in barely a moment. A small distance, admittedly, extremely small in the beginner stages. The tech got its name from the fact that when mastering it at first, it allowed its user to go just about one pace, something like a foot and a half.

Obviously, more experienced warriors could use the tech much more effectively. For example, the famed Theophane, when he'd demonstrated it to me, could move one pace or a whole fifty feet without breaking a sweat. In his words, it all depended on the amount of energy put into it.

Dodging a couple of strong punches, I tried to jump to the side and formed a Spirit Shield, which was then shattered by a Battering Ram from Mr. Viktorov's foot.

"Stop!" he commanded, extending his hand and helping me get up.

"Excellent," he said. "Not as bad as it seemed to me at first. Despite your lack of constant sparring this summer, you've still become more technically skilled. It's clear the practice that's been hammered into you has started to get results. I'm wondering — after our fight, do you know what tech we're going to work on together?"

"Yes." I gave him a tired nod.

After our fight, it felt like every cell in my body hurt.

Yeah... with Yamashita I never worked out this hard. He was always careful. But this guy, and Theophane... demons' sakes! My collarbone really hurt!

After the defensive barrier was down, I looked at the captivated faces of the teenagers and frowned imperceptibly.

I didn't like getting such intent attention from the people around me. I really didn't! One minute the mob is ready to carry you on their shoulders and laud you as a hero, and the next they just tear you apart once they forget the good you've done.

* * *

One Saturday, I was comfortably set up in the gym trying to meditate to the peaceful sound of the rain.

There's energy around me, it's everywhere, if I inhale all the life force in the air it will stay in me, so it can then go to the source, I repeated to myself internally for the umpteenth time. Demons' sakes! I'd read somewhere that magical energy could be called "life force," and it stuck! Ah, yes, life force.

While trying to master the second step of my magical education, I'd had to try a lot of different methods that my mage teacher appointed by George had recommended to me.

I read mantras, I reproduced all kinds of mental images in my head, and at a certain point it seemed to me I'd discovered a narrow path that would finally lead me to success in the end.

If I went off the assumption that some portion of magical energy was present in every atom, then it was in the air too, and it turned out that it was in the same air that — when I inhaled — saturated my blood with not only oxygen, but tiny bits of magic! And that same life force could then accumulate at the source — that is, in my core! It was only logical. Could I build a self-sufficient magical energy absorption process for my core from my outer surroundings based on this particular peculiarity of the body? It was fully possible!

So for half the time I spent doing exercises on my own, I tried to sense the smallest particles of energy I soaked up when I inhaled. After that, I imagined these little particles diffused through the air, like George's dark cloud of magic, constantly seeping into my body.

Of course, I wasn't able to notice any particular results from this method right away, but it began to seem to me that my core had started to refill itself quicker.

After a quiet knock on the door to the gym, it opened, and George came into the room.

He was wearing his comfortable at-home clothes — gray knitted clothes and soft slippers on his bare feet.

"How have you been doing with mastering the magical sciences?" he asked in a cheerful tone, sitting down next to me.

"Oh, you know," I answered evasively, opening my eyes. "Did you want something?"

"Why so unfriendly?" George seemed perplexed. "Maybe I just decided to find out how my favorite youngest brother is doing?"

"Kinda seems like before today you didn't care at all how I was doing," I noticed.

"Are you mad at me for something?" asked George. "I thought you prefer it yourself if I'm not all over you with excessive overprotectiveness. You've been trying to act like an adult, after all."

I wasn't acting like it, I *was* an adult, I thought

as usual, but I gave him a different answer.

"I'm not mad at you — I'm just sharing my own observations."

"Well, that's all good," said George, not wanting to continue on this topic. "So do you need help?"

"Sure, why not?" I answered after a short pause. "How exactly can you help me?"

"Well..." Now it was his turn to think. "As far as I know, right now you're working on the second stage of mastering magic. That is, absorption. I'll try to infuse a small portion of my energy into you. I think that'll allow you to grasp the principles of absorption yourself and get the ball rolling, and then you'll feel for yourself what to do next."

"The mage teacher you gave me already tried to test out something similar, more than once, but he didn't get any results."

"Hey, don't compare the two of us," said George, offended. "Me, a hereditary noble mage, and some commoner who can't do anything without a staff! Besides, I'm your brother — we have the same blood. I think my magical energy has to be similar to yours in some way. So that's why you'll be able not only to feel it, but to absorb it."

"You're a Temnikov, and I'm a Morozov. Darkness and Cold. Are you sure our magic is all that similar?" I added some skeptical notes to my voice.

"Despite that. We do have the same blood, and Mama was a Morozov — she was my mother too. So if we don't try, we won't know."

How interesting... I sighed, staring at George

thoughtfully. For the first time in a long time, he'd come to me himself and wanted to help me however he could. He was even persuading me to take advantage of his kindness. He was sweeping aside his doubt without even thinking about it, and he wasn't even trying to take offense at my skepticism. I'd bet anything that he needed something from me...

"What do you want?" I asked instead of agreeing to work with him.

"To help." George seemed surprised. "I told you, just to help."

"Let's be a little more specific," I suggested. "You want to help just like that or do you want some kind of exchange?"

"Just like that, of course!" he replied.

"So you're not going to ask any favors of me?" I said.

George was quiet for a minute.

"You are more grown up than your peers after all," he handed down the verdict. "Death clearly changes a person."

I didn't fall for it. I didn't say anything, waiting for a response.

"Actually, I did want to ask a small favor of you. But I would've done it only after we repaired our relationship. Don't think I was trying to 'buy' you..."

Well, then. He meant to say that he hadn't come to help me for the sake of self-interest, but only out of brotherly love. So I had to act the same way towards him and do what he wanted.

"I need you to accompany me to a ball at the Commandant of Morshansk's estate."

"Do I look like a lady?" I said, mentally rubbing my hands together.

Hey, why not? I'd get help from my brother in my mastery of magic and I'd get to hang out with Godimir in peace — and, possibly, meet someone important. Better than vegetating at home for an evening, after all. My brain would turn to porridge soon from these constant workouts.

George laughed.

"That's not why I need you. I was just hoping that your presence would take some attention off of me and let me settle a couple of issues."

"All right." I nodded. "Only you have to tell me later why you need this."

"Agreed. Now can you explain to me how you managed to keep Father away from the money in the Morozov bank account? Or did you not manage that after all?"

"Oh, you don't know?" I was very surprised at that, I had to admit. "The whole family's been gossiping about it! It's not a secret to anybody here either!"

"I was busy with other things at that time." George got embarrassed.

Yeah... I remembered what those "other things" were. I coughed and replied:

"After I was taken to the estate, Father sent a form to the Imperial Bank in my name requesting confirmation of how many assets I have. I didn't learn about this right away, but when a rep from the bank showed up, he decided that maybe that was for the best. He let it slide…"

"Don't keep me in suspense!" George interrupted me. "How much was there? Well?"

"About five hundred thousand thalers," I replied with a smirk.

George stared at me in surprise for a bit, then started laughing.

"*How* much?" he asked me again, laughing. "Only five hundred thousand? Hah! And Father dreamed of millions! Millions! Hah! He went so crazy over it! He spent so much money searching for you! Hah! He wanted to buy up a factory or modernize some of his big-investment businesses. And it was just small potatoes. About five hundred thousand!"

I, of course, didn't share George's mindset over this. Five hundred thousand thalers was still a lot of money. But, of course, for a princely bloodline it wasn't a serious fortune. Not at all.

"Oh, my…" said George, his laughter petering out. "And we chased that money, you can't even imagine…"

After a short pause, he decided to get back to business.

"So, let's go back to the reason for my being here," he said, calming down.

"Well, you already convinced me to go to the Ogneyers' ball with you." I didn't pass up my chance to drive that home.

"I mean the other thing," said George, smiling, and commanded: "Now close your eyes and concentrate on your magical core.

"Listen to my voice," he continued after I'd ful-filled his demand. "Listen to my voice and try to feel and see... you're a mage... you can clearly sense your magical core... a tiny sun shines inside you with ghostly light... look more carefully, you'll see little streams of energy flowing into it drop by drop..."

After George had repeated that same spiel a dozen times, at a certain moment it seemed like I really was seeing something like what he was say-ing.

I saw my magical core... I saw how a few lines were going towards it, carrying tiny particles of magical energy in them... I saw the little streams starting to fill with magic... saw them start to shine brighter and brighter... saw my core start to grow a little bit... my chest became tight with nasty pain.

The next second, a shield of ice formed around me.

Chapter 9

WE WERE A LITTLE LATE to the Ogneyers' ball. All because I had to clean up after my prematurely ended lesson with George...

After he, seated in a relaxed pose, had hit his forehead against the hard surface of my defensive ice dome, he'd profusely cussed out a certain Morozov, quickly inspected the shield, and yanked it out from under me. I'd lost consciousness.

"I didn't think it would go like that," he'd said quietly after I'd woken up.

"What happened to me?" I'd asked, feeling an unpleasant stretching sensation in my core. "Were you trying to kill me?"

"No, you dope!" George immediately leapt up from where he was sitting and started pacing back and forth nervously. "You just turned out to be right. Darkness and cold — they're two completely different forces. I think in that moment when your core had some of my energy in it, a particular defense mechanism kicked in."

Straining to overcome my weakness, I tried to sense my magical core. I managed it, but on far from the first try.

Thank the Savior, I thought, wiping cold sweat from my forehead. I hoped nothing bad had happened.

Going into my internal world, I noticed a couple of changes. The ghostly fire inside the ice slab had started to deaden, as a result of which the open space around it had gotten smaller. The darkness swirling around it, on the contrary, had gained some intensity. I still didn't feel like getting closer to it and getting cut off from my magic source when I did.

What was this? Was it all happening because of the Temnikov magic? I glanced around. How could I cleanse my body?

"What's going on? You going to lie there without moving for much longer?" I heard George's voice as he tugged at my shoulder. "Is everything okay?"

"Okay?" I bellowed at him, opening my eyes. "I can barely feel my core! Everything's somehow muddled! There's so much Temnikov energy in me that it's suppressing the Morozov magic! You idiot! You couldn't have thought of the consequences earlier?"

"Shut your mouth!" George snapped immediately. "You're not old enough to take that tone with me! No, I couldn't have known that your body is so susceptible to our magical power orientation! Besides, when I helped Ruslan and other people, everything turned out very well!"

"What in the Dwarf Saws does that nonsense have to do with me?" I said after I'd calmed down a little.

"Hell if I know!" George got upset. "That's the honest truth!"

After doing a couple more rounds of nervous pacing, George turned to me resolutely.

"I know what it could be!"

"What's that?" I asked, surfacing again from my internal world, where I'd been trying to herd the darkness into one spot.

"It's most likely because you only had your initiation recently! Your innate Morozov abilities manifested themselves, but since the ritual defining your bloodline membership isn't complete, you're still open to Temnikov magic."

"That's some BS!" I cursed sharply, and said in a mocking voice: "*Most likely, the ritual, the Temnikov bloodline...*" Then I continued speaking in a normal tone: "Are you serious? Father did the ritual, and it showed that I'm a Morozov."

"Then I don't know!" It was George's turn to snap at me. After a bit, he asked, "How do you feel?"

"Like crap." I frowned. "It's like some pain I can't understand is pulling at my core. How in the world could it hurt, if it's not part of my physical body? And I feel weak, too, of course. How else would I be feeling?"

"Your core is a part of your astral body," said George, rolling his eyes, "so you can absolutely get nasty feelings in your chest or your stomach. Oh, yeah! And how can you be feeling pain in your core and having trouble feeling it at the same time?"

"Because something's tight in my chest! But I can only use magical energy one time out of three! If not five!"

"Well, how was I supposed to know that this was how it'd turn out?" George started making excuses for himself again. "I really didn't want anything bad to happen — I thought I was helping! Nothing like this should have happened."

"Shouldn't have." I mimicked him. "Now I have to worry about this nonsense!"

"It should all pass quickly." George decided to be an optimist. "The unpleasant feelings will go away soon. Well, or you can get rid of all the negative effects yourself."

"Of course," I hemmed, sitting down. "I'll get rid of them. You think it'll work?"

"Of course! You just have to use energy from your source in spells, and there you go! It'll get better right away."

Logical, I judged. There wouldn't be a source of toxic energy, and it would improve immediately.

After meditating for a bit, I directed my magical energy into my palms with great difficulty. The process dragged on. The energy didn't want to leave the limits of my body, like it was clinging to my core.

I had to concentrate all my will to gather enough energy for a spell. Sweat poured out of my eyes, my hands started to shake.

"Cast it!" said George at a certain point. "Cast it, or you won't be able to hold it in."

Parting my hands to either side on intuition, I let loose a spell, mopped up the sweat, and opened my eyes.

"Whoa!" said George, surprised. "That was a Shaft of Darkness!"

"What?" I said, lying down weakly on the floor. "What Shaft of Darkness? I thought I was making an icicle."

"So he thought," George snorted. "And what kind of energy did you use for that spell?"

"I used whatever I could get." I knitted my brows.

"Well, then," said George thoughtfully. "I wonder — if you had fire-oriented energy inside you, would it have been a fire shaft?"

"No experiments!" I replied immediately. "Do some on yourself if you want."

"Yeah, don't worry, I just thought..." George brushed it off, and I asked:

"Everyone told me that when I let magical energy flow through my body, I reconstruct it as my own. Why didn't that work in our case? Why was there so much Temnikov magic?"

"That's what I was saying about your initiation," said George. "You and your nature as a mage are still on conditional terms. Your body hasn't learned how to alter that natural energy, at least, so with mine having a clearly expressed power orientation, you're going to process it worse. Good thing we at least managed to master the second stage."

"Master?" I said in surprise. "Seemed to me like we accomplished nothing! And what do you mean by power orientation?"

"Of course we accomplished something!" said George indignantly. "Just with a few unexpected consequences. You started off extracting energy at a very slow pace, after all, and then at a certain point you filled right up! You started pumping out everything I gave you. I didn't even have time to be surprised before I took a big old hit from your ice shield. And that was very unpleasant, don't you know!"

"But what do you mean by power orientation?" I reminded him.

"That's all very simple," George hemmed. "You could've guessed it yourself. Especially since I already threw you a couple of hints while answering your earlier questions. Magic is everywhere, it's around us, in varying amounts, in various elements. That kind of energy is called natural energy — that is, energy without an orientation. When a mage transforms it, it forms that orientation. If members of the same family constantly perfect a certain type of spell, then over time it turns into their so-called family magic. What we start to become better at than anything else. That's what power orientation is."

"So your power orientation is darkness?" I

asked.

"Well, yeah," said George. "Are you feeling better?"

"Much better," I replied, coming back to my senses. "Like a mountain fell off my shoulders."

"In that case, you should go to your room and take a good nap — we're going to the Ogneyers' tonight."

"Tonight?" I exclaimed, lifting myself up a bit. "I didn't agree to that! I'm totally not ready!"

"Sometimes life presents us with serious trials, and we must overcome them with our heads held high," said George, raising his finger, and with an idiotic grin he left the room.

Screw that, I thought, getting up slowly. That was no way to go about this.

*　*　*

"Why're you so bored?" said Godimir, walking up behind me. "Why're you so sad? Did something happen?"

"No, everything's fine," I brushed him off. Taking a glass of juice from a passing waiter, I added, "I over-trained a little today."

"I thought you said Theophane wasn't around right now? That he left the city on some business?"

"Yeah, and?" I didn't understand.

"Then who's training you? Somehow I doubt that you're training all too hard with your own regimen."

"You know what?" I said with indignation in

my voice. "I've been working really hard, actually! I'm really slogging away, so I can get results."

"I believe you, I believe you." Godimir laughed quietly. "You ready to prove yourself at the imperial tournament?"

"Why wouldn't I be?" I winked. "I train with one of the warriors from security every morning, with Mr. Viktorov at lunch, and by myself every night. When I'm overloading myself like that, my stats have gotta be going up."

"So strong..." Godimir shook his head thoughtfully. "Meanwhile, I train exclusively with magic in the evenings. Incidentally, how are you liking it here?"

"Great," I said, shrugging. "I've had occasion to be here before. Where's this question coming from?"

"You were just the ordinary Ivan Frost then, but now you're the heir to a princely bloodline. Are you seeing a difference?"

"I like your house in various states of being!" I giggled. "Just one thing I'm not used to — there are almost no women here today."

"Well, that's because this isn't a ceremonial ball." Godimir coughed. "Just a small gathering of a narrow circle of individuals."

"You make it sound like it's a group of revolutionaries," I said. "And who's been invited to this momentous event?"

"You don't know?" Godimir raised an eyebrow in surprise. "It's a gathering for the people who are going to participate in a large-scale campaign against the demons."

Ah, so that was it! Now I understood why George had taken an interest in this, I thought, mentally dubbing him a jerk. If he wanted my help, he could've not only described the task to me but even told me the point of the event! I wondered — would I see anyone I knew here?

"Remember how you said your group ran into Cross-Spiders in the fourth circle of the Wastelands?" Godimir continued. "Here's the thing, I found out that you weren't the first people to see something like that. A lot of hunter groups started to go missing, too. So passage to the Wasteland was closed for a while, they sent members of the Mage League there with various gadgets and started gathering strength."

"And what were the mages able to discover?" I was curious. "Or do you not know?"

"I know," said Godimir, glancing around. "They determined that there's a spiderweb border that runs all along the fourth circle, and the demons are starting to actively settle there."

"How's that?" I didn't understand. "That's where the weak demons have always fled! What do you mean they're settling there?"

"They're relocating," said Godimir enigmatically. "I heard my father saying that the stronger demons are migrating closer and closer to the border."

"That really does explain a lot," I said thoughtfully, looking around at the mix of people here.

That meant old man Taras had been right

when he'd said the demons were getting stronger and stronger every year. I wondered — would this news force the emperor and other big names in playing around with infernal business to stop and think? Everyone who made a profit from selling ingredients?

"Good evening, Ivan." I heard a voice I knew well and turned around.

"Good evening, Colonel, sir," I greeted Boemir Gurinov — the commander of a special operations forces unit.

"Godimir." Boemir nodded to Godimir and turned back to me. "You don't have to be so formal — I'm not in full dress, after all."

"That hasn't stopped you from being a special ops colonel and a Hero-rank warrior at the same time," I said, giving his warrior ring a pointed glance. "Congratulations — turns out I wasn't the only one working on my warrior skills!"

"A warrior must be growing constantly, or else he'll start to regress," said Boemir. "How are you doing? Is everything all right? Theophane asked me to check in on you."

That was good! I thought of my mentor gratefully. He'd talked to everyone beforehand.

"Does that mean I can head over to the base and practice my shooting?" I asked Boemir.

"And keep prepping for the next rank. I don't know about you, but my boys are sweating away so that you don't mop the floor with them next time you happen to stop by."

"That's an exaggeration," I said. "I don't think

I could make a good showing right now. The amount of practice I've had has decreased significantly."

"We'll see one way or another," said Boemir with a grin, not believing my words.

"Good evening, Colonel, sir." George greeted Boemir pretty loudly as he approached us.

"I can tell right away that you're related." Boemir glanced over George. "Nice to see you, George, sir."

"Likewise," replied George. He glanced at me and Godimir. "I didn't think I'd find you in this company."

"And for good reason, I dare say." Boemir grinned. "These young people are very richly gifted, and young sir Ivan and I have spent quite a lot of time together. I think you had a chance to evaluate his qualities as a warrior on your last trip to the Wasteland. I'm not wrong, am I? He's the one who took on a Betlor one-on-one, right?"

"You're not wrong," said George soberly. "I don't think it's a secret to anyone who brought that demon's wings to customs."

"That's exactly who I mean." Boemir nodded.

After a few seconds of silence, George continued:

"And perhaps you can dispel my curiosity? Are the details of our upcoming operation already known to you? Commandant Ogneyer wouldn't have started gathering us here just for discussion. Am I right?"

"Commandant Ogneyer," said Boemir, looking

askance at Godimir, "prefers to discuss such questions with his staff. Which has enough experience to resolve any type of problem."

"You won't share any interesting details with us?"

"I don't think that'll do any good," said Boemir. "But I can tell you one noteworthy thing."

"And what's that?" said George curiously.

"Along with the subdivisions from the city's power structures and the groups of nobles, several large groups of free hunters will also participate in the operation."

"Groups of free hunters?" George gave him a questioning look. "Has the matter turned out to be more serious than we initially thought?"

Boemir didn't have time to respond. A servant, who'd approached us inaudibly, invited the men to a meeting in a special room.

Deciding not to loiter purposelessly around this fairly large house, Godimir and I also headed to the meeting.

"You don't think they'll kick us out?" he asked quietly.

"You're the head of the estate's son, and I'm a guest of your father and the heir to a princely bloodline," I said just as quietly. "If we don't get in the way or behave improperly, it'll all be fine. Let's just sit quietly and try not to stand out."

The meeting took place in a fairly large room, one wall of which was covered with a huge white linen cloth that took up the whole wall. Comfortable armchairs were set up across from a large screen, like an amphitheater, and there was a multimedia projector hidden on the ceiling.

"Sometimes Papa and I watch the newest movies in here," said Godimir quietly as we fought our way to the back row along the wall. "Well, if something interesting comes out."

"Not a bad setup!" I grinned. "So we simple mortals have to go to the movie theater and stand in line for tickets, and meanwhile you watch movies here in comfort?"

"It's more fun to watch at the theater than here anyway," said Godimir. "It's just that Father doesn't have much time for all sorts of entertainment, so he watches when it's convenient for him."

"In that case, why did we go to the theater to see *The Foreigner?*" I asked with some feigned indignation in my voice. "If your house has such marvelous things in it?"

"I'm telling you, Father's the one who decides these things. Although we can watch the sequel here. And we'll call the guys, of course."

After a bit, the lights in the room turned down. A map of the Gorbovich Wasteland and the adjacent territories appeared on the screen, and a man in an imperial officer's uniform walked up to the podium near the linen cloth.

He waited for everyone to be quiet, then introduced himself and started to tell those present about the order of operations to be carried out under the code name "Cleanser." After explaining the goals of the operation and general matters to the attendees at great length, he moved on to explaining the duties of each specific subunit, nobles and hunters alike.

Slides flashed by one after another, allowing him to more clearly make the task understood to those present.

From all this I understood that the government had managed to determine the length of the demons' defensive spiderweb border, and they wanted to know why this peculiar wall was being built. What were the beasts hiding from us?

When the officer started getting bombarded with questions, I wasn't even surprised. A lot of experienced warriors and mages were here, people who'd been in all sorts of scrapes numerous times and had a ton of fighting experience. It was understandable that they'd want to get a better personal understanding of some things...

After the meeting was over, all the attendees were invited to a small dinner, and Godimir and I also headed to that event.

"So what'd you think? You weren't bored, were you?" George asked us as he approached us, giving the agreed-upon signal.

"A little," I said, looking with curiosity at the elderly mage standing next to George with a Professor of magic's ring on his finger.

"Then I think you'll be happy to meet the head of the Morshansk Mage League — Oleg Albertovich Berezov."

"It's an honor to meet you," I said.

"This is my youngest brother." George introduced me in turn. "Ivan Yegorovich Morozov."

"Pleasure to meet you," said the man in a pleased voice. "I saw your self-initiation — it was an impressive sight. I think you're going to become a pretty strong mage."

"Thank you, sir," I replied. Remembering my agreement with George, I added: "And why did my self-induced initiation seem impressive to you?"

"What do you mean?" Berezov smiled. "It's a fairly rare occurrence."

"Oh?" I was surprised. "I was told things like that happen pretty often."

"I beg your pardon, Professor," said George, not giving Berezov a chance to respond to that question. "Commandant Ogneyer asked me to find him after the meeting. You wouldn't be against that, would you?"

Incidentally, why wasn't Godimir saying anything? What, was he afraid of this old guy?

"I have to go too," said Godimir quickly from behind me, and he practically vanished into thin air.

"Ivan, *you're* not casting me off, are you?" asked Berezov with a grin.

"And deprive myself of an interesting conversation? Certainly not — I'm not letting myself do that!"

"In that case, Mr. Temnikov—" Berezov turned to George. "It would be my pleasure to speak with Ivan. I don't dare keep you."

"Thank you, sir!" George nodded and turned to me. "And don't you dare pester the professor with stupid questions."

"Shall we go to the food table, perhaps?" Berezov suggested when we found ourselves alone.

"With pleasure," I agreed contentedly, barely keeping myself from rubbing my hands.

Look at that, I'd found someone who could competently answer a few questions about formation for young mages!

Chapter 10

"SO HOW ARE YOU doing?" I asked the five exhausted men sitting on massive benches.

They'd returned home not long ago after a serious skirmish in the Wasteland, which had been done under the leadership of the commandant of Morshansk, and they looked a little worse for wear.

"Fine," said George, leaning back and adjusting his blanket, which had fallen to the side. "We're just a little tired. We just need to wash up a little and everything will be great."

"A bath is a wonderful thing." I nodded in agreement, examining the fresh scars on the family's warriors and mages.

The men were sitting there wrapped in blankets, not hiding how serious the fight had been. Only George looked like he normally did. As it turned out, he hadn't participated in the fighting, but his entire appearance spoke clearly to the fact that he'd really given his all magically speaking.

"Come sit," said George, patting an empty spot next to him.

Sitting down next to him, I adjusted the blanket I'd managed to throw on in the changing room and poured some fresh rye kvas into an empty mug.

"Can you share the details with me?" I asked once I'd finished the preparations. "What was behind the spiderweb wall? Did you find out?"

"This wasn't our mission," said one of the mages abruptly. "It was the demons'. They were clearly waiting for us, so there was a real party waiting for us. I've never seen so many demons in my life! There had to be thousands! A lot of people were killed."

"It's not really right to ask about such things," said another mage, who up until then had been fixing an unfocused stare on the ground. "We spilled blood there, did battle with evil..."

He wanted to say something else, but a jab from Yamashita made him be quiet. I figured if I weren't the son of a nobleman, the mage would've babbled on even more.

"Thanks for reminding me," I said to him, drinking a little of my kvas. "And here I was thinking people go to the Wasteland for mushrooms and berries, not to kill demons."

I firmly met the mage's furious gaze.

"What, you went to the Wasteland a few times in a big group and you're already a hero?" I shot out before I could stop myself. "I practically lived there for two years!"

Lowering my blanket a little, I showed him my huge collection of barely visible scars that nonetheless covered my whole body.

"I can't get most of them to go away even after a year. And you're telling me about doing battle with evil."

The mage shut up right away, and George coughed and said:

"There was nothing there but hordes of demons. A few thousand strong creatures, and that's all."

"Yeah?" I was genuinely surprised. "And no other surprises?"

"If you don't count the fact that half the demons were sixth- and seventh-circle," Yamashita chimed in, "then no."

"That's very strange," I noted. "With a horde like that, they could've assembled even without the Cross-Spiders' help. Something about this smells."

"Definitely smells," George agreed. "That's why Commandant Ogneyer sent a report to the emperor with his conclusions about what's going on. The imperial bloodhounds will try to find out what all of our attention was being diverted from."

"It would be interesting to get even one little glance at their reports!" I had to agree.

* * *

A middle-aged man with unmemorable facial features, without taking his eyes off his reading, once again adjusted his glasses and nervously drummed his fingers on the table.

Our sleeper agent disappeared again, he thought with a frown. *This is really starting to irritate me.*

There were no traces left of his recent satisfaction. Yes, he'd managed to adroitly deflect the attention of the imperial powers onto what was happening near Morshansk, and even carry out all of the actions he'd planned without interference. Which wasn't surprising, since the government couldn't ignore the strange behavior of the demons near a city where a Soul Stone had been found not long ago. The Order's higher-ups could turn even defeat to their advantage.

However, despite that welcome news, it was concerning that four agents had already been found dead.

There's no such thing as coincidence, thought the man gloomily yet again. These events were leading him to think some bad thoughts. Someone had taken them on, and done a good job of it. Even eliminating a few agents hadn't helped.

Once he'd finished studying the report drawn up by the Order's analytical center, the man returned to his interrupted musing.

He wondered if this was the gendarmes or the

clergy after all. This didn't look anything like work from the private sector, he thought, rubbing his neck, which was covered in a lot of unsightly scars. It was more likely the clergy — those beasts knew how to get results. Especially if demons were involved.

With a passing glance at his expensive platinum watch, the man nodded to himself.

He'd have to call the council and bring them the latest news. Then he'd have to personally see to the agents who'd been killed, or else the next phase of the operation would be threatened.

* * *

In the second half of the third school trimester, all the schools in the Nosiriansky Empire held one of the most important events of the year — the rite of testing for magical strength.

Being in a country that was in a constant state of war with the demons made a systematic influx of new mages necessary. Since people with these talents were born not only to noble bloodlines, but also to commoner families, the government's top priority was the timely identification of untrained mages. After they'd been identified, they started their education in the local branches of the Mage League, where their preparation also took place. According to the Empire's stats this year, about two thousand mages had been identified. Hardly a small number, so the government devoted a lot of attention to this event.

For the students at the Imperial Academy, the testing ritual didn't reveal anything new. It was pretty much just members of noble families who went here, after all, and noble children traditionally did tests like that at an early age. So most of the students at our branch not only knew that they had magical abilities but could also use them.

I had just joined a group of students like that, although admittedly, great achievements in the field of magical arts couldn't be expected of me anymore. This was according to Professor Berezov, who had confirmed it — because I'd become a pretty strong warrior at a young age, and my body was used to working with Shiki-Cho. It was precisely that energy, in Berezov's opinion, that was preventing my magical talent from fully developing, and the more I studied magic the harder it would be for me to get to the higher ranks.

Overall, our conversation had turned out to be pretty educational. Berezov, among other things, had been able to shed light on my biggest mistake in casting spells. Now that I knew about it, I was stupefied and didn't understand why I hadn't known about it. As it turned out, during this whole phase of my education, not one of my so-called "teachers" had told me that you were supposed to hold a concentration rune in front of yourself when doing spells! Dwarf Saws take it! How angry I'd been in that moment! I wanted to rip someone apart! That was basic stuff! That was the first thing that stupid Simmeron guy Petius had assigned should have taught me! Demons' sakes!

"What's with you?" Vladimir Ischezov asked me, touching my shoulder lightly. "You have some kind of anger radiating from you, like you're gonna attack someone at any second. Look, everyone's already turning around."

"Sorry," I said, returning to reality and trying to calm myself down. I explained, "I just remembered something unpleasant."

Ignoring Ms. Dashkevich's gaze as it followed me attentively, I started looking around.

They'd taken us — the seventh graders — into a special circular hall on the first floor of the school. The ceiling, walls, and floor were covered with inlaid white tile and red rune designs I wasn't familiar with.

How beautiful, I thought, activating my Eyes of the Wolf tech and looking around on all sides.

I could see a few dozen other magical symbols behind the bright red runes.

"Are those real runes or just dummies?" some maverick asked quietly.

They were real, I thought, but I didn't say anything. I already had such heightened attention on me from my classmates and the other students from our branch — there was no need to remind them of me more than necessary, or else they'd start giving me funny looks and getting distracted again.

When the testing ritual finally started, I realized that it was radically different from the ones that took place in noble houses. At least, the Temnikovs did it completely differently.

Although it wasn't surprising, because as far as I knew, the ritual that was done in this hall was needed to identify magical talent or reveal its absence, while noble families' rituals showed other parameters too. Additionally, today's "magic show" was being done for a lot of people at the same time.

The first participant in the ritual was invited to the center of the room, where there was a short pedestal standing on a small dais. He approached and placed his hands on a small glass globe on top of the pedestal. After a few seconds, the globe started to glow with dim white light.

He returned to his seat to the applause of the attendees, and the vice principal noted something in a folder and called up the next person to the pedestal.

I didn't know how these things were done in other schools, but at our branch that was how the ritual looked. It happened pretty much the same way every time. The participant approached the pedestal and laid hands on the globe, and after a short while it would start to glow. The applause for each new participant got weaker and weaker, but the students approached the dais more and more confidently each time. Incidentally, the time it took for the globe to light up and the brightness of the light were the same for everyone. That was exactly how I figured out that I had the right idea — this ritual could only determine the presence or absence of magical talent.

It was surprising, but every seventh-grade student who did the ritual that day turned out to be a mage. I'd thought for some reason that we had at least one or two Normals among us. Non-mages were sometimes born even to noble families. I was living confirmation of that... or I used to be... now the ritual showed that I was a mage, and I got my share of applause.

After the ritual, everyone was invited to a celebratory lunch, and later we were dismissed to go home, so there were no classes planned for that day.

As I watched the students rushing for the school doors, I was once again convinced that children were still children, even if they were mages. Just as long as they didn't have an adult from another world occupying their bodies...

* * *

I spent the rest of the time until break doing intense workouts with Mr. Viktorov, and also trying to fully master my ability to absorb and transform magical energy while using a concentration rune. It was the same rune that a hereditary mage was supposed to use while casting any spell. At least at the beginner level.

My break didn't start off very well. On the very first day, George greeted me with the revelation that we had to go home.

"To the estate?" I was surprised. "During my break? And you're coming too? Is your exile over?"

"Yes, I'll have to come," said George, seeming satisfied. "But the matter of my exile isn't certain yet — we'll find out when we get there."

"Seemed to me you weren't burning with the desire to go back home," I noted cautiously, "and talk to Father, even less so to Galina."

"I'm not. I have nothing to speak about with that creature," said George, becoming serious. "But still, in the time I've spent in Morshansk, I've started to miss it a little. I need some down time, and to meet up with my friends."

"As if home would be a super fun place for you!" I said sarcastically. "All your fights with Father — now that's a good time!"

"Anyway, we're going to the estate, and then after a few days we'll head to the capital. I've managed to start missing it."

"This really is much more interesting, then," I said thoughtfully in response. "And what are you planning to do in the capital? Why are we going there?"

"For a traditional imperial ball." George winked at me and headed for the room's exit. "So get packing — we're leaving in an hour."

I didn't have time to ask him what he meant by imperial ball.

Oh well, I figured I'd ask on the road. With some sadness, I said:

"I wonder who these friends of George's are? And why, in a whole year, did only one of them come here to visit him?"

"So what's with this imperial ball?" I asked once our helicopter had taken off. "I've never heard about something like that."

"It's a New Year's Eve ball," George explained. "His Majesty holds it once a year, at the Romanov Palace."

"And what in the world does that have to do with us?" I asked, puzzled. "As far as I know, our family's never gone to parties like that before."

"Up until now, when Father started taking interest in politics again," George explained, annoyed. "And what do you mean we've never gone? I've been, and so have Theodore and Ignatius."

Not surprising he sounded so annoyed, it occurred to me. George probably hadn't planned for Father to be able to change so much in such a short time. He'd already been preparing to take the reins of the family into his own hands, and here was this setback. Not only that, but he'd had the riot act read to him just when he thought he was going to win.

"You, incidentally, made a lot of noise too with your self-initiation," George continued in the meantime. "So it's not at all surprising that you didn't have to wait long for an invitation to an imperial ball. All the more so an invitation for the whole family."

Anna, Maria, and Ruslan met us right away after we landed.

"Hi!" shouted Maria, trying to yell over the noise of the helicopter's propellers, running up and hugging me.

Anna approached George. Then they switched places, and once we'd exchanged hugs, they finally joined us in heading towards the entrance to the house.

"So? How are you two? Tell us!" said Maria. Looking at me, she added, "Ivan, have you done the magical strength testing ritual at school yet? Are you ready for the academic stage of the imperial tournament?"

"I did the ritual, but I'm not ready for the academic tournament," I reported with clarity, laughing. "I'm prepping for the warrior tournament."

"A warrior, not bad!" said Ruslan, who'd finally approached us. "Would be even better to prep for the mage tournament!"

"Hi!" I greeted him and explained: "I started studying magic not long ago, but I've been studying martial arts for a few years now already."

"Weakling," Maria declared immediately. "It's better to learn proper magic, if your strength allows it. Leave the fist-flailing to the commoners — anyone can learn to do that!"

"You think the path of the warrior is somehow bad? Or worse than the path of the mage?" I decided to ask, a little hurt by those words.

Not long ago, after all, I'd thought magic was completely closed off to me.

"Well, it's not *bad*..." said Ruslan, joining the discussion. "But mages are much stronger than warriors. There's just no contest."

"I might disappoint you," I said, smirking. "If a mid-level warrior would lose to a mid-level mage, that doesn't say anything. It all depends on the specific warrior or mage's level of mastery — only that and nothing else."

"Oh, come on." Anna looked at me skeptically, and explained like she was talking to a little child: "Mages are still stronger than warriors."

"What about you, George, what do you think?" Maria asked George, who'd been quiet. "Who's stronger, warriors or mages?"

George stopped for a moment, gave me a side-long glance, and said:

"I agree with Ivan — I think it all depends on a specific person's skills. One person's mastery versus the other person's mastery."

Peering at their three discontented faces, he chuckled.

"You know what, though? You're all going to cling to your own points of view anyway, you can't see the other side yet, and if you never do, it'll cost you dearly. I think a sparring match between Ruslan and Ivan will help you see that I'm right and look at the situation seriously."

"You saying Ivan could beat me?" Ruslan was surprised. "No offense, but that's impossible. He's no Knight or Hero — just an ordinary Soldier."

"Let's find out!" Anna declared. "I'd be curious to see what a warrior can actually do against a mage."

"Me too," Ruslan chimed in resolutely. "So, this evening we'll see which of us is right."

If George is the ref, then why not? I thought. Besides, it had been a while since I'd practiced with a mage.

The atmosphere at lunchtime was neutral. Father crawled out of the woodwork, reluctantly talked to George for a bit about some general matters, and then left again. He favored me with a nod of greeting, and that was all.

Now that wasn't actually too bad, I thought as I ate my food unhurriedly. It would've been significantly worse if he'd called me right into his study for a conversation…

That evening, our merry band met up in the mages' hall. I, much like Ruslan, was wearing light gym clothes.

"Well then, shall we begin? Or do you need to jog around a little and warm up first?" asked Ruslan, grinning and taking his place about ten yards from me.

He was clearly confident that he'd win.

"I don't need to jog." I smirked in response, and as I let my spiritual energy circulate, I explained: "That's only needed for the lower ranks."

"Just make sure you're careful," said George, stepping back sensibly and covering the girls with an aura shield.

"I'll be careful as can be," said Ruslan, thinking that warning was addressed to him, but George was looking at me.

"Ready?" asked George.

"Yes," I answered drily.

"Ruslan?"

"I was born ready!"

"Then go!" George commanded, and Ruslan immediately sent a spell at me.

"You wanna get your staff before it's too late, maybe?" I asked, taking a half-step to the side as an Air Fist missed me by half an inch.

"I can fight without it too," said Ruslan, and hit me with something that was already more serious — two wide-range spells.

This wouldn't work, we'd just volley things back and forth forever, I thought. I started to make moves.

Waiting for his Wall of Fire to hide me from his view, I took a couple of quick Spirit-Steps and — finding myself behind Ruslan — hit him in the back with a Battering Ram. It immediately broke through his weak shield, knocked him to the ground, and backed up.

"One to nothing, Ivan," said George, looking at me in surprise.

He hadn't seen Spirit-Steps in my arsenal yet, I thought with satisfaction. And it was pretty striking to watch.

Enraged at his failure, Ruslan immediately attacked me with a couple of strong spells.

Dodging them, I put up a Spirit Shield, tanked a weak Air Fist, got closer to Ruslan, and hit him with a couple of Power Whirlwinds.

This time, he hadn't underestimated me, and he'd put up a couple of truly strong shields. So I had to dodge the spells that came after my move, once again using a Spirit-Step.

I used that trick repeatedly, circling around Ruslan and testing his shields' stability.

The pace of the fight was really fast. One of us would have to slip up soon. Either I'd get hit by a powerful spell from him if I couldn't disappear into a Spirit-Step in time, or I'd finally manage to break the shield he was constantly restoring.

Luck was on my side. Another series of blows shattered the shield and threw Ruslan to the floor. And that was taking stock of the fact that I'd only recently learned to use Spirit-Steps confidently.

It was a really difficult tech — it required outstanding skill and constant concentration. All the better that I'd practiced the tactic I was using today with Mr. Viktorov. It consisted of a Spirit-Step, a couple of blows, and another Spirit-Step, and then a couple more blows.

Judging by how this fight was going, I'd gotten a pretty good handle on it.

"Two to nothing," said George.

"Dwarf Saws take it!" Ruslan beat his fist against the ground and stood up. "What in the world is happening? How is he doing that?"

"What's happening is what should be happening! You're underestimating the path of the warrior, and you're being punished for it," said George coldly. "Were you expecting it to be a walk in the park? Did you think you could beat Ivan just like that? Yes, of course he's not a simple warrior at all — he knows a lot and is capable of a lot. But you're losing to him not because you underestimated him specifically — it's because for some reason you considered yourself stronger on principle."

I looked at the girls' surprised faces as they stood behind George and added:

"The path of the warrior can actually do a lot of good for its adherents. But I also wanted to note that Ruslan was making almost no use of his advantage and wasn't using his wide-range spells — instead, he was using one-off spells."

"Exactly! What kind of mage are you without wide-range spells?" George continued to scold Ruslan sternly. "He dodged everything you cast without breaking a sweat because he's so fast!"

Then George turned to Anna and Maria.

"This is relevant to you too! It's never any good to underestimate your opponent. Every fighter has an ace up his sleeve, and pray to the Savior that you can avoid surprises like that."

"Wide-range?" said Ruslan resolutely, looking at me. "Well, then, let's try again..."

For the next few minutes of battle, I had to dodge beautifully to get away from all kinds of spells.

In the brief moments when I managed to get a little closer to Ruslan, he cast an encircling spell around himself, forcing me to step back.

Finally I noticed that he was exhausted, and I exposed myself to his spell on purpose.

"Stop!" George commanded instantly, ending the fight. "That's one for Ruslan."

"Finally!" said Ruslan, trying to catch his breath and sitting down on the ground. "Man, you're spry!"

"You bet!" I said, following suit. "But not as spry as I'd like to be. You caught up with me in the end. And I'm tired too. Got nothing left in me. That's enough for today, then."

I really was tired, fittingly — we'd used a lot of

techs, after all, and we'd had to do a lot of jumping — but I had about ten more minutes' worth of fumes to run on.

I'd lost for another reason.

I hadn't felt like beating Ruslan a third time and humiliating him even more. He'd lost to his little brother, who hadn't even been using magic, twice already. A third loss could've made him really angry, and I would most likely have been the focus of his negative emotions. It wasn't hard to predict how things would've gone from there. We would've gotten colder towards each other, and possibly a little hostile. I didn't need that kind of thing one bit. So I'd had to set myself up and let Ruslan vindicate himself. At least in his own eyes.

"I'm shocked!" Anna admitted honestly, coming closer. "I never expected anything like this — they're always telling us that warriors are much weaker than mages."

"It all depends on individual mastery," I repeated, shrugging. I stood and helped Ruslan get up.

"So." George turned to all of us and looked at his watch. "It'll be dinnertime soon, so go to your rooms and get ready."

After dinner, a servant summoned me to Father's study.

Nothing to be done — I had to go, I thought, and I told George about it. Savior only knew what was going to happen in there. I'd better have him standing by just in case.

"I know you're not ecstatic about frequent one-on-one conversations with me. So I'll cut to the chase," said Father when I'd entered his study and taken the chair he indicated. "At the imperial ball, you'll be presented to his Highness Prince Vivovt, and I don't want you to dishonor the family."

Aha — he wanted to make sure our agreement regarding the interpretation of several events was in place, I thought, and answered:

"It's in my best interest more than anything. I don't understand why we're having this conversation."

"I need you to understand the importance of this situation and take this task seriously," Father replied. "I would like to warn you not to chatter about what's going on inside the family in front of people."

"I will honor our agreement," I said instead of making unnecessary excuses.

"Glad to hear it." Father nodded, then added after a short pause, "The ball is in a week. Tomorrow I'll send a tailor and Elvira your way — you must be fully and completely ready."

I nodded.

"In that case, if everything is understood, you may go." I nodded again and left the study wordlessly.

As I returned to my room, I got lost in thought and almost walked past George, who was leaving a dark alcove.

"Dwarf Saws!" I cursed. "Don't scare me like that! I thought you were another murderer."

"I'm not gonna murder you." George smirked,

then got serious all at once. "What did he want?"

"He said that I'll be presented to Vitovt at the imperial ball, and that I need to be prepared."

"And bite your tongue," George chimed in.

"Obviously," I said.

The next three days flew by for me as if in an instant. Elvira really knew what she was doing and couldn't allow me to go to the imperial ball unprepared. Thankfully, this time Ruslan and the girls shared my torment, so it wasn't quite so rough.

We headed to the imperial capital, the city of Marigrad, ahead of time in the helicopter I knew so well. The family also had a big house there, where Theodore and Ignatius were living at the moment. That was where we'd leave for the imperial ball from.

All right, good. I'd find time to prepare. We weren't jumping straight off the helicopter into the ballroom, I thought as we touched down on the landing pad at the house in the capital.

Chapter 11

THE TEMNIKOV FAMILY headed to the imperial ball in a luxurious limo that was parked in the garage of the house at the capital. As far as I remembered, there was no such car at the family estate. Although I figured there was nothing surprising about that. Where would noble families be able to demonstrate their wealth and their place in society to others and show everyone else up, if not the capital? No point doing that at home, in your own city! Everyone back there knew what was what, after all.

For that matter, status wouldn't allow a princely family to arrive at a ball at the imperial palace in a cheaper car. Not with our standing — they wouldn't accept that, no sir.

After sixteen hours, the limo left the property with a few security off-roaders escorting it, and within about an hour it stopped near the red-carpeted road leading up to the imperial palace.

"The most important thing is to keep it together and not be nervous," Father said as his last word of instruction, and stepped out through the door opened by an obliging porter.

We could immediately hear the sounds of cameras clicking and the noise of a lively crowd.

"Prince Yegor Dimitrievich Temnikov with his wife and family," proclaimed an emcee over the enthusiastic shouts of the gaping masses, who for reasons I couldn't understand had come to the imperial palace to gawk at the nobility.

Getting out of the car last, as was customary for the youngest, I waved to the large crowd behind the barrier. I got my own helping of the applause, and I followed the rest of my family unhurriedly.

Despite the fact that we'd arrived a little earlier than usual, since Father had to explain a few things to the local clerical office, there were already a lot of guests at the palace.

"Sweet digs," commented Ruslan, standing next to me and looking around a bit.

"Would be weird if they weren't," I said, sizing up the unobtrusive splendor of the palace.

"We got here early, but it seems like there are too many guests here at this point." I heard Theodore's pensive voice. "Is something unusual happening today?"

"No," said Ignatius lackadaisically. "Take a closer look, why don't you — most of the people here are guards and government courtiers. They always get together before events like this for various meetings and conferences. It's just that we used to get here a little later, and it wasn't quite so in our faces."

Turned out his constant partying had a use too, I thought unexpectedly, watching as Ignatius took a champagne glass from a passing server's tray with a natural and well-practiced movement. He probably knew a lot of interesting gossip about high society at the capital.

"Isn't it a little early to start drinking?" Father asked him calmly.

"No." Ignatius waved him off calmly. "I need to wet my whistle."

Father didn't say anything, but his eyes, clouding over with darkness for a moment, spoke for themselves.

"I'll be very careful," said Ignatius a bit more seriously.

"I'm counting on it." Father nodded and, turning to the rest of us, added: "Galina and I are leaving you by yourselves for a while, so for now you may walk around the palace for a bit and look around, but on the condition that everyone meets back here in an hour. Understood?"

"The old man's finally gone," said a satisfied Ignatius, watching Father's back as he walked away. Taking a big swig of champagne, he turned to George and Theodore. "Shall we go and see who's already here? I swear I saw the Olechnovich family and the Malinovsky family, and I think the Sokolov family is here too."

"Let's go," George agreed after a bit. He turned to us and said, "Act civilized. We'll be back soon."

"What, are you leaving us alone?" said Anna indignantly to the older brothers.

"Why not?" hemmed Ignatius. "This is the imperial palace! The safest place in the country! Besides, Ruslan will look after you."

"Me?" Ruslan exclaimed. "I'm plenty grown up already, but Ivan will look after the girls too."

"We believe in you." Theodore gave him a clap on the shoulder. "Don't let us down."

"You should be proud of the honor you've been given," said Ignatius. "Take care of them and keep them safe."

"Don't worry," said Anna after the older boys had left. "No matter where you go in the capital, you'll have a good time in their company."

"It's gotta be boring for you hanging out with them," I noted. "You have completely different interests, and you don't know their friends."

"You're not super fun to hang out with either," said Ruslan, upset.

"Oh, I dunno," I chuckled. "I just have to be personally presented before the Nosiransky Empire's imperial heir today. You think I don't want to introduce him to my brother?"

"And your sister," Maria chimed in.

"Your sisters," Anna corrected her.

"No, of course *you're* fun to hang out with." Ruslan immediately backpedaled. "I was talking about the girls."

* * *

The great hall that we were in started to fill with people gradually, the music got louder, and the number of servers rushing around with trays increased.

Father, Galina, and the three oldest got to the meeting spot almost at the same time, and we all looked around with extreme satisfaction.

"So here's what's happening," said Father to me, Anna, and Maria. "Ignatius is about to take you to the next hall over, where Imperial Prince Vitovt is supposed to make an appearance in a short while. Try to get acquainted with him before the official presentation, which will take place at the end of the evening — this is important to me."

After that, a displeased Ignatius led us to the other room — a fairly large hall which, to our surprise, was no less populated than the first.

It seemed that young nobles from all over the country had come here today. Although I figured that was just how it was, to some extent. The Temnikov family wasn't the only one that had decided to gain the upper hand by meeting the emperor's heir.

Anna, Maria, and I immediately noticed a few people we knew and headed in their direction. After spending a while having conversations about nothing in particular and listening to the gossip and the news, which turned out not to be childish at all, I noticed Godimir approaching us.

"I'm glad to see you," I said after we'd exchanged hellos. "I just knew you'd be here too."

"Well, I *am* the son of a commandant," Godimir replied. Coming closer, he said to me quietly, "I'm also one of Imperial Prince Vitovt's potential classmates."

"That's really great." I looked at him curiously and added: "C'mon, I'll introduce you to everybody. They're good people, not one arrogant snob to be seen among them."

"Listen," Godimir whispered to me after a bit. "Are they seriously discussing the border conflicts with the kingdom of Tanzin and the Koga Republic?"

"Uh-huh," I replied just as quietly. "I'm shocked myself, but it's interesting information — I didn't even know that we had tensions with them. Turns out they've had their sights on our Wastelands for a long time now. You see, we Nosirians have strategic access to infernal territory! I never would've thought that Wasteland spoils could be a reason for conflict between nations."

"It sure is," said Godimir. "If only they lived in Morshansk and fought off some demons for a while. I'd watch that."

After some time, I noticed without any particular surprise that the not-unfamiliar Oleg Glinov was at the ball. He was surrounded by a lot of people, looked content with life, and was looking in our direction haughtily.

When our gazes met, I nodded politely to greet him, but I got nothing but a contemptuous grimace in response.

Jerk! I thought indignantly. Here I was behaving properly towards him, one could say trying to smooth things over, and he was acting like this? Was last time not enough for him?

"Friend of yours?" asked Godimir, noticing us exchanging glances. "Somehow I don't get the sense he's ecstatic to see you."

"That's Oleg Glinov," I explained. "You remember I told you about him at the snack bar?"

"Oh yeah!" said Godimir. "That's the same jerk who gave you a hard time at the Beregov estate! I was wondering why his insolent face looked familiar to me!"

"Very insolent," I said. "I wanted to say hello to him so as not to aggravate the conflict any more. To show him that I have no intention of initiating confrontation here, and he..."

"You saw Grease-ov too?" Maria asked quietly, walking up to me. "He's been staring at us for half an hour now. Clearly he hasn't gotten anything out of anyone for a while."

"Grease-ov?" Godimir chuckled, looking at my sister curiously. "That really suits him. It's original."

"Nothing too original, a lot of people call him that," snapped Maria, not looking at Godimir and turning to me. "Be careful. That jerk loves to get up to all sorts of dirty tricks. I wouldn't be surprised if that's why he's so smug. He's definitely cooked up something bad."

"Based on what he got up to at the Beregov

estate, his dirty tricks are a little underwhelming," I said calmly, but I decided to heed Maria's warning anyway.

On the one hand, setting traps at the imperial palace was really stupid. Everyone here, after all, was a guest of the emperor, and if you offend those, you unwittingly put the leader of the country in an uncomfortable position. On the other hand, though, only reasonable people understood that — idiots were totally unpredictable!

As it turned out, Glinov and the guys from his entourage were in the second category. They caught me when I was in the bathroom. Or, to be more specific, they caught us. Remembering Maria's warning, Godimir and I headed to the bathroom together.

"What do you think, could I get her to like me?" Godimir was torturing me about Maria. "She's not even noticing me!"

"That's just it — she's trying not to look at you," I explained, drying my hands on a paper towel. "That just shows she's interested in you. It'd be worse if she didn't notice you at all. Although, of course, I won't get your hopes up — it's all up to you. I suggest you don't be shy and make the first move. I think asking her to dance will be..."

I didn't manage to finish my sentence. The door to the bathroom opened, and in came a group of boys with Glinov in the lead, chattering loudly.

"Well, well, well," said Glinov with satisfaction. "What do we have here?"

I had to admit, I didn't know what he expected

me to do. Get scared? Say hi to him? Start bab-
bling incoherently? Or start behaving strangely?
Honestly, I had no idea! It even started to seem
funny to me for a little bit, but then I decided to
avoid reacting and continue our interrupted conversation.

"Anyway, like I said, it's all up to you."

"That's actually what I was planning to do,"
said Godimir, understanding. "I'll try."

"What, you too cool for us?" One of the boys
flew into a rage, not tolerating being intentionally
ignored. "S'been a while since anyone taught you
how to be polite?"

"Were you speaking to us, messieurs?" said
Godimir, turning and making a surprised face.

"Don't play dumb, you," said the boy even
more angrily, and the others around him chimed
in. "Who do you think you are?"

"Watch how you're speaking," Godimir replied
sharply. "I'm not a close enough friend of yours for
you to talk to me that way! Not at all! We're at a
reception at the imperial palace, not a backwater
nightclub! So behave yourselves properly."

"You're gonna teach me how to be polite? Who
do you think you are? I'm only gonna ask so many
times!"

"So you've decided to get to know us better?" I
asked calmly, deciding to interfere. "And why did
you choose the bathroom for that?"

"If only there were someone here worth knowing," one of the boys announced.

"In that case, we have nothing to talk about,"

I asserted, moving towards the door.

However, we didn't manage to make it out. The boys were still standing in our way, blocking our path.

"Are we in kindergarten, Oleg?" I asked Glinov, glancing at him.

"That's Mr. Glinov to you," he answered. "And no, we're not in kindergarten, we just want to know if Ivan Morozov is actually who he claims to be or not. And if that internet video everyone knows about is true."

"You could just ask. Why start the conversation with confrontation?" asked Godimir, shaking his head. "Especially in the bathroom? Are you guys right in the head?"

I glanced around at the angry boys and thought about how we could best get out of this situation. Not pushing past them, right? Not fighting? They'd say I started it, and there could be problems.

"This other guy's a lot more insolent than Morozov," said that same guy we didn't know. "We need to teach them a lesson."

"Fighting in the bathroom?" Godimir got even more surprised and turned to me. "Tell them I must be having a nightmare — these aren't real nobility."

"What did you say? Who's not real nobility?" fumed another boy, and at that moment the we heard flushing sounds from one of the stalls.

"It's just, there are more suitable places for a duel," said Godimir, getting worked up. "Don't disgrace us with such suggestions."

"Besides," I added, also a little angered by this whole idiotic situation, "a fight at the imperial palace is hardly the greatest undertaking."

Despite how I was feeling, I still wanted to hit the brakes on this conflict.

"A fight?" Glinov repeated curiously. "Oh, no. I just want to see you and your little friend appear before the imperial heir covered in mud."

With those words, he stretched out his hand in front of him and started to form that swamp spell I'd already seen once.

I was forced to take a few steps back so I wouldn't get all gross, and I got even angrier.

Trying to trip me up? This boy really thought that he could cause me any problems?

The magical energy inside me boiled over, demanded an exit, and it was like when I mentally so much as tapped my magical core, the valve came loose and let my body free itself of all the energy overcrowding me.

The room abruptly got colder.

The tiling and the little patch of swamp that Glinov had left behind quickly started to become covered in frost. I remembered how easily I'd hacked up the lesser demons that had gotten in my way when I was in a state like this.

The boys standing across from me looked around and blanched.

My triumph was spoiled by a stall door opening and someone coming out.

In no hurry, as if nothing unusual was happening here, the unidentified party washed his hands, wiped them off with a paper towel, and walked up to us.

I didn't understand right away why Glinov's friends were saying nothing and staring at the guy in horror; however, when he came closer, everything became clear.

The stranger was a tall boy with slicked-back black hair. He was wearing something that looked kind of like the ceremonial regalia I'd seen on Boemir, with a light blue ribbon going across his shoulder that had the signs of belonging to the imperial family.

"Well, well, well. This evening is no longer boring," he said with satisfaction, and after a bit he continued: "But I dare not distract you — continue. I'm curious to see how this all ends."

"Your Highness." Glinov immediately bowed, and the boys from his entourage did the same. "Please forgive us. It was just a little squabble. We'll settle it later."

"Oh?" Vitovt hemmed. "I thought you wanted to teach someone a lesson."

Apparently, Glinov was trying to find a way out of the situation that had formed. No matter how you looked at it, after all, he was guilty. Evidently, though, he wasn't having any ideas.

Father wanted me to get to know Vitovt, right? Well, then — this had fallen into my lap, so why not?

"Your Highness," I said cooly. "The bathroom is hardly the best place for a clarification of relations, especially between members of the Empire's noble families. Perhaps we should find a more suitable place?"

Vitovt looked at me for a bit silently, then spoke.

"Glinov, Zateikin, Morozov, and Ogneyer, stay here. The rest of you are dismissed."

He'd clearly been prepared well, I thought. He knew everyone on sight, even Godimir.

Seeing how quickly the pallid boys from Glinov's entourage left the bathroom, I chuckled.

No longer as tough as they were a few minutes ago.

After waiting till the unwanted parties had left, Vitovt nodded to the door.

"Morozov was right — this isn't the best place for a conversation. So everyone follow me."

We sat down in armchairs around a small table in the smaller hall, which drew a lot of people's attention to us.

"Now then, let's introduce ourselves," said Vitovt once we'd gotten settled comfortably. "Vitovt the Second, heir to the Nosirian throne."

After Godimir, Glinov, and I had introduced ourselves, Vitovt turned to the last of our group of four.

"Zateikin, when I saw you back there, I was very surprised. How did you wind up in that group?"

"You won't believe it, your Highness — I was just going to use the bathroom," said the boy, laughing. "I went in, and a crowd had gathered there blocking the door. They were standing there and fighting — I started to get curious about what was going on and decided to watch."

"So you were a victim of circumstance?" Vitovt chuckled. "You didn't manage to accomplish what you came for? Well, go then, and I'll talk with the others for now."

Zateikin nodded, got out of his chair, and left. The four of us were left alone.

"So, what interesting news can the last Morozov bring me?" Vitovt looked at me curiously.

"It's a lovely evening, the music is nice, the food is delicious, and the company is interesting," I said after a short pause, trying to work out my style of communicating with Vitovt, to understand what kind of person he was and whether I was setting the right tone for conversation.

If I did have to take classes with him, after all, tonight could determine the next few years of my life alongside him.

"The company is indeed interesting, especially for you," Vitovt agreed, and added more coldly, "but you didn't answer my question, although you knew exactly what I meant."

I shrugged.

"I may not have been the instigator of that situation, but it's not very pleasant for me to think about it."

"Did I ask you if it was pleasant to you or not?" Vitovt asked even more coldly.

The situation was changing every minute, I thought tensely. Just now I'd been in a winning position compared to Glinov, and now it was the other way around.

"You asked me what interesting news I could bring you," I answered, avoiding having to answer, which would put me in even more of a losing position. Not waiting for Vitovt to say anything else, I continued, "But you were there, and you were a witness to what happened. The only thing I can add is gratitude towards you for peacefully resolving the conflict. It would have been extremely unpleasant to start a fight at the palace."

Hearing the word "gratitude" from me, Vitovt assumed a dignified air. He clearly liked what I was saying. The storm was breaking.

"May we, your Highness?" said Zateikin as he returned with a few more boys standing behind him.

"Sit, all of you," said Vitovt, and all the empty chairs were taken.

Ah, so here was Vitovt's retinue, I realized, noticing how unconstrained these boys were as they spoke to the imperial heir.

"What can you tell me about Vitovt?" asked Father when we were left alone in his study one-on-one.

"Authoritative, ambitious, a little arrogant, pays close attention to the opinions of his retinue," I said without taking time to think.

"A little arrogant..." Father coughed. "Not surprising — he's the emperor's son, after all. It would be strange if it were any other way. And what can you say about his circle? About this retinue?"

"The children of high-ranked officials, warriors, and mages can get into his retinue," I answered, remembering the guys who'd approached us alongside Zateikin. "They obviously weren't happy to see new faces popping up next to Vitovt — which, based on my observations, he noticed himself. I'm guessing that when we meet again, I can expect some kind of payback from them."

My conversation with Father didn't last long — it took up about ten minutes. I quickly described everything that had happened at the reception — my argument with Glinov, and all the rumors and gossip I'd heard. Then I answered a few questions.

If an unwitting observer had been watching us from the sidelines, it might have seemed that things were truly picturesque between the two of us, and a well-raised child was obediently responding to all of his father's questions — that trust, love, and mutual respect prevailed in our relationship.

However, it wasn't like that at all. I may have been carrying out Father's mission, but I was doing it because it was to both of our advantage, and he wasn't demanding anything unseemly of me. Besides, I couldn't let myself forget what he'd done.

As I left the study, I took note of the sunrise and decided:

Enough, Ivan! Go get some sleep!

* * *

Raven, as she was accustomed, watched the passersby through the backsight of her sniper rifle and waited for the signal to start the operation. She was especially restless, so she was constantly looking for ways to entertain herself during the long wait.

She finished curiously watching a young couple kiss, tried to guess the cost of a passing woman's designer coat, and sighed deeply.

Where has that loser gotten off to? she thought, irritated. He should've been home long ago! If only he'd get here like usual, take a bullet, and that'd be it. She and the gals would already have cleaned up the evidence and be on their way home.

Moving her sight a little to the side, Raven found her best friend at a glance.

Svetlana, whom simple peasants knew by the name Crimson Fury, was sitting calmly on one of the benches at the nearest park.

She'd masterfully transformed herself into an elderly noblewoman with a cane and was ready to help the snipers take out the target if necessary.

Sensing her familiar gaze, Svetlana made a hardly noticeable show of her fist to Raven, hinting that she shouldn't be getting distracted.

Raven let out a barely audible giggle and grinned.

She found me out! And how come only she can do that? she thought. Svetlana hadn't made one mistake yet! She always knew when Raven was watching her.

Going back to surveying the locale, Raven realized with surprise that Svetlana had been becoming more lively lately.

On the day they'd met, she'd been like a talking robot, but now she could already feel weak emotions and display them completely appropriately. Of course, to the ordinary person it wouldn't seem like much at all for a normal life. However, for Svetlana, it was already a big achievement that had taken her seven long years to reach.

Everything would've been easier if we'd managed to meet right after I got into the League, thought Raven. *But for three years she didn't pay attention to anyone else at all. Not even her sister Elizabeth, although she's a real swine!*

Remembering the joy that had gushed forth from Elizabeth after their failure, Raven screwed up her face. Thankfully, Elizabeth had thought not to say what she was thinking aloud — she understood that her squad, which had lost seven people, would take badly to her badmouthing.

Raven frowned again.

The bungled mission had pretty seriously increased the spectrum of emotions Svetlana could feel, but she wasn't too happy about it. Neither were the others, for that matter.

Everyone had been dumbstruck when the Crimson Fury had arrived at the base calmly and then smashed the training hall to pieces.

Nothing surprising — that had been her first

botched assignment, thought Raven. And the losses were a heavy burden on everyone.

Remembering how that little boy had appeared out of nowhere, killed a couple of her people, and saved the target — Raven got angry herself.

C'mon! Calm down! You're on the job! Raven ordered herself. Despite everything, the client had contacted them personally and given them a two-year deadline extension.

"Ready number one," a dry voice resounded in her earpiece, and Raven pushed her unwanted thoughts aside and clung to her backsight.

Chapter 12

AFTER FALL BREAK, school graced me with a bit of goodwill. My classmates somehow managed to discover that I'd personally met the heir to the imperial throne at the reception at the imperial palace, and that it was possible I'd be studying alongside him very soon.

"Well? How does it feel to be a real star?" Constantine asked me sarcastically after class. "Your demon hunting, your self-initiation video, and your return to your princely status weren't enough for you — you decided to make friends with the heir to the Nosirian throne too? Just to go the whole nine yards?"

"Oh, shut up." I brushed him off, shaking hands with him as he approached me, then turned curiously to Godimir. "And how are you doing? People aren't on your case too much?"

"Business as usual for me." Godimir smirked. "I'm the son of the city's commandant, after all. The other kids always pay extra attention to me at this school. So meeting Vitovt hasn't changed any of that — but for you, it's probably excessive attention."

"If, of course, by lots of attention we mean love letters." Ilya cuffed my shoulder.

The boys burst into laughter.

"The romantic hero... the stealer of girls' hearts... a real catch..." they all chattered in chorus, clearly having a good time.

"Are you guys spending time in your own class or in mine?" I said indignantly. "Where did you get all that intel?"

"Well, it's not every day a whole mountain of love letters tied up with silk ribbons turns up on one kid's desk!" said Sergei.

"By the way, the air around you is simply fragrant from the boatload of perfume on them," Constantine noticed. "Do you still have all the envelopes with you?"

I nodded.

After popping into the math teacher's office just before class started, I'd noticed a lot of little envelopes piled in a heap on my desk.

As I'd approached my desk, I'd had one question in my mind:

What was I supposed to do with all these?

When Ms. Dashkevich had showed up at that point, she'd watched me with laughter dancing in her eyes, and then she'd advised me to hide them in my bag and start preparing for class. I'd had no choice but to listen to her.

"If they're still with you," Constantine interrupted my reminiscing, "then can we perhaps help you with them? Let's read what our gals wrote in them. Don't just say no right away — you're going to have a rough time getting through so many letters by yourself."

"No thank you." I coughed. "I can't allow confidential correspondence to fall into the hands of young donkeys."

"Donkeys?" snorted Sergei. Supporting me, he turned to all the others: "Have you all forgotten that someone here has to prep for the academic phase of the imperial tournament? There's not much time left — the participant selection starts this trimester. So I don't know about you guys, but I'm going to go study some more. Ivan can deal with his letters on his own."

"For sure," Constantine agreed, looking at my bag with pity. "The tournament really is starting soon, so I'm going to go study too."

"I'll come with you guys!" Ilya chimed in. He narrowed his eyes at me and Godimir and explained, "We study for the academic tournament together after class. We even did some serious studying over break. Unlike some people who did nothing but run around to balls!"

"Balls are great," said Godimir, grinning. "Entertainment, dances, new friends. It's much better than wasting away over textbooks for the whole break. Besides, we'll see the results of your work after academic regionals. It'll become immediately obvious there who really studied and who goofed off..."

After break, during which I'd allowed myself to relax quite a bit and openly loaf around, began a period of more intense workouts.

I had to admit, I'd been impatiently awaiting it myself — my body was used to heavy workloads and seemed to have stagnated. It demanded movement, it needed a strong and skilled opponent. So during our first workouts of the second school trimester, led by Mr. Viktorov, it was like I was walking on air.

"Oh-ho-ho!" he exclaimed after our first sparring match. "You're really raring to go! Your speed! The strength of your blows! Your reaction time! They're all at their peak! Why is that? Were you that inspired by meeting Imperial Prince Vitovt personally? Hmm?"

"Don't tell me you believe any gossip you hear too!" I said, surprised in turn. "Someone as wise and respected as you!"

"Curiosity is a terrible thing," he admitted, embarrassed. Nonetheless, though, he went on confidently, "That, and all kinds of rumors are going around the school, so I decided to learn everything from the primary source."

"Then here's my report. I did personally meet Imperial Prince Vitovt. We talked, we got acquainted with each other, but nothing more," I admitted honestly. "I think, as you already know, that starting next year I might be studying in his class."

"I heard, yes," admitted Mr. Viktorov, smoothing down his disheveled hair.

"But that's not why I'm feeling inspired today. It's because of my extended rest time. I sat around at home and didn't do anything for the whole break. So my body is demanding a serious physical workload, and I can't get those anywhere but from your workouts. My father called my only sensible sparring partner back to the estate. I really just missed my workouts."

"Now I understand." Mr. Viktorov nodded. "But unless my memory fails me, you have the ability to train with Colonel Gurinov's people. I don't think it's a good idea to let such a magnificent chance to gain experience slip away."

"Did Theophane tell you that?" I said, unsurprised. "Well, yes, I did have that. Theophane wanted me to circumvent the Warrior League to get Militant rank, and that was only possible in a military environment. That's the only place with as many warriors as I needed, and where competitions are constantly being held and ranks are conferred. Besides, Colonel Gurinov was extremely interested in having me motivate his fighters. So he scratched my back, I scratched his."

"I think Boemir's new rank also played a role," Mr. Viktorov agreed, chuckling. "That clearly didn't come about without Nur-Kulsaan pollen and some help from your mentor."

Oh! I had a chance to get some information that Theophane didn't want to share with me! I could barely keep from rubbing my hands. I hoped Mr. Viktorov wouldn't consider this critical information.

"I haven't heard much about this pollen stuff," I said, not showing obvious interest. "Is it really that effective?"

"More than anything," said Mr. Viktorov. Coming closer, he added in a whisper: "I even used to think that you were training under the influence of exactly that. But then I realized it wasn't true — the pollen can't guarantee such stable and extended growth in a warrior's strength, and other indirect signs showed me that I was mistaken."

"How?" I didn't understand and asked him my question. "How does this pollen work, in general? Do you dissolve it in water? And just drink it? Or do you inhale it through your nose?"

"Dissolve it in water and drink it?" Mr. Viktorov repeated, laughing. "Inhale it through your nose? Where did you get ideas like that? Hah!"

"What's so funny?" I didn't understand.

"It's just that it's not all so simple," said Mr. Viktorov, not laughing anymore, and warned me: "Don't even think of doing that under any circumstances. Either inhaling it or dissolving it in water and drinking it. You'll get such an influx of spiritual energy that your circulation channels won't be able to sustain the power and will start to destroy your body, and you'll simply die. Generally, Nur-Kulsaan pollen is taken only by being added to one very complex and expensive potion. Even then, a warrior who takes it must know the right dosages and maintain a strict schedule for taking it, or else it could all end tragically."

"Wait." I decided to confirm something. "You're saying that if you take the pollen, then your body fills up with an incredibly large amount of Shiki-Cho in a matter of seconds?"

"That's right," said Mr. Viktorov. "It's just that the volume will be so great that it'll kill you."

"So, maybe, do we need to supply our Heroes with pollen when they're dealing with strong enemies?" I asked. "For instance, when a Hero is out of energy, he needs to be given a few grams of Nur-Kulsaan pollen, and there you go! He'll be in great shape and continue the fight!"

Sheesh, I might break my tongue with all these infernal names!

"It's an interesting idea, of course," said Mr. Viktorov. "Although it's not a new one. Many fighters have tried to make it happen. The thing is, no one has managed it. It's all because after pure pollen enters a human body, in addition to a large amount of energy, the person also gets incredible bloodlust. There hasn't been much investigation into how much of it is innate and how much of it is foreign, when this happens. Only Knights and Heroes have a ghost of a chance at surviving after taking pollen. Because of that, and because they know techs that can quickly deplete their magic reserves as they're bursting from the excess."

"That is, if a low-ranked warrior using pure pollen could get rid of the excess Shiki-Cho quickly, he'd survive?" I said, remembering my "flamethrower" and "spirit arm" techs.

"Generally speaking, he'd live, but that's admittedly on the brink of fantasy," said Mr. Viktorov doubtfully. "Anyway. Enough chattering. We've had a brief rest, talked a bit, and now the time has come to return to training. This round, I'll allow you to use Shiki-Cho and all the techs in your arsenal."

I nodded in agreement, stood up, and got ready to fight, but my thoughts were somewhere far away.

It seemed I'd figured out what I'd do in a situation with no way out, when my strength was at its end and there was an enemy nearby. Maybe Mr. Viktorov was mistaken, and I'd be able to survive after all...?

Day by day my routine, which had suffered changes after the start of the new school trimester, settled in. On weekdays were classes, workouts with Mr. Viktorov, and lessons at the Mage League of Morshansk, which I'd been invited to personally by Professor Berezov.

Training and school were something I was used to, but the lessons at the Mage League brought me a sense of novelty. However, as it turned out, nothing happened there that could have merited my fixed attention. Young Acolytes on the path of the mage, who'd only recently awakened their abilities, studied basic theoretical knowledge and meditated under the leadership of an experienced mentor. Thankfully, after it became clear that both my meditation and my absorption of magical energy were in proper order, my mage mentor started giving me more serious material, and I focused on studying the simplest runes and trying to reproduce them with the force of my thoughts. Although at first, those lessons were planned the same way for everyone.

My weekends were booked solid too. On Mr. Viktorov's recommendation, I did reconnect with Boemir. As it turned out, he himself had been waiting for a call from me for a long time, so that he could suggest returning to our workouts at the military base.

In a short span of time, he organized a gathering at his base for all the Militants of the Morshansk garrison who were trying for the next rank, and he got to work on giving them intense workouts.

In the time that had passed since my last visit to the base, many of my former opponents had grown significantly in their mastery, but as I discovered, I hadn't lagged too far behind them either after all the sparring I'd done.

My progress was linked not least to my having mastered the Spirit-Step tech. That tech sapped a ton of spiritual energy, of course, but its usefulness couldn't be overestimated. So I started beating Militants significantly more often — or, more precisely, almost always. I started losing only on the tail end of a lot of nonstop sparring at the end of the day. It was even better that this world had healing potions, otherwise after a couple of workouts like this my fists would've been smashed up and bloody.

Noticing my obvious progress, Boemir invited me to train with a couple of Veterans. At first, it seemed for some reason that I was roughly at the same level as them, because I was stronger than most of the Militants here. However, as it turned out, that that wasn't true at all.

In sparring matches with Veterans, I always got the feeling that if I pushed just a bit harder, just a little bit more, I'd be able to fight with them like an equal! Our speed, at least, was on the same level, Dwarf Saws' sakes! I didn't manage to win a single sparring match out of a dozen, however. Although maybe that happened because Boemir had forbidden me from using Spirit-Steps while fighting them.

My intense preparation for the warriors' part of the imperial tournament, my interesting lessons at the Mage League headquarters, my constant sparring matches with high-ranked fighters at the military base, and my independent exercises with my family magic in the evenings all kept me so occupied that at a certain point I started paying less attention to my education at school.

It didn't affect my grades, but Ms. Dashkevich noticed the downtick and reacted extremely negatively. She started having additional educational conversations with me, calling on me in every class session, came to my classes with other teachers, and promised to complain to George.

I had to assure her that I wasn't going to lose

ground and that I'd keep studying persistently. I reminded myself that in studying my school subjects to the best of my ability, I'd train my memory, and that would undoubtedly serve me in life.

During this series of changing events, I didn't even notice how fast the academic tournament came up. Ilya, Sergei, and Constantine did manage to prove their worth to our school's judges and headed to regionals to defend our branch.

Admittedly, I hadn't been planning to give in to the excitement over the tournament and keep track of how the competitions were going, but Godimir insisted that we meet up at the snack bar like we used to. Besides, Sergei, Ilya, and Constantine were participating in the tournament, and it wouldn't be right not to support them at a time like this. Mr. Viktorov also went ahead and told me we'd be stopping our workouts temporarily so I could recover.

"I remember how starved for workouts you were when you came back from break," he noted. "So rest at least a little bit and relax. In the end, go root for the kids from our school! As far as I know, you're pretty close to a couple of them."

In general, after hearing the opinion of my wise trainer and weighing all the pros and cons, I decided to relax a bit after all. So on the day the competitions started, Godimir and I sat at our favorite table at our snack bar, ordered food, and started waiting for the broadcast to begin.

"Are these seats taken?" I heard a familiar voice and noticed three girls standing next to our table, one of which turned out to be my classmate Nadezhda Zorin.

"Of course not — have a seat, ladies," said Godimir with a broad grin and glancing at me slyly. "But you do understand Ivan's admirers will never forgive you for this?"

The girls blushed and giggled sweetly.

"Neither will yours," Nadezhda teased Godimir. Not giving him a chance to put in a word, she added, "Actually, we just want to root for our people, and all the tables are totally full except yours. Besides, I sit next to Ivan at school lunches, so I was hoping he wouldn't turn us away."

While the girls settled in comfortably, Godimir decided to prove that he was a gallant gentleman, asked them what they'd like, and ordered for them.

I didn't get on well at all with the girls I didn't know. It wasn't even because they were too young in comparison to my psychological age, since I felt completely comfortable with both Godimir and Nadezhda. It was that after every question I asked or answer I gave, they giggled idiotically and turned their eyes aside shyly.

Geez! Why are they doing this to me? I thought after half an hour of drawn-out conversation. I hoped it wasn't on purpose. Were they actually like this? Was it not a game? An attempt to trick a young, naive, defenseless boy in such an idiotic way?

Of course, the only one of the girls who talked to me normally was Nadezhda. So I figured it was no surprise that it was mainly the three of us who talked at the table — me, Nadezhda, and Godimir. We almost didn't notice her cronies' rare responses. They were so uninteresting that I didn't even remember their names, and I wasn't ashamed of it. Almost.

"Hey, look, it's Xenia Ognev!" Nadezhda exclaimed happily, turning the attention of everyone around her to the TV. Our class prefect was being shown. "She's already secured three sure wins!"

"That's great, of course, but next round she's getting a tennie." Godimir noticed the line of running text. "It's gonna be cutthroat."

I agreed with him completely. A "tennie" was a part of the academic tournament where each of the contestants in turn was asked ten questions, to each of which they had to give a correct and complete answer within ten seconds.

If a contestant slipped up, fumbled, or didn't have time to finish a thought, that meant that contestant wouldn't get the deserved point. In addition, the most difficult thing was that the contestant wouldn't know if one answer or another had counted until the end of the competition. Contestants who gave fewer than eight correct answers were eliminated from the tournament.

"My older sister said," one of the giggly girls cut in, "that a few years ago, because all the participants got eliminated on the tennies, the organizers couldn't even nominate winners."

"Don't worry," the other brushed her off. "Have faith, Xenia will come through! I sit next to her in class and I know how she slaves away at her work."

"No matter how you look at it, tennies are the toughest round. And I doubt any of the participants in the tournament don't slave away at their schoolwork," Godimir noted. "It's just that that round itself is really hard. I don't really understand when the tournament hosts make the decision to include a tennie in the contests for one subject or another. As far as I remember, last year there wasn't a tennie for language arts."

"That's nothing surprising," said Nadezhda. "They do them if there are a lot of participants left after a few rounds of a given subject, and it's pretty hard to single out the best. After all, many students can allow themselves to be good individual students in one subject or another and prepare splendidly. So they came up with a harsh selection process like that, that lets them not only test the student's knowledge but also see if the student is capable of giving answers in a stressful situation, when hundreds of thousands of people are watching them on TV."

"It's just cruel," I had to admit. Curious against my will, I asked, "And what if a participant would have answered correctly, but the answer wasn't counted for some reason? Could you prove that you were right? There's probably scandal after scandal going on over there, huh?"

"I don't know." One of the giggly girls shook her head. "But I've heard that things like that happen, and if they do, the judges explain right then and there why the answer wasn't counted. I don't know if it goes further than that."

"We'll ask Constantine later," said Godimir, pulling us away from the conversation. "On that note, he's doing a tennie right now."

"Right on!" exclaimed Nadezhda. "Great job, Constantine! You made it to the tennies too!"

It seemed like our friend was staying pretty calm, but Godimir and I — as people who knew him better than the others — could see that he was panicking. Not surprising, since his first two answers hadn't been counted for some reason, and apparently he knew it. So he knew that he couldn't slip up or cut himself any slack. However, to the universal jubilation of the Morshansk fans, he gave the correct answers to all the other questions and became one of the two lucky participants to move on to the next round.

"I never thought I'd be this worried for someone over an ordinary academic tournament," Godimir admitted to me, moistening his dry throat with juice as Constantine — white as a sheet after the contest — disappeared from the screen.

"Agreed," I replied, following suit. "That was really something! Seemed to me like they weren't going to count his third answer, but obviously he made it through."

"Well, great job to everyone!" Nadezhda declared. "He did so well! I didn't even know Constantine was so good at math. If his first two answers had been counted, he would've had ten correct answers."

"No one knew," Godimir admitted, puzzled. "I

didn't think he'd be able to get so far."

When the final results were announced, we found out that Constantine had completed regionals successfully and, having taken third place, would be heading to the capital.

The school rejoiced, the teachers walked around happy, Ms. Dashkevich wouldn't stop showering us with good grades.

Unfortunately, Ilya and Sergei didn't get any especially good results and had to return to school. After that, they joined us in rooting for Constantine. He got tenth place and subsequently received his share of applause, admiration, and love letters.

*   *   *

Meanwhile, Godimir and I continued prepping for the warrior tournament.

"Ivan, sir, we're here," said the elderly man driving the Temnikovs' armored car, pulling me away from texting my sisters.

"Thank you," I said, sending my goodbyes to them. I left the safe interior of the car and came face-to-face with my former shooting instructor Dennis Ilyasov.

"Hi," he greeted me. "The Colonel is already sick of waiting for you."

"Hi, Dennis," I said. "Has he really been waiting that long? I haven't been to training for two weekends, and he went right to being bored?"

"He has a lot of troubles," said Ilyasov offhandedly.

"I understand everything and speak without reproach. I'm just drawing attention to the fact that his concern doesn't check out with his absence at the previous training sessions. To be honest, I thought he wouldn't be there today."

Ilyasov gave me some kind of shrewd look, but he didn't say anything.

"Well?" I said impatiently.

" 'Well' what?" he said with a confused look.

"First pull a simpleton face, then make yourself out to be innocent," I chuckled. "What did he prepare for me this time? Has he brought in someone new? Not a Veteran already, or a Knight?"

"How should I know? I don't know anything!" said Ilyasov, laughing. Opening the door to the training complex, he whispered, "You'll see it all for yourself now."

"Well, good," I said curiously in reply.

Finding myself in the hand-to-hand combat practice hall, I witnessed an interesting scene.

In the ring was a young, barefoot girl around seventeen years old in close-fitting shorts and a short, bright-colored top. She was in the ring clobbering one of the stronger Militants pretty skillfully.

Lightly dodging a counterattack with a step to the side, she broke through his Spirit Shield and knocked him out with a confident blow to the back of the head.

Now I'm in for it! I understood immediately. Wasn't it shameful to use a trick like this on me?

Boemir noticed me and gave me a beastly smile, beckoning me over.

"Do I have to go?" I asked Ilyasov in a sad tone.

"What else can you do?" he said merrily. "You're not the only one who didn't want his lunch handed to him by a little girl, but you can't argue with the commander."

"Well, I can still try to run away," I said, heading towards Boemir.

"That's not how you do things," said Ilyasov, laughing. "Don't worry, if you get it bad once from her, maybe you'll have the motivation for further self-improvement."

"I constantly work myself to the bone," I said indignantly. "I don't need another stimulus. Especially not ones like this."

"You tell that to the conscripts you beat up during your training," Ilyasov noted fairly, and headed for the viewing platform. "They didn't want to get beat up by a little boy either."

"What's going on over here?" I asked Boemir after we greeted each other. "You looking for new ways to heighten your soldiers' motivation?"

"Not just for my soldiers," he replied, "but for more experienced warriors too."

"And have a lot of them already sparred with the new stimulus?" I asked.

"Almost all of them." He chuckled. "I sense that you're not against joining in the shared activity either."

"I can't say that," I said, watching the speed of the girl's blows and the techs she was using. "I don't need another stimulus for my training."

"Everyone needs a stimulus," said Boemir. "You first of all — or else, don't you see, you've decided that you're too strong for your age."

"Why shouldn't I?" I was even indignant.

"Well, in general, of course you are," Boemir agreed, backpedaling. "It's just that your development could stop at that point. And this adorable Ivan-hunter is already almost a Knight."

"*What?* Almost a Knight?" I couldn't believe it, and I looked at my future sparring partner with new eyes. "How is that possible? So she's a strong Veteran? At her age? I can't believe it!"

"You're talking just like the Militants I chose to train with you, when they realized their opponent was only twelve years old," said Boemir with a smirk. "So go on, warm up — it seems it'll be your turn soon."

Diving into the locker room, I got changed quickly, and as I started warming up I noticed a familiar feminine figure on one of the viewing platforms. Boemir's wife was sitting next to her.

Somehow sensing my gaze, she turned her head, and I saw the surprised face of Ms. Dashkevich.

I waved to her, and at that moment the girl in the ring sent another Militant flying with a beautifully technical blow.

"Maybe it's already time for you to take a break?" Boemir asked her. "You've been fighting without a break."

Noting her head-shake of refusal, however, he

turned to me.

"Let's go, Ivan, you're up."

Jumping into the ring, I froze in place, looked at the girl's emotionless face, and — hearing the sound of the gong — leaped aside by some miracle, dodging her instant attack.

Spirit Shield. Spirit-Step. Hit. Spirit Shield. Hit. Spirit-Step. Spirit-Step. Spirit-Step. Spirit Shield. I dodged all of her powerful blows quickly, trying to carve out time for a counterattack.

Apparently, she wasn't a fan of talking.

After taking two hits, one of which sent me to the ground, I rolled to the side and got to my feet using my "flamethrower" tech. However, she'd thrown up a Spirit-Shield over herself and didn't intend to give me time to recover. She attacked me through my "flames," which held her back for maybe a second.

With no time to dodge her series of attacks yet again, I used multiple Spirit Shields, then took a bad hit anyway.

She was quick, strong, and very skilled, not giving me a single second to think, which provoked quickly growing irritation in me that turned to anger.

At some point I found myself on the floor again, taking a couple of nasty hits from this girl who was now even faster. Intensely angry, I threw myself into an attack, not sparing my Shiki-Cho.

My opponent, who'd been fighting with an emotionless face, as if nothing unusual had happened, easily dodged my torrent of blows and got a read on the full picture of the fight. Then she went on the counterattack and slammed my head against the mat.

I sprang back up in a second, and without paying attention to the intense pain in my head, I attacked her even more furiously. However, I got the same result. A counterattack and wild pain in my skull.

Just one more time, I thought. Just one more time.

For some reason I was incredibly insulted that I was losing to some girl I didn't know, though she was so strong. However, it was even more insulting constantly winding up on the floor and hitting my head every time it happened, which was already giving me a splitting headache.

The next moment, with the last of my strength, I took a Spirit-Step right off the ground, appeared behind her, and dealt her a powerful blow to the top of the head.

She tumbled to the floor, and when she turned her head, for just a moment it seemed to me that I saw a surprised expression on her emotionless face. The next second I blacked out.

Chapter 13

I DIDN'T FEEL THE GREATEST when I woke up.

The cotton ball covered in liquid ammonia that had been shoved under my nose had such a sharp smell that I involuntarily jerked my head back and felt a sharp, unpleasant pain in my head.

When I opened my eyes, bright lamp light immediately struck my eyes, an unpleasant sound rang in my ears, and I got nauseous.

"Here, drink this." The healer who'd been present at the training held out a small flask with some kind of potion in it to me.

Opening it quickly, I brought it to my lips and forced myself with difficulty to drink its contents, which tasted just as horrific as they smelled.

"Ugh! What is *that* crap?" I said, wiping off my lips and feeling a tight lump in my stomach begging for an exit.

Keep it together or I'll puke, I resolved mentally with all my might. I'd never live that down.

"It's a standard healing potion," said the healer, looking at me doubtfully. "In all your fights here, have you really never tried one even once?"

"Not once," I brushed him off, feeling the slicing pain in my head starting to lighten up a little. "But why does it taste so bad? I'm all nauseous now! And it's clearly not from the concussion!"

"It shouldn't make you nauseous." The healer shook his head. "The taste itself is as ordinary as can be. I'm telling you, it's a standard healing potion. It's just meant for an ordinary soldier who'll use it during a fight or right after. When you compare the price and the quality, it's the best of its kind. It heals wounds pretty quickly and effectively, and it's made from the simplest ingredients. So who cares about its specific taste? Besides, the military department spends so much money on potions, and improving the taste makes that too expensive. It's irrational. Better to make cheaper potions, but more of them. So it's good that our soldiers have that, at least."

This healer on duty was all wound up — I'd clearly offended him with what I'd said. Because really, why was I reacting this way? Well, because of the horrific taste. Or was it? Hadn't he given me what he gave everyone, after all? Or had losing to that girl made me so angry that I was harping on every little thing?

"I'm sorry," I said, still with that foul taste in my mouth. "Thank you so much for your help. The potion is terrific, it's just that I think my headache made me a little upset, and I'm used to other potions, so I wasn't expecting one like that."

"Well, yeah, for training we only use the cheapest, worst-tasting potions, so people stop getting hit," said Boemir, walking up to us. "Besides, even some nobility can't afford your potions."

"I don't know how expensive my potions are, of course." I thought of Marissa, who'd made them. "But they're not made with the most expensive ingredients."

"Well, it doesn't matter, actually." Boemir brushed me off. "Tell me instead — how do you feel? I won't have to report to the emperor that from my carelessness came the tragic death of the last member of a princely line?"

"I'm fine," I said, feeling that my head hurt much less.

"Excellent." Boemir nodded. "Not a bad fight, and despite the questionable strategy you chose, the end of it turned out just great. I thought you'd lose much faster."

"I kinda didn't want to lose at all," I said, getting up. "But as it turned out, our strength levels were truly uneven."

"How are you feeling, Ivan?" I heard the familiar voice of my lead teacher and turned my head in her direction.

"Good afternoon, Ms. Dashkevich. Thank you for your concern. I don't feel bad, although of course it could be better," I said, turning my gaze to the girl who'd been my opponent not too long ago, standing next to Ms. Dashkevich. "I wasn't expecting to see you in a place like this."

"I was just as surprised when I saw you here." Ms. Dashkevich laughed. "Olga invited me — she's an old friend of mine." She gestured to Boemir's wife. "We happened to cross paths in Morshansk. And Svetlana came here too, to visit me on break. One thing led to another, and we somehow wound up here so we could test her skills in battle with experienced warriors."

"Is she your daughter?" I asked, raising an eyebrow. I couldn't get it through my head that Ms. Dashkevich had a daughter that age. However, after a bit, I noticed to my surprise that there was a pretty serious family resemblance between mother and daughter. At first, because of Svetlana's lack of emotions, it was completely unnoticeable. Because Ms. Dashkevich, on the other hand, excelled in expressing her emotions.

How could a living being have a daughter like that? Interesting... she probably got her emotionlessness from her father.

"Oh, yes," said Ms. Dashkevich in the meantime. "Allow me to introduce my daughter Svetlana to you."

"Nice to meet you," I said, nodding unhurriedly.

I had to be careful because of the pain in my head.

"Nice to meet you too," replied Svetlana emotionlessly, her face not changing for a moment.

"All right, enough dragging our feet," Boemir

declared. "Ivan, go drink your potion, get yourself in order, and we'll continue training. We have a lot more to do today."

Saying goodbye to the three women, I headed to the locker room for my things.

I couldn't drink Marissa's potion fast enough to get away from that horrible taste! I had to pull myself together and get some good work done at the same time.

In my mind's eyes I saw Svetlana's emotionless face, impossible to understand anything from.

No matter what, we'd meet here again one way or another, and until then I'd try to become much stronger. I could even turn to old man Taras for help. Was he a Hero or was he just goofing around? We'd see who had the last laugh.

* * *

"Are you sure you want to go here?" asked my driver with obvious doubt in his voice, looking with surprise at the good-quality but at the same time very simple house in Morshansk's residential sector, amid buildings that likewise didn't stand out in any way.

"I'm sure," I said, climbing out of the car and throwing my bag over my shoulder. "I'll be a while."

Opening the wicket gate, I found myself in a driveway that had been painstakingly cleared of snow. Internally praising old man Taras for his hospitality, I walked up to the house and knocked resolutely on the door.

"Ivan is here!" I heard the cheerful voice of Marissa, who somehow knew I was the one standing on the threshold.

I heard the sounds of the locks being undone. The next second the door opened, and the stout figure of Marissa, with a huge smile and an anorak thrown over her shoulder, embraced me.

"It's been so long since you've been here..." she said warmly, then pulled me inside. "Come on, follow me. No good freezing to death outside."

As always, she smelled unbelievably good, like various wildflowers and fragrant herbs.

"Hi!" I said just as warmly once we were in the front hallway. "So how are things here?"

"Oh, like always." She threw up her hands, hung up her anorak on a coatrack, and added joyfully: "So! We can save all the taking for later. First take off your jacket, hang it up, take off your shoes, and go to the kitchen — I just mixed up batter for pancakes, so we'll have a little something to eat. Now I have to run off before something burns."

Marissa hurried to the kitchen, from which the delicious smells of fresh pancakes were indeed emanating, pretty quickly. My stomach rumbled, and I hurried to head after her.

I saw old man Taras at the table with a sleepy face — he had his back comfortably pressed up to the warm stove and was slowly drinking something out of a big mug.

"Hi, Ivan!" he greeted me right away, smiling. Gesturing to an unoccupied chair, he said,

"C'mon, sit down and tell me how you are. It's already been a while since you've come to visit us."

"I'm here on the sly," I answered, feeling a prick of conscience. "I'm studying and training. A little bit of everything. I really haven't come to visit you in a long time. My fault — what can I say?"

"We hope that you'll stop by more often." Taras smiled contentedly. Narrowing his eyes shrewdly, he added, "So why aren't you bragging about how you recently made the acquaintance of Vitovt?"

"Is that really a reason to be proud?" I shrugged. "That's just how it was. It was nice, of course, and possibly useful for the future..."

"He's the heir to the Nosirian throne," said Taras indignantly. "What are you on about? Most people haven't seen him up close even once, and never will. And you spoke to him personally! In an informal setting!"

"And where did you learn that?" I reacted instantly, looking at him suspiciously. "Has the gossip really gotten around the whole empire already? And not just to the nobility, but to commoners too?"

"Well, of course not to the whole empire," said old man Taras enigmatically. "It's not the entirety of the commoner population that knows it, but no one who's interested is being left without food for thought."

"Very curious." I shook my head pensively, reflecting on what this palace gossip could get me into. "Especially if you take into account that that information was for select ears."

"It's just gossip." Taras grinned.

"What are we going on and on about me for? How are *you* doing here?"

"Oh, just fine." Taras shrugged. "We're old folks, we have nothing to say about ourselves. Everything's like it always is. While it was warm we worked on the farm, stocked up on food, got ready for winter. I went to the Wasteland a few times for its local goodies — herbs that no one else collects, as you know. Now that winter's coming, there's almost no work left to do, so it's just watching after the livestock, since we've stocked up on fodder just like we should! In general, we've been resting. I can barely get away from this furnace right now — I'm warming all my old bones."

Once again examining his completely happy but still somewhat sleepy face, his loose-fitting embroidered linen shirt and the neat tile-covered stove behind his back, I decided to ask one question that it seemed I wasn't meant to learn the answer to.

However, curiosity was consuming me — besides, if he didn't give me an answer in this situation when he was at his most relaxed, then he never would.

"Old man Taras, how did it come to be," I began, choosing my words carefully, "that you — a Hero-rank warrior — live in the residential sector of an imperial outpost, doing your housework, drinking the hard stuff all day, lying around on a stove and feeding livestock? Somehow I got the impression that warriors of your rank meet their old age in more comfortable conditions. Besides, even now you're still strong as can be — which you haven't failed to demonstrate."

"Erm..." Taras sighed heavily, running his hand over his face hard a few times — he was perking himself up. "See here," he said slowly. "On the one hand, you're asking question that I don't want to answer at all. But on the other hand, it would be dishonest to hide the truth from you. Besides, a few things that've happened make me obligated to go about this the opposite way and answer your questions."

Marissa chuckled unexpectedly.

"It's not just you," said Taras, turning his head in her direction. "You know that yourself."

Taking a big swig of his mulled wine (that was what was in his big cup) and smoothing his beard, he squinted at Marissa anyway and asked her:

"So you think I can tell him?"

"Why not?" She shrugged. "Sooner or later, Ivan will find out everything anyway. And it's better if it's from us — besides, given recent events, it would be good for him to trust us and not treat our warnings with skepticism."

"What's this you're on about?" I frowned. "Why these riddles? What's with the winking, intrigue, and skeletons in the closet? Where are those sweet, kind, and sharp Avtiukians I once knew?"

"We're here, we're here." Marissa smiled. "Soon you'll understand everything."

"You asked me why I — a Hero-rank warrior — live like an ordinary citizen of the empire? And what's more, not among the wealthiest?" said old man Taras, taking another swig of his heady drink. "Here's the situation. The main reason is that I like it this way. In theory, this kind of life. We Avtiukians are the kind of people who love puttering around on the homestead. And no matter how you look at it, no matter what kind of an education we were given, the homestead calls out to us one way or another." Pausing briefly, he continued: "The second reason is no less important. One could say it's the defining reason. Besides, Marissa insists that I tell you how this all started. Are you ready?"

I had only to nod. They were making this all complicated, but what was I supposed to do? Refuse? No, I should listen to what they had to say.

"I was born in an ordinary family," old man Taras continued in the meantime. "Or to be more precise, in an ordinary rural Avtiukian family. My parents had their own big house, an allotment of land, and a robust homestead. One of the worst misfortunes that haunted ordinary folks in those days was the pretty frequent appearance of demons not far from undefended settlements. The demons slaughtered entire villages and farms, the Hunter League didn't always get there in time to help, and we peasants had to pay the hunters a lot of our hard-earned money so that they'd stay in one area or another.

"It was exactly that childhood desire to defend my loved ones that put me on the path of self-improvement, and when an old warrior came to our neighborhood looking for students, I was ready. By the will of fate, it turned out I had a natural aptitude for using spiritual energy, and after only a few years of intense training, one fairly powerful viscount house noticed me as a young Veteran." Taras fumbled his words, but with a look at Marissa, he continued: "Under the guidance of the local warriors, I became stronger and stronger. Then I grew up a little more, settled down, started a family with a lot of children, and despite my pretty tense relationship with a couple of opposing houses I believed I had a bright future.

"At that time, I'd already gotten my Hero rank, and I could only see life through rose-colored glasses. But in one moment, everything changed. House wars that erupted took the lives of not only my family, but all the members of the noble family that was sheltering me.

"By some incredible chance, I was the only survivor of that whole massacre. At one time, I wanted to die. But my heart was thirsting for revenge.

"I don't want to get into the details, but my hands ran crimson with the blood of my enemies. I avenged my first family magnificently, but when I realized that I'd be destroyed before I finished my revenge, I retreated temporarily."

I stared with surprise at this kind, familiar jokester — old man Taras — who was now sitting before me and telling me a story that didn't match his outer appearance at all. It seemed like it was carrying him many years into the past, and now with his eyes wide open he stared at his wrinkled hands as if they were covered in blood.

Is this all really true? I thought, looking from old man Taras to Marissa.

"For a while I hid," he continued in the meantime. "I settled down next to the Wasteland, became a free hunter, and earned a living by going to the Wasteland — it was a workout and a proper living, which I squandered in bars and eating houses. One day, I met a remarkable man who'd been throwing away his life just like I had, and he agreed to teach me his 'drunken master' style for a couple of daily bottles of wine. I discovered my fate, and this man suggested I join an organization that would allow me to destroy all my enemies in the future.

"I stepped over corpses with the persistence of a wild boar, went on through the pain, suffering, and many wounds so that I could learn the high art of covert killers. Over the long years of waiting, I'd realized that revenge is a dish best served cold. The skills I'd gained allowed me to constantly and almost unnoticeably annihilate everyone involved in the death of my family.

"At a certain point, the last of them understood everything and started a chase for me, but by the will of fate I managed to kill them and survive."

At that moment, Marissa coughed expressively, ruining the whole mood of the story. Old man Taras, paying her no attention, continued.

"And there I was — I'd gotten what I was after, lying there barely alive on the brick fragments of that small estate, trying to stop up my punctured lung with my hand, staring at the corpses of my dead enemies, hearing the cries of their children, and instead of the relief I wanted I felt emptiness. The lust for revenge, death, and destruction that had led me that whole time fled away somewhere.

"When I came to my senses, I suddenly understood how many people had died at my hand, how much grief and suffering my revenge had brought. I was ready to die, but..."

Taras fell silent, took another swig, and continued.

"But I was saved. Or rather, she saved me. She was like an angel sent to me from Heaven by the Savior, an angel who helped me to survive, fake my death, and then hide so that I could start a life with a clean slate."

She'd saved him? She'd healed him? Her? An angel? He wasn't talking about Marissa, by any chance? I watched her skillfully remove another pancake from the frying pan.

"It was a long time ago... yes... about sixty years ago... We hid well... No one probably remembers us anymore..."

"And why have you lived here all this time? You're hiding? Living an ordinary life? And is that why you have such a magnificent beard? So no one can recognize you?" I peppered old man Taras with questions thick and fast.

"Not just because of that," Marissa replied instead of Taras. "This is just the kind of life we like. As you know, I'm an Avtiukian too, and as the rumors among the people go, working on the homestead is in our blood."

"You're an Avtiukian yourself, and you couldn't just walk past an Avtiukian like him?" I said with a shrewd wink.

"Something like that," Marissa chuckled.

"But how did you meet?" I continued trying to get answers.

"We'd been working together," she said simply. "For that same organization. And I admit it, I'd been chasing after that tall, broad-shouldered man with deep-seated pain in his eyes." Marissa chuckled after a short pause. "It seemed so romantic to me then! Dwarf Saws take it! What a fool I was! A revenge-seeker, a Hero! The head of the league! I was just enamored with him!"

The head of a league of killers? I thought in shock.

"And what now? You're not in love with me anymore?" Taras winked.

"What do *you* think?" said Marissa, turning and putting her hands on her hips. "You're wearing a simple shirt tied up with a belt, your head's already bald, your beard is uncombed and unshaved, you drink constantly! Eh! You're a total mess! But what a man you used to be!"

"When you healed me at the ruins of that estate, crying and confessing your love to me, you said something completely different!" said old man Taras indignantly. "You said you'd love me when I was old, and when I was sick!"

"I'm telling you, I was different then." Marissa laughed and turned back to her cooking.

"What organization were you the head of?" I crept cautiously into the dialogue, trying to find out if the guess that was starting to appear in my head was right or not.

"Head of the Assassins' League," old man Taras responded drily, taking another swig of his mulled wine.

Despite the fact that I'd been expecting it, that bit of news seemed fantastical to me anyway.

"No, well, all right!" After a bit I put my shock aside and gestured to old man Taras, then shifted my gaze to Marissa. "But how did *you* end up there?"

I looked at the short, plump, and incredibly kind little Marissa as if for the first time, somehow unable to believe that she'd once been part of an organization of hired killers.

"Who, me?" she said indignantly. "You think I'm worse than him, or what?"

"Well, he's a fighter!" I explained. "A Hero-rank killer! A warrior! And what were you?"

"I was a healer and an alchemist!" she said proudly, puffing out her chest. "Hardly the worst in the League, by the way. I could treat people, and make poisons, and even add a little something lethal in. I was a Master-rank mage, after all."

"Why did I ask this question?" I said with anguish, raising my eyes to the ceiling. "They really mean it when they there's grief in knowing too much. I could be living with myself peacefully right now, remaining in blissful ignorance and not knowing about your sorrows! A simple answer would've been enough for me. Like, 'Ivan, I went through a lot in my time, I got tired of bloody fights, and now I'm living out my days on my own little piece of land. I like taking care of the farm.' That's it! That would've been enough. And you laid out this whole drama for me, and what a drama it is! Now I don't know what to think."

"See, that's just what I'm talking about!" exclaimed old man Taras happily. "Our life now is peaceful and stable. Everything is in order, and we can rest as we please, tending to the land and working on our farm."

"I'm still shocked," I admitted to them, and in the meantime Marissa started setting the table and noticed the bag I'd brought, which was lying nearby.

"Now why did you climb into your seat with your bag?" she asked. "Put it aside for now. If you stain it by accident, it'll be no good."

"It was because I brought you some little gifts," I said in dismay, undoing the clasp and putting some treats I'd bought at the store on the table.

"Now, what did you go and spend your money for?" Marissa threw up her hands. "We have everything here!"

"I didn't want to pay you a visit with empty hands." I shrugged. "You always feed me all I can eat. I wanted to show you some kind of hospitality too."

"Thank you, sonny," said old man Taras, gazing at the expensive bottle of good whiskey with love in his eyes. "He knew what would make me happy."

"You've got nothing to do but get drunk, huh?" Marissa yelled to him, putting saucers of jam and sour cream on the table.

"By the way," I remembered. "What *did* you tell me that story for? You know, about the Assassins' League and all that? You said that if you didn't, I wouldn't believe you or something like that."

"Understand this." Taras sobered up immediately and, moving the bottle I'd given him to the side, he said, "Based on our experience and a few indirect signs, we have reason to suppose that a few squads from the Assassins' League have started working in Morshansk. And since they tried to kill George earlier, we believe that you're in danger too."

"Is it that serious?" I asked cautiously.

"Very much so," replied old man Taras, sighing deeply. "We can't tell you the secrets of the League, or we'll most likely die. However, we certainly can warn you about what might happen."

"What do you mean?" I was curious about that. "How's that? 'We can't tell you or we'll die?' What does that mean?"

"It means that we took part in the magical ritual Golden Silence," said Marissa. "Look it up in your family library or ask your brother. I'm sure he probably knows that ritual."

"Understood," I said thoughtfully, giving a melancholy sigh. "I just wanted to wheedle old man Taras into giving me some extra training, and I learned all that."

"What do you need that for?" Taras was surprised. "You've been working out with Leonid, and training with Boemir's boys, and visiting the Mage League headquarters — how would you find any more time for me?"

"I'll find it." I knit my brows. "Not too long ago I lost to a certain young lady and now I have a really strong thirst for revenge."

"Well, there you go," old man Taras coughed, turning to Marissa. "The young man is growing up! He already found himself a lady! And apparently one who fights!"

Then he shifted his gaze to me and said:

"Never fear, Ivan, I'll help you. Especially with something like this. A lady should know her place!"

"I'm about to give it to you with this towel!" said Marissa, quietly but threateningly. "So you don't teach the child nonsense!"

"But what about the training?" I asked. "I need old man Taras alive, after all."

"First have something to eat, and then you can get to your training!"

"But I can't train with a full stomach!" I said. "You should know that as a healer!"

"And I'm telling you that after lunch, you can go straight to your training," said Marissa. "First, tell me how the imperial ball went, what news and gossip you heard there, and then do what you want."

Chapter 14

IT WASN'T UNTIL AN HOUR LATER that old man Taras and I finally broke free from the house.

A light snow was falling. The neighboring buildings were covered with little white caps, and puffs of black smoke were slowly coming out of the pipes. I didn't know why, but I was overwhelmed with a sense of some kind of light tranquility. I figured the delicious homemade lunch played no small role in that.

"Lovely," I said after a bit. "I think I understand why you and Marissa settled down here in particular."

"You're still too young to understand," old man Taras noted philosophically. "For that, you have to not only be smart, but also live a good while and gain your own experience, so you can understand afterwards that the homestead is calling you, that your forefathers, your grandfather, and your father did just that, and now you will. Although, pardon me, that most likely isn't for you to understand, my dear Ivan. You're different. Why, you have such strong heritage! And you're a good warrior, and you most likely won't be last among mages. I haven't seen anyone like you in a long time. That wasn't your family's trade."

Actually, my ancestors were from Belarus, I wanted to say. So I knew how to dig up taters and do stuff around a farm. I didn't love it, but I knew how.

However, I said something different.

"I still feel some kind of peace here. And you're making it sound like only Avtiukians are capable of understanding the quiet beauty and charm of one's own home."

"Heh," Taras laughed. "It's not just us, you're right there, but later on after many, many years, believe me, you'll understand what I'm talking about."

"It's entirely possible." I shrugged, not wanting to argue over such a trifle.

"Now come on, Ivan, follow me," said old man Taras after a short pause. "I have one cozy little nook here where I sometimes reminisce about the old days and limber up. It'll be just right for our purposes."

Crossing the yard and finding ourselves behind the first line of the farm's premises, we ducked into a pretty spacious shed.

"We used to have eight cows," old man Taras

explained into the void, looking around warmly at the space that smelled pleasantly of hay. "This is where we kept the food for the whole winter. Later on, the number of cows on our farm kept getting smaller every year, until in the end there was just one left. Her name's Little Lady. It's her milk Marissa's always treating you to."

"It sounds like you still have a goat, too?" I frowned, remembering.

"We have both a goat and a cow," said Taras. "So, will this shed work for us?"

"I think so." I nodded, looking around again at the large space with a high ceiling.

"Then for starters, show me what you can do," said old man Taras, settling down comfortably on an oak-wood chock that had appeared from who knew where near the walls.

"I can't show you everything," I noted, remembering a few of my techs. "Showing you certain things would just be dangerous."

"Don't worry," he brushed me off. "I already know all about the capabilities of your 'Globe of Fire.' But that won't factor in much — you and I are going to train entirely different qualities. Right? I just wanted to assess your current speed and level of control over the techs you know."

"And how am I supposed to show you that?" I didn't understand.

"Show me a fight with your shadow, just don't get carried away — I still need this shed."

After a few minutes, old man Taras yelled:

"Defend yourself!" and jumped right up from

the chock at me.

Despite having seen him fight the Assassins' League warriors on the day of the murder attempt, I still wasn't used to how this man carried on a fight. Something felt wrong about this jovial and perpetually drunk old fellow becoming so skilled, strong, and dangerous. Things like that didn't happen in real life. Cognitive dissonance at its most jarring.

Old man Taras wasn't fighting in the "drunken master" style right now. His blows were sparing but very precise. Without straining himself at all, he figured out the places where I was appearing after taking Spirit-Steps and dealt me an annoying blow to the forehead. And I was moving without much constraint myself.

As I watched this ordinary and completely awkward-looking old man with a bald head and a disheveled beard, wearing felt boots and black coat tied with a simple belt, effortlessly drag me through the mud, I unexpectedly fell into depression.

First I got my lunch handed to me by a pretty and very striking girl, now a seemingly feeble old man. What next? Would a kid beat me up? Maybe I shouldn't be going to the imperial tournament.

"Stop!" Old man Taras stopped me, jumping aside to his chock. "What did you just do?"

"What do you mean?" I didn't understand. "I was fighting. I put up a Spirit Shield and blocked you, and then after you attacked I ducked and hit you with a Battering Ram."

"I got that." He nodded. "What I want to know is — why did you become several times more dangerous in the last ten seconds? You easily dodged a few of my attacks, switched to the offensive, then put up a Spirit Shield, blocked me, and counterattacked again — in the same place where I'd just moved with a Spirit-Step, no less! And what's most interesting — this is the first time you've truly been a match for me!"

Old man Taras thought about something, narrowed his eyes, stared at me, and then said with a nod: "Hold still!" He walked around me in a circle a few times.

"Well? What did you realize?" I asked impatiently when he returned to his place.

"I realized this!" He looked at me gloomily. "That you think a lot!"

"I'm sorry, I think a lot?" I didn't understand at all.

"You think a lot in a fight, of course," he explained. "Where you need to act intuitively, on your reflexes, you prefer to think first and then hit. That is, how to hit, where to hit, and so on. It seems to me that Theophane worked a lot on this problem of yours, but apparently, since he's been gone the problem has returned."

"Well, of course I think about how to fight!" I said indignantly. "How else am I supposed to get a read on where the fight is going? To understand what kind of enemy I have in front of me? To see his weaknesses and take advantage of them? If I don't think, I lose fast."

"Hmm." Taras scratched his head pensively. "When Theophane comes back, I'll give him a thrashing over your education."

"What's wrong?" I didn't understand. "This happens automatically for me. And I don't have to stop moving to figure everything out."

"Not so automatic, based on what I saw," old man Taras explained. "Just answer me honestly about what you were thinking about just before I stopped the fight. Those last few seconds."

I sighed heavily, but I decided to answer honestly anyway.

"About how I'm losing not only to some teenage girl, but an old man too."

"I'm not that old yet," said old man Taras indignantly, chuckling. "There you have it! I was right! When you weren't thinking about the fight, about where specifically to hit next and what you needed to do, your body did what you needed it to do faster and with more precision. When your body acts without getting your brain involved, you become a more dangerous enemy."

"So what am I supposed to do now, not think at all?" I gave him an outraged look. "That can't be it!"

"It can," he replied. "That's precisely what we'll start our lessons with."

When after a few hours I managed to break away from the clutches of the hospitable Avtiukians, who invited me to dinner too, my driver looked a little anxious.

"Let's go home," I said, collapsing into the back seat with no strength.

Old man Taras was a real wolf in sheep's clothing!

"I was already starting to think that you'd been kidnapped," said the driver with a chuckle, swallowing frantically.

"There are just some good people living there who are pleasant for me to talk to," I explained. "Besides, I did tell you right off the bat that I'd be a while. Get used to it — this won't be my last trip here."

Once I got home, I found out where George was and headed straight for him.

"Come in, sit down," he said, not getting up from his chair and not tearing himself away from his papers. "Do you have something urgent?"

"Very urgent," I replied, taking the seat he'd indicated. Once I'd settled in comfortably, I continued. "For whatever reason you've been sitting around in your study a lot recently. Did Father give you some new homework?"

"No." George rubbed his eyes in exhaustion. "I'm trying to squeeze into the local trade market for ingredients, but it's not going so well."

"Oh?" I was genuinely curious about that. "Can you give me more details? It's just that before I got my name back, I wanted to get one interesting thing out there via the Ogneyers and earn a lot of money."

Incidentally, why am I not working on that now? I asked myself. After all, now I had both the resources and the connections, and it could turn out to be a wholly advantageous project. Some money certainly wouldn't hurt me.

George laughed.

"You had some kind of project?" he asked. "When you were thought to be a commoner? Doing something with your ingredients? C'mon, don't make me laugh. Here I am with the status of a noble heir, and I can't do almost anything — only my alliance with the Ogneyers is allowing me to expect at least something. And you... the ingredients market is already so oversaturated with different players, you can't even imagine how hard it is to earn at least something there and find a new niche."

"Well, okay." I narrowed my eyes. "If you feel like joining my team in the future, your cut will be a lot less than it could've been."

"Fine by me," said George with a grin. "So why did you come to see me?"

"Oh, that's small potatoes." I grinned in response. "I have some information that the infamous Assassins' League has started working in Morshansk."

"Are you sure?" George immediately sobered up. "If this is some stupid joke, then..."

"A joke?" I interrupted him unhappily. "What, don't you know me? Or do you think I'm inclined to joke about things like that?"

"As it turns out, I have absolutely no idea," said George after a bit, and explained, "If you have access to sources of information for that kind of thing. Or, perhaps, is this how you're trying to tell me that Theophane is back?"

"This information isn't from Theophane." I shook my head. "Even I don't know where he is yet."

"Then where's this gossip from?" George asked me in a skeptical tone. "Or is there a whole network of agents working for you, and it's anyone's guess?"

"The information is from a reliable person who cannot divulge more detailed intelligence. He said that you'll understand if I tell you that it's all because of some 'silence' ritual."

"Silence, you say," said George pensively. "I know a little something about it, of course. People who've gone through that ritual can't speak about things they've been forbidden from disclosing. But if this person is really from the Assassins' League or a former member of it, then I'm actually surprised you managed to learn so much. Could I meet this person, perhaps?"

"That's out of the question." I shook my head decisively.

"You don't understand." George frowned. "If the Assassins' League is really at work in this city, then they've most likely come for my head, so I'd like to personally communicate with this person. If this could be shared with you, then I think I can ask the questions I need to and get more detailed information about what's happening."

"You can't," I replied, remembering how I'd tried for half an hour to get old man Taras and Marissa to tell me anything more specific about the killers than just warnings.

We don't know them, Taras had answered me. The specific killers, I mean. However, based on several indirect signs that we can't tell you about, there is a way to be absolutely sure that there are two or three small groups of killers working in Morshansk. Believe us, we have no reason to lie...

"I'm going to insist anyway." George frowned. "Or do you think I need to send my people over to that sweet old couple you visited today in the residential sector? Maybe they know something? Huh?"

"Just try it." I frowned, and it got colder in the room. "Then you won't have a brother or another source of information. And besides that, I won't lift a finger to help you in any way. Last time, my ice globe couldn't have turned out to be more to your benefit, and now you'll have to find a way out yourself."

"What an interesting guy you are!" fumed George. "You came here with news like that, told me about some source of information you have, and you won't let me talk to them! What am I supposed to do here? Expect a strike around every corner? Huh? Maybe you have a suggestion? Since you're so smart? This is still a threat! You little louse!"

"Well, I do know something about this, anyway," I noted, calming down. "Usually, if the Assassins' League doesn't manage to fulfill an order openly, then they either pay back their fee or they start putting roots around the target so as to kill him when he's not expecting it."

"So is it possible we need to start with that?" George muttered with dissatisfaction. "Now I'll have to re-check all the new servants."

"Maybe," I agreed. "But you got me to digress from my business with the ingredients."

"Okay, okay." George brushed me off exhaustedly. "That's enough, get out of here, I'm going to work and think. A lot."

"Happy working," I said, getting up and heading for the door.

We'd see if I managed to earn more from ingredients than he would or not.

*   *   *

During school break, I kept working on the three things that were most important to me at the same time. I trained with Boemir's soldiers at the base, where Svetlana appeared periodically; I trained with old man Taras, who tried to wean me off of thinking too much while fighting; and I worked on actualizing — I wasn't afraid of that word — my brilliant plan for enrichment. Although, of course, only time would tell whether it was brilliant or just wishful thinking. Despite belonging to an ancient princely bloodline, I didn't have all that much money left in my bank account. I could live on it, of course, and I could pull the wool over everyone else's eyes if I needed to, but it might not be enough for a project that required big investments.

In general, because of my busy schedule, I had

almost no time for anything. All the better that the mage league made accommodations for school-age students and announced its break at the same time as the school, so that its Acolytes could get at least a little time to rest. The boys from my friend group also treated my busy schedule with understanding and weren't too zealous about insisting I come to various hangouts. So I did have some time to work on my project.

A few years previously, when I'd officially been considered dead and seriously reflected on my future, one interesting idea had come into my head. It was linked first and foremost, of course, to what I had to deal with every day. More precisely, extracting and reselling ingredients I got in the Wasteland.

Even then I'd understood that the market system for the riches that could be found there was extremely imperfect. You could sell something at the Free Hunters' Exchange if, of course, you weren't worried about finding a buyer in advance. Various industrial giants would take something. However, they could buy things for peanuts at the customs points for the benefit of the state. In general, the system needed some real improvement. It should've been set up so that individual people could be allowed to distribute information about their goods at will through information networks, on a website, or in a catalogue. And so that buyers could know where they needed to go if they needed one item or another.

At the same time, though, I understood that

some kid showing up out of nowhere with that kind of idea wouldn't get anything but a jab to the ribs and a lot of attention. For my plan to be carried out, someone had to have my back. I'd even started looking into the Ogneyers. However, as I knew now, everything had gone sideways after I'd met up with George.

Now, as it seemed to me, everything would turn out much better. I had status, a bloodline, and the chance to register my business in the legal name of the Morozovs while I was still a minor. I'd studied the special laws.

I'd devoted quite a lot of my free time to my project. I'd pored over the legislation, studied information about this world's technology, and investigated how phones, computers, and servers worked.

It was all at a basic level, of course, and superficial by a long shot, but this knowledge allowed me to understand exactly what I needed to implement my project and how I needed to do it.

I dedicated more than a little time to working on the design of my future website and catalogue. It wasn't thorough, of course — there were graphic designers for that — but I laid the groundwork. How I envisioned my project, where the pages should be, what their functions were. The procedure for charging clients, ratings for hunters, personal profile designs, and a lot of other stuff.

A few days before the start of the new school trimester, Ms. Dashkevich's daughter said her farewells to the whole team at the military base, not forgetting about me. Then, promising to return after a few months, on her next break, she left the city.

Right, yes, Ms. Dashkevich had said that Svetlana was just in town visiting someone, I thought as I looked after that lovely girl. In a few months we'd see how much stronger I'd become, I promised.

The new school trimester — the last one for this year — seemed to sneak up on me, and I had even less time. Because I'd continued training more intensely, working out at school and at the Mage League headquarters, and also working on my future enrichment. Thankfully, I was almost finished with my project and returned to it only when I thought of something new and interesting.

At the beginning of the school trimester I already knew exactly what I wanted to do and how I could do it. I'd already realized that the level of programmers I needed could only be found at the capital of the Empire. So I decided to set the project aside until nationals at the imperial tournament. I didn't even doubt that I'd get past regionals.

The selection for our branch's warrior and mage teams, like last year, took place in a pretty big basement room under the gym. True, this time I was there not as a spectator, but as a direct contestant.

The people who wanted to participate in the warriors' tournament were divided into two age groups — middle schoolers and high schoolers.

From the name it was clear that in middle school, where I was, were the fifth to seventh graders, and in high school were the eighth and ninth graders.

I didn't think that was totally right, since a difference of one year between students in the younger classes was pretty substantial, but of course the powers that be didn't give two cents for my opinion. So I didn't voice this to anyone — what was the point? It wouldn't change anything either way!

It was a little different for the mages, though. For them, duels between participants happened without any age restrictions. That is, everyone who wanted to participate fought in the same group. This was obviously because most of the participants were in fact high schoolers. Full-fledged study of magic began in seventh grade for children, after all — a little earlier for some — so only the older kids could show anything off.

To my mild surprise, just about half the school decided to participate in the tournament selection this year. So all the seats in the basement were taken, not only by students but also by parents who'd come to root for their kids.

"Look at that, that guy's trash!" I said in surprise to Godimir, who was standing next to me. "A first-level Junior who can't even sense spiritual energy. Where does he think he's going? Huh?"

"Don't you worry about him," Godimir brushed me off. "You can see for yourself that he understands his position, or else he wouldn't be behaving so nervously. You should just remember that the imperial tournament is wholly a status thing first and foremost, and a lot of the nobility force their children to at least test their strength, just in case they make it."

"Yeah, this is almost the first time I'm seeing a lot of the participants in the selection process," I muttered unhappily in response. "Apparently, this is going to drag on because of how many people are trying out, and I'd like to have time to get other places."

Good thing old man Taras wasn't as strict of a teacher as Theophane, and he'd be understanding about this situation.

"Agreed, but believe me, not everyone here's as much of a wimp as you think," Godimir retorted. "A lot of kids train at home with private tutors. So they can totally beat the ones who train with Mr. Viktorov."

"Have you seen how many girls there are?" Vladimir Ischezov asked us, approaching us quietly.

"You don't stand a chance, most of them are high schoolers," Godimir noted quietly.

"What about the redhead?" said Vladimir, gesturing to our class prefect. "But you got me all wrong — I'm saying our branch has quite a lot of magically talented girls, but there's not one among the warriors."

"Because they're physically weaker," I said weightily, and immediately frowned in dissatisfaction as I remembered how strong Svetlana was. "And besides, their kind hearts clearly don't want to solve problems with raw strength and fists. Now with magic, that's a different story."

There were in fact quite a lot of girls hoping to prove themselves in the magic tournament. I looked at them pensively as they exchanged glances gloomily. Certainly no fewer than the boys.

Exchanging glances with the warrior candidates, I sighed heavily. Because there were so many people, I started to associate this event with aimlessly wasting time. I knew full well that I was stronger than any student at our branch, but rules were rules, and Mr. Viktorov — who also knew this — simply couldn't register me for one of the slots without the selection event.

I didn't waste time with any one of the first four opponents I was put with. I preferred to finish those fights pretty quickly. I was really irritated and had no intention of being diplomatic — there was no comparison between our ranks, after all, even less so our skill levels. Now, at regionals and nationals I was expecting more skilled opponents. From Mr. Viktorov, after all, I knew that there were a lot of strong fighters there.

After the scores were added up, it was announced that the ones chosen for the tournament were me, Godimir, and three other students who'd been training under Mr. Viktorov's guidance.

The mage selection that followed was more interesting to me. Before I left, I even watched a couple of matches.

As I'd guessed, the strongest turned out to be only ninth graders — that is, high schoolers.

* * *

"You're late," said old man Taras to me, looking at his watch theatrically. "That's not like you."

"I'm sorry. The tournament selection just ran late. I didn't even anticipate that there would be so many kids among the nobility who wanted to wag their fists around."

"I see," said Taras, putting on his outer layers, then decided to tease me. "I hope we're not training in vain? Did you make the cut? Otherwise, it'd be insulting to waste so much of my personal time on a talentless hack."

"And how would you spend your time then?" I smirked in response. "Wallowing by the stove all day and pumping yourself full of booze? Such an important task."

"Yeah, if only." He screwed up his eyes dreamily. "On the other hand, you wouldn't have to get your caboose out in the freezing cold every day."

For today's training, old man Taras decided to introduce a few changes to our usual routine and started with a question instead of harsh Shiki-Cho-less sparring at the limit of my strength.

"Show me, Ivan — how do you use the Spirit-Step tech?" he asked. "Move back and forth ten times, and then do it while mimicking a fight."

Tracking my movement as I skipped around the shed chaotically a few times, he decided to stop me and asked me his next question.

"Now tell me, Ivan, what do you think — if I

move and take a Spirit-Step at the same time, will I be able to get to a new spot? Or no?"

"I think you will," I replied, remembering what Mr. Viktorov had said when teaching me this tech. "Although for me, I have to stand still for at least a moment in order to take a Spirit-Step."

"There you go! You're absolutely correct," said Taras with satisfaction, stroking his beard. "I don't need to stand still to take a Spirit-Step."

He showed me a Spirit-Step combined with an attack.

"That's how it's done."

"But that's completely above my level," I said indignantly, shaking my head. "When I become a Knight, then I'll think about improving my technique. For now it's too early for me to be thinking about that. I know, I tried it already."

"There's a lot there you're right about, of course, but not everything." Taras grinned slyly. "Of course what I just showed you is Knight- and Hero-level — you have long years of training ahead of you yet before you get there — but you can still improve the tech a little." He stroked his beard again and continued, "Here, imagine two situations. In the first one you block, then move with a Spirit-Step and attack, and in the second one you block, then wind up, and only then take a Spirit-Step and finish the punch. In which of those two scenarios will your punch get to the target in the majority of cases?"

"Well, the second one, probably," I said pensively, trying to picture all of those actions in my mind.

"Why's that?" he probed immediately.

"If I act like in the second scenario," I started answering him obediently, "that is, winding up after blocking — I've shown the enemy the beginning of my attack, and I might deceive him about what I'm doing and force him to block or put up a Spirit-Shield. But then I'll move to a different spot, and before he can react, I'll get him. If I do that the blow itself will be quicker than in the first scenario, since I'm eliminating the wind-up time."

"Right," said Taras, chuckling in satisfaction. "Right! That, I admit, is a fairly difficult use of the tech, but a very useful one. So, you can start practicing in the following sequence: block, wind-up, Spirit-Step, strike. Got it?"

I nodded.

"Then c'mon, let's start by doing it ten times."

Chapter 15

SERGEI DIACHENKO — the Temnikovs' head of security — walked with quick, confident steps towards the head of the family's study, where Yegor Temnikov had been spending practically all day and all night lately.

After knocking briefly and being invited in, he opened the door and entered the room.

He found Temnikov at the study's open window, through which he could watch his daughters taking an unhurried stroll through the gardens.

"Did you get them?" he asked, not taking his eyes off the window.

"Only one," said Diachenko drily, a bit irritated by his lack of success.

After he'd finally settled confidently into the unsteady position of head of security and secured a stable and satisfying life for his family, all of his attention had been wholly and completely directed at fulfilling his official duties and resolving the Temnikov family's problems. Of which, as it turned out, there were more than enough. Lately, Diachenko had gotten so used to reporting the successful completion of his operations that any failure evoked a whole storm of negative emotions in him.

"That's bad," said Temnikov, turning around and fixing an intent gaze on Diachenko. "What's the reason for your failure? Do you recall that you assured me everything was under control?"

"At the present time, I don't have the necessary information for a report. My operatives are trying to investigate that now. They're taking the records from the nearest security cameras, studying the assault crews' actions, and searching for where we might have slipped up. According to the preliminary reports, the crews' actions were beyond reproach, but one of the detectives somehow managed to sense danger anyway, and thanks to that he was able to hide."

"If the assault crews had worked strictly according to protocol, no one should have sensed danger," Temnikov noted weightily. "The Prischepkins, the Chesnokovs, and others might suspect us — they've experienced it themselves. But, of course, you know all that."

"Yes, it's true," Diachenko agreed. "But I didn't notice any mistakes either. And I believe the reports from my group commanders."

Lately, Diachenko's relationship with Temnikov had undergone a few changes. Diachenko had started to take advantage of Temnikov's trust and support. Their communication remained businesslike, but now Temnikov could allow himself to speak with less constraint.

"So far it looks like you're trying to cover up for your people," said Temnikov. "Either that, or something that sounds even more far-fetched — the detective you let slip was a high-rank warrior or mage. Do you believe that was the case?"

"As practice shows, people like that are extremely ambitious and occupy themselves with more important things than surveillance," Diachenko admitted, trying not to show that Temnikov's words bothered him, and concluded: "However, we can't strike that theory from the record."

"I suppose not," said Temnikov after a bit. "And how did the first one behave? I mean the one you caught."

"Going by his facial expressions, right before we got him, he also sensed something — either that or he got a signal from the second one through some kind of channel, but despite that we succeeded in capturing him fairly quickly. It went off without unnecessary casualties, but only because each group had a healer."

"Such interesting spies out there these days! Masters of not only espionage, but battle too. Although, if there had been someone truly strong there, then we wouldn't have gotten away without losses," said Temnikov thoughtfully. "Where is the prisoner now?"

"In the cellar, in a cell. He's unconscious," said Diachenko. "He was injected with a large dose of sleeping potion. So he'll wake up in somewhere around an hour."

"Sleeping potion, that's good," said Temnikov, then said resolutely, "All right, it is what it is. We may have only one spy in our hands, but for now that's enough for us. Take the reagents you need — let's go talk to our prisoner. We'll finally learn who's had it out for us so long and so stubbornly, and how long this has been going on."

*　*　*

On the floor of the prison cell in the cellar room lay a young, thin man. His hands were bound with an imposing-looking rune-covered chain, the end of which was tightly embedded in the equally imposing wall.

"And you mean to tell me that he was the one creating serious problems?" Temnikov said in a skeptical tone, looking at the unkempt man lying on the floor. Then, stopping Diachenko as he stepped forward with a syringe in hand, he listened for something and tossed the prisoner's body into the air with a spell.

The prisoner, coming awake instantly, pressed himself up against the wall and stared at the two men in terror.

"Who are you? What do you need from me?" he cried somewhat hysterically. "I'm an ordinary man! I have nothing to give you! I beg you! Let me go!"

"You're putting on a show for nothing," said Temnikov calmly, sitting down in a chair obligingly carried in by one of the guards. "Someone unprepared could never feign sleep so skillfully."

"Besides, his body couldn't shake off the influence of a sleeping potion that quickly," Diachenko added, setting his unnecessary syringe aside. "Especially not at that deadly dosage."

The prisoner didn't move for some time. Then, calming himself in an instant, he sat up more comfortably against the wall and stared at Temnikov.

"Good afternoon, Prince Yegor," he said, and added as if inviting him to a dialogue, "I suspected, of course, that it was your people who were involved in my capture, but I didn't really believe it up until the end."

"And why is that?" asked Temnikov, crossing his legs and settling more comfortably into his chair.

He decided to play by the other guy's rules for now and see where that could lead. What if the loquacious young man didn't hold his tongue?

"Well, if nothing else, because your security team's standards are extremely low," replied the prisoner impudently. Seeing Diachenko frown, he continued with satisfaction: "Of course, I must admit that since your new head of security arrived, its standards have increased significantly. There's no use in doubting that, but you have a long way to go before you're truly robust security professionals. You hardly have any experience. Not everyone can recover after almost losing a war. Wouldn't you say? We on the same page here?"

"But nonetheless, here you are, and those *were* my people who took you," Temnikov noted calmly, paying no heed to the improper tone of the conversation.

"Believe me, it won't be for long," replied the prisoner in all seriousness. "Just as soon as my employers become aware of where I am, they'll be here right away. They've probably sent someone after me already."

"Are you so sure that some detective could mean more to someone than making enemies with a princely house?" said Temnikov, surprised. "And they'll storm the place? That declaration seems a little too self-assured to me."

"I think that a specialist who's been able to conduct surveillance on a powerful house almost unnoticed for the span of a few years is an entirely valuable individual. And if that person has also been able to tie up a few loose ends for that family's security that could've led the gendarmes and the clergy to them, then his value would increase exponentially."

"What do you mean?" Diachenko spoke up immediately, suspecting the worst. "We haven't broken the law, and no one gives a damn about the rest of our doings."

"Now there, Sergei, you're as shady as your master's magic," said the prisoner, chuckling at his spur-of-the-moment witticism. "Yes, shady. Everyone in this room knows full well why those organizations would take an interest in what's been happening in one of the country's notable noble families. A younger-looking Yegor Temnikov, whose power has grown to the level of a strong Archmage even outside the bounds of the family estate, will catch their eye instantly."

"These statements can only speak to your level of incompetence," said Diachenko, not intending to lose this round. "Prince Temnikov has been at such a high level for a long time."

No, I won't let you catch me so easily, thought Diachenko, calculating what he was going to do next after hearing THAT information. He had no intention of even indirectly confirming that they'd taken part in blood rituals. Although the prisoner clearly knew about it. It was probably better to put a stop to this nonsense and get down to business quickly — the executioner would teach this idiot to tell the truth right away.

"How old are you?" Temnikov asked unexpectedly, directing an intent stare at the prisoner.

"I'm much older than I look," replied the prisoner, staring just as intently at Temnikov. "We know how to make our fighters and mages stronger too — it's not just the Temnikovs who know the forgotten rituals."

"You're too calm and cheerful," said Diachenko threateningly. "Aren't you afraid that we'll start torturing you? Your surveillance on our house is already a crime. You can stay cheerful for now, but soon you'll find out what pain is."

"Well, I was hoping to avoid that," said the

prisoner seriously. "I'm ready to work with you and tell you everything I know. As someone with experience, who's seen a lot in my day, I realize that everyone breaks under torture. So I'll talk."

"In that case, you have one minute to prove your usefulness," said Diachenko. "Your time starts now."

"Then I'll start from the beginning. It became known to our organization that an unknown party had started kidnapping citizens of the Empire. Those who went missing were primarily people linked to the criminal world. Some time was spent on searching, and a car full of captured prisoners led us to the estate of an influential family. The character and number of those affected clearly spoke to the fact that someone was conducting forbidden rituals with the aim of strengthening his personal magic. We couldn't allow any outsiders to find out about the disappearances, and although the rumors went around anyway, we cleaned up your warriors' tracks. After that, my coworker and I were appointed to do surveillance on your house."

"Why did you need to do that? And what kind of organization are we talking about?" asked Diachenko calmly, keeping himself together even though everything inside him was simply snarling with anger.

"I'm incompetent and can't assess the motives behind our leaders' actions," said the prisoner. "As for our organization, it's a secret order. You can be sure that soon, one of its emissaries will be here for me, and he'll tell you everything."

"Do you mean to say that all this time we've been watched by some secret order that managed to find out what I was doing?" said Temnikov coldly.

"It wasn't that hard," replied the prisoner with a bit of self-satisfaction. "You don't think that when various members of ill-reputed classes start disappearing in a certain place, no one notices? Au contraire! That was your biggest mistake! Many of the powerful in this world need people like that, and their disappearances don't happen without a trace. Without them you can't launder money, you can't fake documents, you can't frame competitors. So, admittedly, we had to do quite a bit of hard work to cover your tracks."

"Clearly, your order has some decent expertise in covering tracks," said Diachenko. "You can only notice such imperfections if you're running operations like that yourself. And if your order is allowing itself to do similar rituals, it's becoming clear that you do a lot more kidnapping than we do."

"Not bad," admitted the prisoner, looking at Temnikov. "This young lad is truly your greatest success. His head works right, and he's much more competent than the last head of security by a long shot. Although I think I just said I'm much older than—"

He didn't have a chance to finish. A powerful punch from an invisible hand in the solar plexus knocked all the wind out of him, and he was caught up by the neck in a dark aura and hung in midair.

At first, he didn't react to this at all — only struggled to say something. However, his strength started to fade pretty fast — you can't last long without oxygen, after all, no matter how prepared you are.

He beat at the dark fog with his feet and his shackled hands, trying to weaken it and gulp in at least a little bit of air, but nothing worked. He grew weaker and had almost stopped moving already when Temnikov finally let him go. Collapsing to the ground, he started frantically gulping in life-giving air, but before he had time to enjoy the oxygen, he was lifted up off the ground by the neck again.

"Don't you dare speak to me in that tone," said Temnikov calmly once he'd finished this punishment.

"Y-yes, y-your G-G-Grace," said the prisoner once he'd caught his breath a little, squeezing the words from his throat with difficulty. "I beg you, forgive me for my discourteousness — I was insolent."

At that moment there was a knock on the door to the cell, and it opened.

"Prince Yegor," said Yamashita, coming in. "A few minutes ago, a car drove up to the main gates. The driver said that his friend was captured by mistake and is now being held at this estate."

"Invite our guest to the sitting room on the first floor and make sure that no one in my family gets too close to it," ordered Temnikov, and turned to the prisoner. "Your colleague who got away?"

"No." The prisoner shook his head, rubbed his neck, and added hoarsely, "I told you they'd come for me."

* * *

About two hours later, Temnikov finally entered the sitting room and approached the guest, who was examining the family's portraits on the wall with polite interest.

The stranger was a tall, dark-haired man with a neat hairstyle and delicate features on his young face that were vaguely familiar to Temnikov. His stylish dark blue coat stood out on him, and around his neck was a thin, light-colored scarf.

"Good evening, Prince Yegor," the man greeted him politely.

"Whom do I have the pleasure of meeting?" said Temnikov, looking intently into the stranger's serious eyes.

"Alexei Alexandrovich Cibulkin," he replied. "Esteemed actor at the Great Imperial Opera and Ballet Theater."

"Please, sit down," said Temnikov, finally remembering where he'd seen this man, and gestured to one of two armchairs near the fireplace. Taking the open chair, Temnikov continued: "What use could I be to an actor from the GIOBT?"

He examined the man, whom he'd seen more than once onstage at the theater, with some surprise.

Was this man really the emissary of a powerful

organization? Or was the prisoner out of his mind? Hmm. Musn't be. He still had some way to go.

"You see," said Cibulkin slowly, tapping on the armrest of his chair with fingernails covered in a heavy layer of colorless varnish, "the thing is, due to some misunderstanding, my friend was taken prisoner by your people."

"Where did you get the idea that they were my people?" asked Temnikov.

"What do you mean? There were eyewitnesses! As soon as I was told about this, I hurried here right away."

"Oh, that's who you're talking about!" Temnikov pretended to realize. "Do you mean that spy who's being tortured in my dungeon now?"

"*What?* What spy?" cried Cibulkin anxiously. "There's been some kind of mistake! Some kind of mistake! Why torture him? Show at least a bit of mercy! Please?"

"At least a bit of mercy?" said Temnikov pensively. "Can you at least explain to me why I should do that?"

"Aside from the fact that mercy is a Saviorly virtue?" asked Cibulkin. "You must understand that this is some kind of terrible mistake. My friend was simply minding his own business and wasn't following anyone."

"So what your so-called friend is saying now under torture is also a mistake?" Temnikov countered, frowning. "About a secret order? About the surveillance he conducted on my family? Spare me your performance — we're not at the theater.

Speak directly or I'll chat with a different emissary."

Cibulkin was quiet for a for some time, mulling over what he'd heard, then spoke.

"Very well. Let's do this your way, even though I was hoping we could resolve all this peacefully," he said, sighing heavily. "I want you to give the order to have my man released."

"I repeat. Why should I do that?" asked Temnikov, forcing Cibulkin to enter an open conversation and show his cards.

Judging by his heavy sigh, it worked.

"I think you should take into account that our organization has indisputable proof of the Temnikov house's participation in the disappearance of several hundred people. A rumor here, a little suggestion there, a bit of gossip thrown out there, and the entire Nosiriansky Empire will know that a princely house kidnapped people for blood sacrifices. Your glorious house's days will be numbered. And you can be sure that neither our emperor nor the nobility nor the clergy will forgive you for it. Of course, each organization will have its own reasons for being unhappy, but that won't change the fact that you'll cross the line for all of them at once."

"I don't understand what you're talking about," Temnikov objected. "Is this some kind of joke? Or are you trying to defend your spy in such a strange way?"

"You're hiding it well," said Cibulkin. "You wouldn't even know that you've heard a strange accusation that's actually true. According to the opinions of our analysts, after what you just heard, you could've let yourself to fly into a rage and attack me, but clearly, the blood sacrifice rituals not only rejuvenated your body but also saved you from a variety of character flaws."

"If I attacked people every time they started talking nonsense, I'd have no one left to talk to," Temnikov noted calmly.

Cibulkin was silent for a bit, then continued nonetheless.

"Would you allow me to show you a few of the materials I have at my disposal? I have them with me, on a tablet — I think it'll be interesting for you to learn about them."

Taking a small tablet from Cibulkin, Temnikov pressed the "play" button and, not without curiosity, focused on the screen.

In a short video with documentary-style filming played scenes of a few groups of people being kidnapped, and a voice behind the camera explained pretty clearly how the perpetrator's trail had successfully been picked up. Facts, evidence, and proof flashed by on the screen for a few minutes, and at the end the voice revealed who was living behind the high walls of the estate where the kidnapped parties had been taken.

"And what's this supposed to enlighten me about?" asked Temnikov, setting the tablet aside. "That your organization makes crackpot videos? Or spreads false news? Lunatic ravings."

"Maybe you could say that. But only in the

event that you're not connected to what transpired, and that's incongruous with reality. We have weightier evidence that we're correct, and also indirect proof that would allow us to bring it to the public."

"Why are you telling me all this?" asked Temnikov. "What's stopping me from gutting you and your man in my dungeon? Believe me, my people will be merciless in getting the information they need. I'll figure out how best to handle it from there."

"I admit, my main goal is to secure cooperation between the house of Temnikov and my organization. In the event that you detain me, information about your escapades will immediately spread to all interested parties," said Cibulkin. "I must warn you that despite my entirely peaceful appearance, I can be fairly dangerous."

"Is that so?" said Temnikov, not stopping himself from being sarcastic. "Do you believe that you could fight the head of a house at his own estate on equal footing? What a joke."

"You're entirely correct. At his own estate, the head of a house is practically invincible. However, I have my own aces up my sleeve," said Cibulkin, paying no attention to the sarcasm and taking out a pocket watch.

"Is that an artifact?" asked Temnikov, sensing shielding magic.

"You could say that," said Cibulkin. Opening it up, he showed Temnikov that there was a Soul Stone in place of the inner workings. "Our organization possesses knowledge of several fields of forbidden magic. Believe me, the power granted by it could dumbfound you. At times it's deadly. I can't defeat you, of course, but I'd try to get away."

"A Soul Stone," said Temnikov, feeling growing alarm. And you're not afraid that I could outplay you and leave you to the mercy of the clergy with your little rock in exchange?"

"And tell everyone around you about your dirty deeds? I think you're much smarter than that. Even if you manage to secure the support of one of the Empire's central powers, the rest won't forgive such a serious violation of the rules of the game either way." Pausing briefly, Cibulkin continued, "Instead of losing all kinds of things by taking that thoughtless step, my organization is inviting you to do the opposite. We want ordinary cooperation. I think your family's head of security, and you as well, have been able to appraise our people's level of preparedness. Both in surveillance and in covering tracks. I'm certain that we'll be useful to each other. Of course, it's unpleasant for me to play the role of some kind of blackmailer here, or even more so a bandit, forcing you to make a decision you don't want to, but I'm sure that we need each other. For that matter, you still don't know some of the side effects of the ritual you did."

"Side effects?" Temnikov repeated. "And what about your security guarantees? Perhaps in honor of the securing of our alliance, you'll destroy the compromising evidence you have on me?"

Cibulkin smiled.

"Unfortunately, at this time we can't go that far. The materials are our primary insurance, and you're too influential of an individual — we can't act so carefree. Ah, yes. There are always side effects to rituals you've done, but I don't have the right to divulge information while we're still not allies yet."

"I need to think," said Temnikov thoughtfully, then asked after a short pause: "Tell me, what's the name of your organization?"

Chapter 16

I ALMOST INAUDIBLY HUMMED the tune of a song that had been popular once, watching the passersby drift past the window, now and then giving way to views of small villages.

"What're you so lost in thought for?" Godimir, who was sitting next to me, poked me in the ribs. "You haven't said anything at all the whole trip. It's not like you. Did something happen, maybe?"

Hmm. I agreed with him, but only partially. Truly, for most of this bus ride I'd just been sitting in silence, but saying it wasn't like me — nonsense. In our little friend group, I'd always been the least talkative one.

"Everything's fine," I admitted, turning to the somewhat sleepy Godimir. "I'm just in the kind of mood where I don't feel like doing anything."

"What, were you up half the night?" he asked

in a suspicious whisper, and added even more quietly, "Me too."

Now his extended silence made sense, I thought. Chuckling, I said:

"No, actually, I slept, and very well. It's just that while we've been on the road, I started thinking about how I've spent a pretty long time working for good results in this tournament. Constantly perfecting myself and striving forward, overcoming a lot, motivating myself not to stop and to move forward. And today, in the home stretch, I thought to myself: did I really do all this so I could win? Did I really push myself that hard? Not let myself be idle? Could I maybe have done it differently? I started feeling some kind of apathy and having thoughts I don't understand. Imagine, I even thought to myself, did I really have to go so hard for some school tournament? For an ordinary! School! Tournament! Maybe it doesn't mean squat? I mean, you get it."

Godimir looked at me in surprise, and after a bit he gave me a crafty smile.

"Well, if you have this apathy and none of this means squat to you, then my chances of winning are growing fast. I don't know about you, but I'm going to this tournament to win!"

"Go on then, Mr. Winner," I chuckled, turning back to the landscape outside the window. "Let's see how you do this year."

The team of warriors and mages from our school branch were riding to the tournament together on an ultra-modern bus. It had awesome, soft armchairs with recliners, small personal air conditioning units that let you choose the operating mode and the temperature, a comfortable bathroom in the back of the coach, and other blessings of the civilized world. In my world, more often than not, it was star athletes or whatever and really rich tourists who took these kinds of buses. Here it was children, albeit of noble origin.

Mr. Viktorov and his assistants, an experienced elderly healer and two gray-haired members of Morshansk's Mage League, were here along with the tournament participants.

Ahead of and behind us were two escort off-roaders with heavy weaponry on their roofs and mid-ranked warriors inside. To an outsider it might seem like these precautions were excessive, but if you remembered the demons that went for outings in human territory now and then, then it became clear that this security wasn't unnecessary at all. Even with Mr. Viktorov and two mages who clearly weren't weaklings on the bus, it was better to play it safe and entrust the lives of children to the professionals.

For that matter — no use denying it — the Ogneyers, the Temnikovs, and the Morozvs always had plenty of ill-wishers, so it was no good giving their enemies even the slightest advantage.

Exactly for those reasons, Ogneyer and Temnikov warriors were guarding the bus. It was possible that members of other noble houses wanted to object to the commandant, but they'd decided not to draw unnecessary attention to themselves and were driving behind us at a short distance from our party.

I was unspeakably glad about that, because I'd managed to investigate and learn that not all members of noble families were allowed to use one weapon or another within the city limits.

The city of Gomel greeted us with fog. Cold fog that instantly sucked the warmth out of people's bodies. I got that from the other kids' frowning faces, as well as their obvious desire to get inside the nearest building as quickly as possible. For me personally, the weather was perfectly lovely — probably because the cold had been causing me fewer inconveniences lately. And now even when it was fifteen degrees out, I felt fully comfortable in my ordinary school uniform. Evidently, my magic practice was manifesting itself, particularly in its inherited aspect. It was no accident that I could already create icicles about a foot and a half long pretty easily.

Once we'd unloaded our things from the bus, we moved in an organized fashion in the direction of a multi-story building with an evocative name: the Imperial Jasmine.

Walking past the doors as they parted to the sides, we found ourselves in a gleaming white hall of a positively imposing size.

The high ceiling was held up by a couple of beautiful Greek-style columns. To the right and left of us were waiting areas with comfortable sofas and armchairs, as well as small cozy establish-ments seeing to the gastronomic needs of the visitors.

About twenty yards in front of us we could see a wide registration counter for guests, or a reception desk.

"Right before our eyes, dear viewers, yet another team of young tournament participants has arrived at the Imperial Jasmine Hotel in Gomel. Who knows? Maybe the future champion is among them," said a young, pretty reporter girl in a stiff pantsuit, winking at the camera. "I'm sure you're all just as curious as I am to find out."

"That's Vera Poliakova! The host of the show *In Tune!*" whispered one of our mages, inconspicuously sprucing herself up. "And the camera's on us right now! Cool! Wheee!"

The girls immediately put on modest smiles and started looking around shyly. The boys, on the other hand, lazily glanced at the people around them with serious faces.

Children, I thought with a smile, looking around at the other kids. Looking at the camera, I winked, not expecting it myself. Although, if I'd been on the news in my world at their psychological age, I'd probably be on cloud nine!

"Listen up!" said Mr. Viktorov, getting everyone's attention and blocking the camera's view of us with his broad torso. "The warrior team is coming with me now. We're going to settle into our rooms. I'll tell you your room number assignments, give you your key cards, and do a brief orientation for you. The mages are going to follow Master Porkin." He gestured to the mage standing just to the side of him, who was lost in the background next to the huge warrior. "He's also up to speed on where you're going and will explain everything to you. This is where we split up. We'll meet up right before the start of the tournament."

Our team's rooms were on the fourth floor. There was an incredibly beautiful view out the window — a huge, very old park with giant trees.

Once everyone had figured out how to use the key cards, we left our things in our rooms and gathered in Mr. Viktorov's room to continue the orientation.

"Listen up, kids," he said, looking around at all of us with a resolute gaze. "The time we had to prepare for this tournament has passed. We've arrived at the Imperial Jasmine Hotel, we've registered, we've gotten settled in our rooms, and that means there's no turning back now. The mission of defending the honor and dignity of the Morshansk branch of the Imperial Academy lies on your shoulders."

When he'd finished saying that, he looked around at us again as if waiting for objections, and hearing none, he continued with satisfaction.

"The tournament will take place not far from here. Next to the hotel is a fairly impressive building that we walked past — you even paid some attention to it."

"That's the Gomel Arena," Godimir explained quietly.

"Exactly right," Mr. Viktorov confirmed. "The tournament opens this evening — the official ceremony starts at nine o'clock. We have to be there much earlier."

"And what will we do with all that time?" someone asked. "I mean, before the tournament starts."

"Until then, we're going to have a little something to eat, and then we'll at least try to get some sleep."

"And why is the start of the tournament scheduled so late?" one of the boys asked, puzzled. "What, are we going to fight all night?"

"No." Mr. Viktorov shook his head. "Only the official tournament opening and the first round of fights are slated for today. I don't think any of you will do more than one fight."

Thank the Savior, I thought with relief.

I wasn't at all overjoyed at the prospect of fighting all night. We needed to rest at night. And then what was one to do with the whole day? Strange business. Why start the opening ceremony at such a late hour? Wouldn't it be simpler to start the tournament in the morning? Or would the fireworks not be visible? In general, I completely didn't understand the role of the regional event's organizers, who changed the fight rules every year with no rhyme or reason. Bureaucrats, what can you do!

"Do you already know how many contestants are booked for each age group?" it was Godimir's turn to ask, as the most experienced of us. "I'd like to know how many opponents I'll have to fight."

"I don't have that information yet. If you remember, last year we only learned that after all the teams got to the Jasmine. So after the rest of them register, we'll know everything."

Hmm. Too bad. I wished I already knew how many fights I had in store.

The idea that I could lose one of the fights and get eliminated from the tournament didn't even occur to me. I was fully confident in my strength.

"Any other questions?" asked Mr. Viktorov after a bit. He got pensive shrugs in response. "Then get yourselves in order, and we'll head to the hotel restaurant. The quicker we get going, the sooner we can go nap. I hope the hungry crowd of contestants haven't all been so bold, and there'll be at least a few open tables left for us."

The restaurant occupied the top two floors of the Jasmine, so after taking the elevator up, we got there pretty quickly.

Looking around, Mr. Viktorov confidently led us after him, and before long we'd taken one of the open tables by the bay window, which opened up to a beautiful view of the city.

"Surprising that we found an open table by the window, it's usually crowded here," said Mr. Viktorov, looking around with satisfaction. "Not that I'm any fanatic about places like this, but the view here is nice."

"Good afternoon, my name is Olga. Would you like menus?" said a lovely waitress, walking up to us with several leather folders in her hands.

"No, thank you," said Mr. Viktorov. Without a glance at our indignant faces, he ordered efficiently. "Don't look at me like that," he said sternly. "I know you all. If I give you the chance, you'll eat all kinds of junk, and that's dangerous when you have upcoming fights, you know."

After a while, a tall sturdy man around fifty years old came up to our table and said with a crooked smile:

"Why, hello, Leonid. Are your fighters ready to lose to my kiddos?"

"Hello to you too, Simon," said Mr. Viktorov sullenly, getting up and shaking the man's hand. I sensed the tension growing quickly between the two of them. "The fights will settle everything."

"Is that so?" Simon feigned surprise, then added with a smirk, "The fights will settle everything, huh? Don't think you're being too hasty in saying that? Gotten humbler, have you? Maybe you think the commandant's son has grown so much in his skills that you can talk like that? Or have you found yourself a new protégé? Judging by what I've seen, the boy really is something, but will that be enough when he's fighting my students?"

"I'd ask you not to discuss me in my presence," said Godimir, frowning.

For my part, even though they were talking about me too, I didn't say anything. Yes, everyone knew who this unknown trainer had in mind, although neither my name nor my title had been said aloud — everything was within the limits of decorum. He'd really called out Godimir, though. There was no other commandant's son on our team, after all.

Casting a condescending glance at Godimir, Simon didn't respond to him and turned to Mr. Viktorov.

"I agree. Let the fights put everything in its place. Know that I'll be watching your students' fights with interest."

He left without saying goodbye, and immediately after that the waitress we already knew returned, carrying a big tray filled with food in her hands.

"Your 'friend,'" said Godimir to Mr. Viktorov, "really doesn't watch his mouth. I didn't say anything to Father last time, but I won't stand for hearing something like that again."

"You're right," agreed Mr. Viktorov. "Good ol' Simon really overstepped. Last time I only asked you not to do that because his kids were stronger. If we'd gotten your father involved, the situation would've become extremely unsightly. Imagine if with the help of a high-ranking relative, we got revenge on a simple trainer whose student won in an honest match."

After pausing for a bit, Mr. Viktorov continued, looking at Godimir intently.

"I hope you remember that last year, you lost your last fight because of his provocation?"

Oh-ho! I was surprised. What details were coming to light! What was this about provocation?

"I remember." Godimir nodded, not lowering his eyes. "But that's not related at all to last year's situation. He'd better watch his tongue or it'll get cut short."

"Agreed. Don't make a mistake like that a second time," said Mr. Viktorov sternly. Looking around at all of us with a watchful stare, he continued, "That goes for all of you. Don't rise to provocation, keep your heads on straight at all times. Certain interested parties could find some ugly way of getting a strong contestant out of the way."

"Are you really serious?" I didn't believe it. "It's an ordinary tournament, albeit a significant one. Who's going to make a potential high-ranking enemy for no good reason?"

"Oh, anyone." Mr. Viktorov shrugged, digging into his chicken soup and acting as an example for the rest of us. "Bon appetit, by the way. Winning this tournament means respect, honor, and — most importantly — a lot of money, allotted from all kinds of funds. They go to both the trainer personally and the branch that cultivated the best students."

"Still, I can't believe that someone would stoop to such dirty tricks. Even from practical considerations. If you get caught up in something ugly, you'll never live down the shame for the rest of your life, and on the other side of it the people you offended could bring some serious charges against you. Attempted murder, for instance."

"You're right, Ivan," said Mr. Viktorov, finishing his soup and starting on a juicy cutlet. "But there are many, many black marks on the history of this tournament. So it's better to be on your guard, and as I said, no one should leave their rooms unless it's necessary. And if you have somewhere to go, under no circumstances should you go alone."

Is it just me or is he exaggerating? I thought, not distracted from my food.

After our light lunch, I quickly took a shower, set an alarm, and collapsed onto my bed.

Despite Mr. Viktorov's command to rest, try as I might, I couldn't sleep. Although there was nothing surprising about it. In the past week, I'd completely stopped training. Completely. As we'd agreed, I wasn't supposed to do anything in this time — that is, not do any physical or magical exercises.

I'd taken my break, hadn't done anything except study, and I'd very quickly stopped knowing what to do with myself. I wasn't used to letting myself relax and rest like that. Thankfully, I did have some things to do, and I occupied myself with analytical work and planning. For that time I'd lived like the most ordinary person who didn't have difficult trials, challenges, or deadly threats planned for his life.

At first it seemed to me that seven days wasn't much for a proper rest, that I'd need at least a month to fully recover. But after three days, I was already practically out of my mind from the lack of work. Turned out my energy had filled me up like a balloon and was trying to find a way out of its cramped physical casing. I had to get rid of some of the accumulated energy — that was exactly why I could move around normally and not just jump around at every step.

After lying around with nothing to do for a while, I decided to use my free time more rationally, and I took my laptop out of my bag and connected to the internet. After that, I started searching for information about programming companies in the capital.

At a first glance there were quite a few companies of that type, but with detailed analysis of their activity it became clear that each specific company occupied some particular segment of the digital market. For some reason it was believed here that only strict specialization could get you to a high level. Although, of course, there were also those who didn't agree with that point of view and pursued a few different routes from the start.

As I studied the materials on yet another hacker company, I heard the sound of my alarm, notifying me that my peaceful time to myself was over.

Setting my laptop aside with a sigh, I started to gather my things. I obviously hadn't wasted the time, since even though I hadn't found anyone yet who could take care of my brainchild, I'd narrowed my search field by a lot and understood where I needed to dig.

I barely had time to zip up my sports jacket before I heard a resolute knock on the door.

"So, you manage to get some sleep?" I asked Godimir, who was standing in the hallway.

"Of course!" he answered cheerfully. "What about you?"

"I didn't quite get there," I admitted, moving to

the side and letting him into the room.

"No." He shook his head. "That's not why I'm here. I came to summon you to Mr. Viktorov's room — he's already gathering everyone."

We didn't sit around in Mr. Viktorov's room for too long. The standard questions about how we felt, warnings, pep talk, and good-luck wishes. After that, we went down to the first-floor lobby, which had a ton of people in it.

"Let's head for the exit and not get lost," said Mr. Viktorov, moving forward like an icebreaker ship.

Outside, the crowd was even bigger. Huge crowds were confidently moving towards the Gomel Arena from all sides. Infiltrating the hurrying crowd, we went on ahead. We really didn't have far to walk, so we found ourselves in the oval-shaped stadium fairly quickly.

"I hope we won't have to stand in line with everyone else?" said one of the boys in dismay.

"No," Godimir hurried to cheer him up. "There's a separate entrance for tournament participants, arena employees, and media people. If it were any other way, some of the contestants would hardly have time to get to the opening ceremony on time."

We got past security efficiently, followed the volunteer assigned to us, and took our places in the first row of one of the sectors.

Glancing around, I noticed a lot of boys sitting in the first rows of the other sectors. They were separated from the spectators by five rows of seats and thick plexiglass a few yards tall.

"I thought they'd give us some kind of room," I said, surprised. "To warm up and get ourselves in order. We're not going to sit here in the stands like this the whole time, are we?"

"Don't worry about that," said Mr. Viktorov, brandishing some kind of key in his hand. "There's a small locker room just for our team, and as you can see, they already gave me the key."

"And how do we find it?" I asked.

"It's just behind our sector. Besides comfortable armchairs, it also has a few lockers, a shower with a bathroom, and a couple of TVs broadcasting what's happening in the ring. If you want to watch the fights, you can go there. These places are reserved for us, and no one can take them."

"Then maybe it's better if we go to the locker room?" someone suggested. "The stands are just starting to fill up, and there are still forty minutes until the tournament starts. Let's go sit there in peace and come back later."

"That's exactly it — it starts in forty minutes," said Mr. Viktorov, looking at his watch. "So soon there will be whole crowds of people coming to the arena. I don't think there's anything for you to do there for now. But after the first matches start, you can do as you please."

"By the way, where are our mages?" Godimir asked. "Are they planning to root for us or what? Last year we all sat together."

"They should've been here by now," said Mr. Viktorov, looking around. "I did tell Porkin it was better to leave earlier. He probably didn't listen to me and is panicking now."

As Mr. Viktorov had said, the arena soon filled with people, and a little bit later our mage comrades finally approached. They showed up right before the start of the ceremony, a little irritated and staring at their supervisor with clear hostility.

"What a zoo!" said Mr. Porkin indignantly. "We barely shoved our way through! So many people! So many people! And everyone's running here and there in chaos, like they don't know where to go! There aren't enough volunteers for everyone! We had to get our bearings on our own!"

"I told you, you should've come with us," chuckled Mr. Viktorov, and added quietly, "C'mon, be smarter next time."

"We told him it would be better to leave earlier too..." I heard one girl explain something to Godimir, but she was interrupted by the loud voice of the ref standing in one of the rings.

"Good evening, dear friends! I'm happy to welcome you..."

There it goes, I thought as the crowd roared enthusiastically.

"Come down and walk behind me, like we talked about," said Mr. Viktorov, pointing to some unremarkable gates in the barrier, and went on first towards it.

Lining up in single file behind him, we did a lap of honor, slowly walking around the stadium along a wide footpath with the other branches' teams.

Meanwhile, our talkative ref — with a tablet in his hand — listed the branches' teams, named the trainers and their ranks, and didn't even forget about the students themselves. Headshots of us appeared on eight huge screens suspended high above the roof of the arena.

Judging by the applause that some of the students got, I realized that some of them were already pretty well known and loved by the public. To my surprise, I also got a portion of the advance standing ovation — I could practically feel the streams of curiosity rushing towards me from all sides.

Unsurprising. I was doing this tournament for the first time, and I was the dark horse who'd become known throughout the whole empire because of one ill-fated video. So a lot of the people here were dying to know what I'd make of myself in reality.

After we returned to our places, everything started to turn around pretty fast. Brackets with the first participants started to appear on the big screens. Their ranks, last names, and branches were listed.

Within a few seconds, right after the first pair of fighters, the second and the third began to appear.

"Godimir, you're up in the fifth round in ring one," said Mr. Viktorov, narrowing his eyes. "So prepare yourself — you're going up there in about ten minutes."

"And what should the rest of us do?" I asked

just in case. "How will we know when we should come out? Like, after ten fights or five? What if you leave?"

"Easy as anything," said Mr. Viktorov. "Look at the scoreboard and look for your last name. As soon as you see it, you'll know it's your turn soon. It's acceptable to approach the ring two fights before your own, so if I'm not there, try not to lag behind. Get out there and win."

Despite knowing my own strength, especially compared to these ordinary boys, I still felt a little tense. The other kids from our branch were quiet, too. They were also nervous.

Right, they weren't used to fighting in front of a crowd of fifteen thousand people, I thought as I watched the first fight already ending in one of the rings and another immediately starting in the other. Ah, so the fights in each ring didn't happen all at once, but in a lineup, so to speak, so that the announcers could commentate on what was happening without talking over each other. Plus, if needed, the arena could be cleaned up quickly while a fight was going in the other ring if one got covered in blood.

Godimir waved to us and said: "Well, the Savior be with you!" And then, with a confident stride, he headed to his ring.

His opponent was a lanky redheaded boy who held out against him for about two minutes.

"Weakling." Mr. Viktorov commented on Godimir's opponent's preparation and clucked his tongue.

"Do you know yet how many contestants are booked for our age group?" I asked, watching as Godimir left the ring in content.

"In yours, one hundred and twenty-six. For the high schoolers, ninety-four," said Mr. Viktorov, looking at something on his phone. "Are you ready to fight or what?"

"Of course! I'm always ready! Why? Am I already up soon?" I asked, looking at the screen of his phone as he turned it to me.

"After a couple of fights, you're going to ring two," said Mr. Viktorov. "The info will show up on the scoreboard soon."

"Got it," I said, then started to reflect.

So. If I took into account that there were all of two hundred and twenty contestants at regionals — that was the sum of the contestants from the two age groups — and also added in that each contestant was supposed to do at least one fight today, it followed that today there would be one hundred and ten fights. Say we added my knowledge of the average length of a fight to that statistic — two or three minutes. More or less. Conclusion: this event would last about five hours.

"Ivan, you're on deck," called Godimir, who'd already returned to the stands and was watching the scoreboard.

Nodding gratefully, I headed to ring two, continuing to reflect.

Sitting here for five hours — that sure was a lot. The organizers probably had a few short breaks planned. It wasn't an accident that the whole stadium was covered in different shops — I remembered the delicious-smelling hotdog I'd promised to get for myself right after my first fight. That meant the event would drag on, though. No, something was wrong with these organizers!

"Try not to end the fight on the first blow," Mr. Viktorov requested, walking up to me. "I want your somewhat higher level to be a secret, so don't be in any hurry to study all your opponent's weaknesses and strengths, and then attack."

"All right." I nodded, climbing into the ring.

My opponent was clearly sure of himself. This tall, light-haired boy was clenching his fists in a warlike stance, narrowing his eyes mockingly, and trying to throw me off balance.

To my disappointment, he showed no signs of whether the germ of spiritual energy control and all that could be found in him.

The fight was uninteresting, so when I got sick of dodging his slow attacks, I went on the counter-attack and K.O.'d him.

"The win goes to Ivan Morozov! Soldier-rank! From the city of Morshansk!" said the ref, declaring my victory.

"I don't know about you," I said to Godimir after he congratulated me, "but I feel like having a huge hotdog. You with me?"

"Of course. I'm already feeling shot too," he replied contentedly. Heading after me, he added, "Good thing Mr. Viktorov isn't here, or he would've ordered us not to go anywhere without him."

"Agreed." I nodded. "I just don't understand —

what could pose a threat to us? There's security at every square foot."

"Nothing's a threat," Godimir brushed me off, rubbing his hands gleefully. "C'mon, faster!"

Chapter 17

DESPITE MR. VIKTOROV'S FEARS, our trip to get food went smoothly. No one came at us, tried to stop us, or bothered us with stupid questions. Really, we just approached the nearest concession stand, waited in a short line, and placed our order.

After we returned to the stands, Mr. Viktorov's condemning eyes bored into us and he shook his head, but he didn't say anything.

It wasn't hard to understand him — we'd just gone off somewhere without permission, and we'd bought unhealthy food too, which he didn't approve of, as he hadn't neglected to demonstrate at lunch.

He had to understand that kids who'd finished eating at lunchtime would most likely already be hungry by dinnertime. The three high schoolers from our team had a good reason to be staring at us like they were! There was obvious hunger in their eyes! Was Mr. Viktorov one of those people who thought that deprivation made fighters angrier, and having enough made them weak?

Not caring that everyone around me was staring, I tucked into my delicious-smelling bun and smoked sausage with pleasure and squinted contentedly.

Just what I needed! With just a little more mustard, it would've been magnificent, I thought. I started studying the updates to the scoreboard with optimism.

"Anything interesting happen while were gone?" I heard Godimir ask one of the mage contestants from our branch.

The mages, unlike our warrior teammates, were more restrained and weren't throwing hungry glances at our hot dogs, which clearly said a lot about their evening trip to the Jasmine's restaurant.

"I mean, it's the warrior tournament. No one shows off anything special other than speed," one bored boy brushed him off, and added after a short pause, "Although, no, there was one funny thing. A few minutes ago, one of the contestants sent another one flying way out of bounds literally a few seconds after the fight started. And he had to do a simple kick to do it."

"Whoa! One single kick? And his opponent didn't even have time to do anything?" I joined the conversation and turned to Mr. Viktorov curiously. "That's not one of that Simon guy's students who can use spiritual energy like that, is it?"

"That's the one." Mr. Viktorov nodded and added with a frown, "You didn't have to go any-where, especially not to get food like that. You would all have seen it with your own eyes — that guy is from the younger age group, by the way."

"Well, what are you gonna do about it now?" I shrugged. "We missed it. We wanted to eat, and we would've had to sit here for a few more hours hun-gry. Come on! Do you think we need to be afraid of him? Could he pose a threat to me?"

"To you?" Mr. Viktorov looked at me askance and turned back to the fight in the ring. "To you, no, but to Godimir, certainly. Judging by what I saw, the kid is on good terms with his spiritual energy, so you understand the extent of the threat yourself. I can't say any more for now. You can't draw a lot of conclusions from one single blow. Alt-hough, if you remember what he demonstrated last year, I can add that he clearly has pretty good technique, and his speed is decent. Quite a dan-gerous fighter. The most important thing for us is that he was the one who got your friend eliminated from the tournament last year."

"What's his rank?" I asked, glancing at Godi-mir.

"First-level Soldier, almost as high as you," said Mr. Viktorov. "Although, to be fair, I'll note that you've earned a higher rank, of course. Per-haps after the tournament ends, you'll be awarded one. If you become the champion and feel like tak-ing some extra tests."

"Why not?" I shrugged. "It would be a really good test of my abilities and a nice bonus — otherwise, judging by the scoreboard, most of the contestants here are equal to me in strength. And that's clearly not true."

Mr. Viktorov hemmed in approval, but he didn't say anything in reply.

After watching the fights for about two hours, Godimir and I were planning to leave — after all, no one had cancelled tomorrow's duels and rest was truly necessary — but one of our guys was called up to the ring, and we decided to hold out a little longer.

"Dwarf Saws!" Mr. Viktorov cursed almost inaudibly. Looking at the scoreboard, I saw why. The ninth grader from our team had to fight one of Simon's students.

"Do you think Oleg will lose?" I turned to Mr. Viktorov, remembering my teammate's name.

"We'll see. It all depends on him and him alone," said Mr. Viktorov tensely. "But it's worth mentioning that he'll have to spar with one of the prize-winners from last year's regionals."

"They have the same rank." I reviewed the information on the scoreboard and frowned with dissatisfaction.

Really, what was with all this? There were Soldiers everywhere — you couldn't swing your arms without hitting one! Either first-level or second-level! I'd been told before that I was so strong and specially unique, that I was the only one who could use Shiki-Cho so actively at my age. Now it turned out the situation was radically to the contrary. Soldiers everywhere!

"Don't you know that no Soldier is alike?" Mr. Viktorov said in a lecturing tone. "You, for example, can use spiritual energy very well, and you have good control of the simplest techs. By those criteria, you could already be given the Militant rank, and fully deservedly. However, by the rules of the League, Soldiers are required to take tests to get that rank. So, *de jure*, you're an ordinary Soldier, and the rest of the kids of that rank who are here may be much weaker than you, but they're also worthy of being called Soldiers. The main differences in strength between fighters start right after they receive the Militant rank."

"I understand," I said thoughtfully. "I've been stuck on Soldier for a long time, I need to move forward."

While Mr. Viktorov and I talked quietly, a few fights finished up, and the pair of warriors we cared about took the ring.

"The Savior be with you!" said one of my classmates quietly, and when the gong sounded, the contestants rushed at each other resolutely.

They exchanged blows quickly, they sized up each other's strengths and weaknesses, our guy hit his opponent with a Power Whirlwind that ran into a powerful Spirit Shield, and they were off to the races.

After a few minutes of fighting, I noticed that the fighters, who weren't reducing their speed at all, were getting a little tired. Both of them had a couple of bruises and scratches. It turned out they were equal in strength, so the fight dragged on for a while.

"Oleg is good," I noted, turning to Mr. Viktorov. "How is it that he wasn't in the tournament last year or the year before?"

"Because at those times, other kids were stronger," Mr. Viktorov replied. "Oleg started to grow in mastery not too long ago."

To our great disappointment, Simon's student won this fight regardless. He turned out to be hardier, cleverer, and more experienced than Oleg. His opponent wore him out, sped up abruptly, and finished the fight pretty quickly.

"Dwarf Saws!" Godimir couldn't contain himself. "Our first defeat! And we lost to a guy from Podlesk!"

"Simon spares special attention for his students who have no magical gift and no other options for becoming stronger," said Mr. Viktorov pensively. "Other trainers do that too, but several noble families training in the basics of spiritual energy are his direct responsibility. So his kids are a little stronger than many of the other tournament participants. When you have no alternative due to a lack of magical talent, after all, you have to hone what you can."

"I thought everyone did that." I looked at him in surprise. It's only logical, after all. If a young guy has no other options for becoming stronger, he takes the path of the warrior and will be more interested in it than kids with magical capabilities."

"You think that way, but a lot of nobles prefer not to waste their time flailing their arms and legs, and instead to be useful to their families in some other way — in business, for instance," replied Mr. Viktorov, chuckling. "And, I admit, many parents support such aspirations from their young ones."

I wondered why there was such prejudice against warriors. It really was a good chance to become stronger. After all, using myself as an example, I'd proven that a mid-rank warrior could beat a mid-rank mage.

"Let's hope that guy makes it to the finals," said Godimir pensively, sitting down next to us. "Oleg just barely didn't have enough to win, and I think his outlook will be good for the finals."

"And what then?" I furrowed my brows, trying to understand what Godimir was getting at. "What will happen if one of the Podlesk guys makes it to the finals?"

"Then he and the second finalist's opponent will fight for third place," he replied.

"Ohhhh! I get it!" I nodded, remembering that I'd encountered similar rules on Earth, when I'd watched fights in the Olympics or something.

They also had two third places.

Meeting up with a downcast, trudging Oleg, we gave him friendly praise for a good fight and tried to cheer him up a little. After that, Mr. Viktorov put in a word.

"Your opponent was quite strong. Last year he even made it to finals, and I don't think that this year will be any different. So don't lose your spirit. We have to hope that you'll fight in the ring again in this tournament."

After that, Mr. Viktorov had pity on us and sent us off to get some rest. True, it was just the three of us. The other two were left to wait for their turn.

* * *

After sleeping for about nine hours, I got myself in order quickly (since I was already a little late) and went out into the hallway where the other boys from our team were gathered.

"What's up, Ivan? Ready to hand everyone their lunch?" I heard Godimir's cheerful voice.

"Good morning!" I greeted everyone, yawning. "I'm ready, but why are you so cheerful and jolly? You sleep well or what?"

"It's not that," said Godimir, and continued with self-satisfaction, "It's just that it turns out I was the star last night. I was even on TV, unlike some others."

"Ah, and my mistake has now become clear! It's not about sleep, but the lack thereof. Turns out you didn't sleep the whole night — you watched all the news and searched for yourself," I teased him. "It would've been better to rest — today is a really high-stakes day. By the way, how did it go for the rest of you? Did you all win?"

"Everyone but me," said a gloomy Oleg — as it turned out, the only one from our team who'd lost his fight last night. "I hope you don't get put with someone from Podlesk in your first couple fights. If that does happen, though, then smear him all over the ring."

"Don't worry." Godimir clapped him on the shoulder. "You heard Mr. Viktorov yourself. Your opponent last night was really strong. He'll most likely make it to finals. That's when you'll have a chance to fight for third place, and maybe at the capital you'll get your revenge on him. You were almost equal in strength, after all — you just got unlucky."

"You're right." Oleg nodded seriously. "I need to get a hold of myself and not break down, or else I won't be ready for a potential fight at nationals."

"Good morning." We heard Mr. Viktorov's cheerful voice. "Well, kiddos? You been waiting long? Ready to go to breakfast?"

"Yes!" we all exclaimed merrily, and we headed to the restaurant together.

Taking one of the open tables — true, it wasn't by the window this time — we placed our order and got to discussing last night's rounds.

"What are they going to do with our age group?" After a few minutes, I decided to do my bit in the conversation. "I mean that last night our age group had a hundred twenty-six contestants, but today there are sixty-three left. That number kinda isn't divisible by two. What'll happen to the extra guy?"

"The organizers don't have any issues with that. The system was worked out a long time ago," said Mr. Viktorov. "I explained to you yesterday that there's a special computer program that pairs contestants randomly for matches and does that only for the next five duels. It chooses a sixth pair after the end of the next fight. And it works out that none of the contestants can say for certain when they'll be called to the ring and who'll be their opponent. That creates intrigue that keeps both this show's contestants and audience in suspense. The same thing goes for the last contestant in the round, too. No one knows who that's going to be until almost the very end of the event. True, there is one nuance. Then that contestant is required to fight in the first match of the next round."

"Yeah," said one of the high schoolers. "After round two, there will be thirty-one of the sixty-two contestants left, and that lucky kid will get added back in. That way there are thirty-two contestants left. After round three there will be sixteen left, then eight, and then begin the semifinals."

"I have no more questions," I replied, returning to my food.

As we left the building, we almost crashed into Simon and his students, who were purposefully walking in our direction, though there was plenty of room to avoid each other.

"Could that be our biggest rivals walking by?" Simon called to Mr. Viktorov. "Your boy wasn't too upset last night because of the defeat, was he?"

"Not particularly," I replied, walking past. "We're waiting for your guy to get into the finals, so our guy can take third place at regionals and get a chance for revenge at the capital. So good luck, Morshansk is counting on you."

"Bon appetit!" chuckled Mr. Viktorov, and our team hurried to the elevator without waiting for a response.

For me personally, round two of the fights was more interesting. If only because I didn't know until almost the very end whom I'd be fighting. Or would I be fighting at all? Could I be that lucky sixty-third kid? Incidentally, the situation wasn't making me nervous, since I was confident in my strength.

As it turned out, it did not fall to me to become the lucky guy who'd be moving on without exerting himself.

Hey! The second-to-last fight! But there hadn't been a half-bad chance! I looked at the screen and started thinking. Although, on the other hand, almost two hours of waiting were finally over.

The lucky kid getting moved to the next round turned out to be a boy we didn't know, who was congratulated on all sides and was clearly very surprised by what was happening.

Good, at least it wasn't a fighter from Podlesk's team. Better for them to do some sparring and use up their energy. That way it would be easier for Godimir, I thought, taking my place in the ring and preparing to fight.

Unfortunately, my second opponent turned out to be so weak that I didn't even understand how he'd won his last fight.

We sparred for a little bit on pure physical

strength, and I finished the fight off pretty quickly.

This guy was so weak! He hadn't even been using spiritual energy. Were all the fighters in our age group really like this? Dwarf Saws' sakes, in that case this would be my first and last tournament! What point was there in proving anything to anyone here? All I had left was to hope that Simon's provocation wasn't empty bragging, and his students really could do something. There were only two of them in the younger age group, of course, but I should meet up with at least one of them sooner or later!

After a short break, which we spent in the private locker room set aside for us by the tournament organizers, the time for round three approached. In round three, to my delight, I was finally paired with a student from Podlesk.

He turned out to be a sixth grader; he was a completely ordinary kid with nothing noteworthy about him.

Godimir warned me that he was the one who'd eliminated him from last year's imperial tournament, and that even then he'd had good control of the standard techs.

After a fleeting search for information about his family on the Internet, I discovered that this guy was from a family of weak mages that actively practiced spiritual energy. Their talent with magic was pretty modest, so for a few decades now they'd been adapting and trying to use spiritual energy.

If that was how things were, then I'd found a strong opponent. I figured he'd done no less training than I had in my day, and that meant I wouldn't be disappointed by his abilities.

After the gong announcing the start of the fight, the boy rushed towards me strenuously and dove down at the last second, trying to kick me with some kind of strange sliding tackle.

A jump and a Spirit Shield under my feet allowed me to escape a disgraceful fall, as well as a powerful Battering Ram sent up at me from below. That strike, in theory, was supposed to throw me out of bounds. If I hadn't fought Militants in my time, I would have been ignominiously tossed out of the ring in the first few seconds of sparring. Interesting move.

Not losing his nerve at my reaction, the boy leaped closer to me, trying to take advantage of the fact that I had no support under my feet and was still hovering midair, and attacked. Reflexively taking a Spirit-Step, I got out from under his blows, appeared behind him, and went on the counterattack.

The element of surprise played its part — he took a few painful blows and found himself on the ground, frantically defending himself.

I should have finished him off, of course, but I'd deliberately slowed down, showing that using Spirit-Steps was still difficult for me. I hoped the contestants at nationals would make a note of that for themselves.

The boy, taking advantage of my brief disorientation, managed to get out from under attack.

After fighting for a bit longer, I assessed his

high level, then beat him back with a couple of Power Whirlwinds and — closing the distance — K.O.'d him.

"Morozov wins!" I heard the ref's celebratory voice. "From the Morshansk branch of the Imperial Academy!"

"Great job, Ivan," said Mr. Viktorov in a pleased tone, watching as Simon fussed over his defeated student. "You've made this old man happy. You've won a spot as one of the contenders for the medal. Although I didn't doubt you, of course."

I shrugged and nodded in response to his praise. There hadn't been anything complicated about that fight. If, of course, you didn't count how badly that boy had gotten me at the beginning. It was immediately obvious that he'd been training seriously since he was a child, unlike most of the nobles here. Too bad that I'd shown everyone I could do Spirit-Steps, but my reflexes had worked by themselves.

All right. That wasn't important. The main thing was that I'd won, and that meant everything was going according to my carefully devised plan, I thought. Picking up my phone, I started having a look at where I stood.

After round three, there were only thirty-two of us — the fighters from the younger age group — left. Thank the Savior that Godimir had won his fight, just like me. But we hadn't managed to get through without losses — another one of the high schoolers had been eliminated.

There were only three of us left.

"Hey, Ivan," Godimir called to me quietly during the break, his eyes burning with excitement. "I was just talking with a couple of the guys here — it turns out that they bet money on you winning the last couple of fights. Right before this round, I decided to see how it works too, and I earned about eighty thalers! Can you imagine?"

"Congratulations!" I said to him with a slight smile, seeing how happy he was with the first money he'd worked for.

Yes, of course it was an incredibly easy and risky way of making money, and without the money his father had given him, he wouldn't have gotten anything. Or rather, the sum he'd won would've been significantly lower, but still. His first money was his first money.

"That's what I approached you about... maybe you want to bet something on yourself?" he asked, and added in a whisper: "You can bet on yourself, as I learned."

"And which bookie are you working with?" I decided to ask. "Which betting company, I mean."

"Marathon, of course," coughed Godimir. "They're actually the only proper bookies who pay out incredibly big wins! Even the Imperial Revenue Service supports them! So I think you should do it! But it's best not to associate yourself with the others — they're just small fries. Some of them keep your payments, some of them have other kinds of problems. They only give you back your money in installments, for instance. And all their installments are less than fifty thousand thalers. They break it up, you see. They can't give you back everything you've won right away."

"What, do you intend to win more than fifty thousand thalers?" I was astonished.

"I don't know yet." Godimir shook his head pensively. "I wasn't really planning to, of course, but you know, if fortune herself falls into your lap, why not go for it? I'm going to bet on you and me winning. We'll see what comes of it."

Alerting Godimir that I was about to tell him a certain secret, I took my phone out of my pocket and showed him my unlocked screen.

"So you've been hanging out on here too?" exclaimed Godimir in a whisper, seeing the Marathon logo. "And? How much did you win? Spit it out! How did you get to this point without telling me anything?"

"I'm hoping to find out how much I earned after the tournament ends. I had time to place my bets right on the first day of the tournament, when we were sitting in the stands. Old man Taras put me up to it. You know he's an Avtiukian, right? They're clever people, always very tuned in to this sort of thing, they never miss their chance... he said to me that he believed in my victory and would bet an impressive sum on it. I decided there were worse ideas and did the same thing. I didn't tell you because it was a secret, but after the end of the tournament I would have shared the joy with you. And the total from my bets is high, so I didn't want to jinx it."

"And how much is it?" asked Godimir curiously. "Three thousand?"

"Fifty thousand," I replied simply.

"*How* much?" cried Godimir, unable to contain himself. Already quieter, he added: "Where did you get money like that?"

"Well," I said, shrugging philosophically, "I had some of it in my own account, since Father doesn't forget to send small amounts for my expenses. Some of it Theophane and I earned on our trips to the Wasteland. After I legally became a Morozov, that money was transferred to my main account, so I made up my mind. If I was confident in my own strength and knew that there was no one stronger than me here, then why not hit the jackpot? Besides, I'll need that money soon for a certain large-scale operation."

"But why did you say that you'll know the total you've won after the tournament ends?" asked Godimir, frowning. "You bet on yourself winning in the younger age group? There are a whole lot of contestants in it! The coefficient must be around five! You could win about two hundred fifty thousand thalers just like that!"

"The coefficient was about six and a half," I remembered. "But I plan to win a lot more than that. I placed an 'express' bet."

Getting a confused stare from my young neophyte, I explained.

"An 'express' bet is a combined bet on two or more events, where losing either one means you lose the whole of everything you bet, but winning promises you a lot more money. The betting coefficients go up and down, after all. The risk is much higher than with single bets, of course, but the winnings are bigger."

"And what did you bet on?"

"That I'd win all my fights absolutely. And, accordingly, that I'd get first place at regionals and nationals. If I'm not mistaken, that's more than ten bets."

Godimir gave me an incredibly surprised stare, then asked:

"Do you understand how much money that is?"

"Of course I understand." I smirked. "So, no hard feelings, I bet it exclusively on myself."

"Yeah, I understand." Godimir nodded. "It's just that you're going to have so much money! Father sets aside four hundred for me every month, and I never know what to do with it. What are you going to do with yours? Why do you need so much money? Because you're not taking a risk like this just for kicks, right? What if you run into someone stronger than you at the capital?"

Hmm. He'd probably get less from those individual bets than me, I noticed, and I said:

"You're right. It's truly a great risk, since I bet almost everything I have on 'express.' But one way or another, I already have to think about the welfare of the Morozov bloodline. I understand that after some time, Father will stop openly supporting me, and I'll have to survive on my own. So, you know, I'm trying to turn that around somehow. Besides, I already found myself one interesting little project, and I'll need a lot of funds to launch it."

"And what project is that?" Godimir immediately perked up his ears.

"I'll tell you later," I answered him. "Besides, I absolutely have to talk to your father about it. So, believe me, I'll definitely make sure you're in the loop."

"What are you two being all hush-hush about?" said Mr. Viktorov, walking up to us. "Discussing tactics for your upcoming duels, I hope? Because it's time to think about that. There are only sixteen contestants left in your group. The winners of the next round will be fighting for spots in the quarterfinals!"

"We're ready," I said to him. "Godimir was just upping my motivation and reminding me that today I have to fight for victory with all my strength."

"Yeah," Godimir immediately corroborated my words. "It's good that you're here. I just wanted to ask — how are the fourth and fifth rounds going to work between the groups? The number of contestants is getting smaller and smaller each time, after all, and so are the number of fights and the time for breaks accordingly. So are we going to have at least some kind of break between fights? Am I right? They can't just throw us into the ring before we're ready, right? It's just so irrational."

"Don't worry, they'll let you rest. Everything will be like it was last year," Mr. Viktorov reassured Godimir. "After round four of the warrior tournament, the mage tournament matches start.

So you'll have more than enough time to rest."

"That makes me happy," said Godimir. Just then we heard the signal that meant the next round was starting soon. "See, last year the tournaments came one after another, and there was at least a little bit of time to rest. This time the organizers clearly weren't in any hurry to start the mages' fights, so I started to worry."

Round four turned out to be wholly successful for our team, because we all won our fights. The guy from Podlesk who'd beaten Oleg also made it to the next round.

"We're doing well," said Godimir, collapsing next to me. "I hope Simon's student gets it from you, or else he's really just too strong. I wouldn't want to get eliminated from the tournament so close to a prize-winning place."

I nodded in agreement.

I didn't want that either. The contestants who won the next round were definitely going to nationals.

The first matches of the mage tournament, quite honestly, disappointed me. It was all because only a minority of the kids here were capable of anything worthwhile. The rest showed average performance, weaker even than a certain Stanislav I then remembered. The leader of that old gang of silver-spoon kids that Theophane and I had saved in the Wasteland.

Yes, even that gold-covered show-off had turned out to be pretty strong in comparison to the kids fighting here, and even then I'd thought that he was weak, frankly...

All I saw were the simplest spells: weak little lightning bolts, flickering shields, air fists, and fireballs.

I'd been mentally prepared to see something like this at the intramural selection event. There, the understanding was that the best would be chosen from everyone who wanted to try. But here? At the imperial tournament regionals? Seemed to me that the fights should be more entertaining.

True, it was reassuring that many of the kids here most likely just didn't want to expose their true skill levels yet and weren't showing off their capabilities. On principle, just like I was doing.

There weren't many interesting fights — they only cropped up when two opponents roughly equal in strength met in the ring.

It was already near evening when the first round of the mage tournament ended. The time came for the warriors to continue fighting.

This time I was put with a pretty strong kid from Old Streets. His blows may have been weak to me, but his speed and his Spirit Shield tech turned out to be superbly well trained. He was incredibly good at defense and successfully dodged my attacks for several minutes. Of course, I could've finished the fight pretty quickly, but I liked fighting with him on physical strength alone. It allowed me to train up a little more and hide my strength at the same time. I didn't want to show all the aces up my sleeve to everyone around me...

"That was a good fight," I said to the boy when

he was brought back to his senses.

"Thanks," he muttered in irritation, and left the arena with his head down.

Godimir beat his opponent as usual, but this time it wasn't easy for him. A fairly impressive bruise that quickly turned blue confirmed this.

"How are you feeling?" I asked him. "Everything okay?"

"I'm fine," he said, sounding tired and unable to stop touching his face. "The potion is working great, my lips are already fully healed, the blood stopped coming out of my nose, that means the bruise will go away soon too."

"You barely won," I said unhappily. "Your opponent was pretty strong, of course, but why did you take so many hits?"

Godimir rubbed his face in pain again, shrugged discontentedly, and said, "It just kinda happened."

After waiting for everyone left in the lineup to finish their fights, overjoyed at our victories, we went to go sleep, since we were all finished for the day — the rest of it was the mages fighting again.

There were only eight fighters left in our age group. The strongest in the whole region. So this round, the fights were really difficult and entertaining. They were really hard for Godimir and our classmate. And while Godimir still won by some miracle, our other classmate lost to Simon's student just like Oleg had earlier.

"I'm both happy and sad about it," Oleg admitted. "On the one hand, I'm sad that one of our guys lost. But on the other hand, I'm happy that I still have a chance at third place."

The rounds of the mage and warrior tournaments came one after another, so after a few hours of chilling out, the semifinals lineup started.

Mine was the first fight. I proved my right to make it to the finals. Godimir wasn't so lucky — the guy from Podlesk beat him in the end.

After beating Godimir, the boy looked at me and drew his finger across his throat, promising me future defeat.

Judging by the explosive reactions of the audience and the press, they liked that. Strong emotions made a tournament livelier and more interesting, after all.

Oleg, by the way, did get his chance at going to the capital and pretty easily beat his former opponent — the second finalist in the older age group.

* * *

"Final round! In the right corner is Ivan Morozov! Morshansk branch of the Imperial Academy! In the left corner is Podlesk representative Marat Nozhev!"

The gong sounded, and my opponent — like his younger friend whom I'd fought earlier — darted into the fight.

He attacked quickly and aggressively, as if he was trying not to give me extra time to think and appraise the situation. Judging by what I'd seen during the tournament, all of Simon's students subscribed to this fighting philosophy. Force, speed, and pressure were the main peculiarities that distinguished them.

I figured if Theophane could see all this, he would've said a four-letter word. He would've punished the person who'd taught a warrior to waste energy so thoughtlessly. Since my mentor wasn't here, though, I decided to teach him that lesson myself.

As long as my speed was significantly higher, I could dodge all his attacks without breaking a sweat. Which brought him out of his mental equilibrium and clearly made him angry.

When he decided to calm down a little, I started retreating as if by accident and fell clumsily a few times, escaping his especially furious attacks. He caught his second wind. He started advancing even more resolutely, and with my legs tangled up I continued to dodge his attacks in my inconceivable manner.

I hadn't trained with old man Taras for nothing after all, I thought, and when my opponent had really let his guard down, I broke his Spirit Shield easily and sent him flying.

"Ladies and gentlemen!" the ref announced ceremoniously. "The winner in the younger age group at the Gomel regionals of the imperial warriors' tournament is Ivan Morozov! Morshansk branch of the Imperial Academy!"

Chapter 18

"GREAT JOB, CHAMPS!" We heard a familiar voice and turned around.

Our team, located in the foyer of yet another stylish hotel, was approached by a smiling Ilya Zateikin, one of my likely classmates for next school year.

"Hello, nationals contestants!" I replied, shaking his outstretched hand and quickly introducing our guys to the imperial prince's friend. He already knew Godimir, so they simply greeted each other.

"I heard someone got first place at his regional warriors' tournament?" said Zateikin to me, grinning, then added a bit more quietly: "But don't let it go to your head too much — the magical arts are valued above all else at nationals, even more so among the nobility."

What was this? Just a friendly note or a warning? Did he want to tell me something, but he couldn't do it directly? I thought about it, and I decided I'd consider it a warning and start to keep an eye on my surroundings more often. I'd play it safe.

"I'll take that into consideration." I nodded gratefully. "On that note, congratulations on fifth place in your magic tournament."

"Thanks," said Zateikin, narrowing his eyes and looking at his watch. "I need settle a couple of things now, so I'll be going, but I think we'll manage to cross paths again and chat in peace before the start of nationals."

I nodded in agreement.

Indeed, there were still a couple days before nationals. This time was necessary so that all the contestants had a chance to rest and fully recover.

That was how it should be — it was plenty of time to heal wounds with potions and fill up one's spiritual or magical energy. Besides, I myself would have time to do all my business at the capital.

In these free days before the next phase of the tournament started, I actually had very big plans. I'd even say grandiose plans.

I had, of course, communicated my planned absence to Mr. Viktorov well in advance. He clearly wasn't very pleased, but he couldn't do anything about it. Besides, our family had a house at the capital, where according to the tournament regulations I was allowed to stay at during free time. So I left the hotel with a clean conscience.

Mr. Viktorov could only ask me to be more careful, not to take risks, and be mindful of my safety.

"Nikolai, we'll have to go for a drive in half an hour, get the people ready," I said to the leader of the small personal guard appointed for me by George.

Nikolai, after asking a few clarifying questions, left the room.

No objections, no unsolicited advice, no demand for an order from someone older in the family. There was none of that nonsense.

Our little group had turned out with that kind of relationship, above all because I'd chosen the people in it myself. They were also the very same warriors who'd gone to the Wasteland with George and me.

These fighters were convinced of my strength from experience and understood that I had every right to give them any order and wait for its fulfillment. So they most likely weren't going to throw a wrench in my plans.

Although it was possible that another thing playing a not insignificant role in this surprising dynamic was the fact that I'd simply hit one of the guys who hadn't agreed to fulfill my order in time. And pretty hard. After that, I'd forbidden anyone to give him a recovery potion. Incidentally, the fact that he was a mage somehow hadn't helped him much.

Our car cruised confidently through the capital city, and in the meantime I once again studied information on my tablet about a small company that had caught my eye. To be precise, I'd paid attention to it only because its director unexpectedly turned out to be someone I kind of knew.

"Andrei Valerievich Byshkovetz. Twenty-four years old. Single. Currently serving in the Morshansk Special Ops Brigade," I read aloud again in a whisper, grinning.

The information on the site was clearly outdated. This young man had already finished his service in special ops last year, before my fantastical return to the house of Temnikov.

I remembered this guy real well. Calm, self-confident, purposeful. And what was valuable was that he'd made quick progress in the time between our fights. It seemed that at the end of his military service, Andrei had even gotten the rank of second-level Soldier...

No, but this was just lucky, I thought, rubbing my hands. The company was small, although it worked with a few serious clients. It clearly needed good investments to make such a great profit. I figured Andrei was no fool and would want to get the most out of this collaboration. He'd be interested in not only increasing his profits, but possibly getting himself some serious patrons that could be the Temnikov or Morozov family.

It was our chance acquaintance, I believed, that should serve as a good start to the development of my project. After all, if I showed up at a bigger and more specialized company where there were no higher-ups I knew, some of my ideas could go unfulfilled. Or I'd have to use more force to get the results I needed.

"Ivan, sir, we've arrived." I heard the driver's voice, and the car stopped.

"That jerk!" said Andrei quietly yet again, clenching his sturdy fists till it hurt and frantically trying to decide what he should do next.

This young man, who'd graduated with beautiful marks not long ago from one of the most prestigious universities in the Nosiriansky Empire, was now trying to understand how exactly he could take back control of his own creation.

It was all because even in his first year at the computer science department of his academy at the capital, Andrei had been thinking about creating his own small yet profitable business.

To Andrei, who'd been fascinated by programming from a young age, it hadn't been difficult to occupy himself with creating simple sites and doing marketing on the internet.

Of course, he was a young commoner who wasn't from a wealthy family and didn't have the money to open his own business; however, he had one good friend who'd wanted to earn some money. This friend was a philandering playboy with a certain amount of cash and a desire to invest it, and he was ready to offer as much help as he could in exchange for a certain share in the project.

Once their agreement had been made, things had taken off. After some time, the young owners had managed to organize a pretty successful developing IT company with their own four hands. This was not least because of Andrei's business partner — he knew how to find friends and advantageous contracts everywhere.

With a soaring heart, Andrei had handed over the marketing and management matters to his friend, while he himself concentrated on creating projects and training professional staff.

With each passing year, their humble business had grown and developed more and more, until Andrei finally finished his education at the university and received a summons to the military recruitment office at the capital.

His attempts to get out of serving in the armed forces had led to an unexpected consequence — he'd been sent to serve right on the border of the Gorbovich Wasteland! The biggest infernal territory in the Empire!

Pouring out sweat and blood in the training hall and in the Wasteland, Andrei had thoroughly cursed himself for trying to bribe the military commissar — a stern, one-legged colonel with an ugly scar across his whole face. Only after entering the armed forces had he understood the mistake he'd made.

I should have thought to bribe the special ops guy who was maimed in the Wasteland! he hemmed at himself yet again, and again thought of his business partner. Maybe he'd planned to have him sent so far away?

Yes, his business partner had turned out to be a hardened guy. Having somehow gotten out of military service while Andrei spilled blood on the battlefield, he'd managed to take over their whole company, gradually dismissing Andrei's employees and hiring his own protégés for their positions.

Andrei had known nothing about it. He'd had no time to look into the details of what was happening at the company, since he'd been required to concentrate on training and surviving. Money was also deposited in his account in good order. True, the transfers had stopped two months before he'd been transferred to the reserve.

That had been his first wake-up call, and shortly thereafter he hadn't had long to wait for the others. Andrei had received a letter from a judge saying that he was being removed from the position of director due to his failure to perform his official duties.

His business partner had refused to pick up the phone, and there had been no one left at the company who was loyal to him.

After receiving his documents for his transfer to the reserve, Andrei had headed straight to his office and seen that he was being legally forced to sell his share of the company.

If only he'd been able to participate in the company's work while he'd been in the army! Those scoundrels! He hated corrupt courts, thought Andrei angrily.

At some point his business partner had decided that he could handle leading the company himself just fine, and that also meant he alone could get all the profit...

Next to the business center where his office was, a very expensive off-road military vehicle abruptly came to a halt. It clearly belonged to one of the nobility, which brought Andrei back from his unpleasant thoughts.

As far as he knew, as a rule, it was members of noble families who got around in cars like that, if not always. The thing was, armed transport was forbidden in the capital city, and special permission was needed for a car like that to be within the city limits.

So it was probably a member of a prince or marquis's family, thought Andrei. But what could he have forgotten here?

Andrei's curiosity chased his unpleasant thoughts out of his head instantly, and he remembered a princely heir who used to get around in a car just like that — George Temnikov, before hitmen had blown up his car.

That young nobleman had cleaned out the first few circles of the Gorbovich Wasteland almost singlehandedly, demonstrating not only extraordinary magical talent and strength, but clearly proving the right of princely families to occupy a privileged place in the imperial hierarchy.

Even Andrei himself had had occasion several times to see a display of a hereditary mage's power, when the commander of his brigade — Colonel Gurinov — had sent out his security company.

A quick glance at the small coat of arms on the door of the car, and Andrei froze in astonishment.

It actually was the Temnikov family!

The back door of the car opened, and a little boy in an expensive suit with a tablet in his hands got out. Not tearing himself away from the screen, he said something offhandedly to his guard, walked up to the door with quick steps, and vanished into the building.

Ivan! Unable to believe his luck, Andrei leapt up from where he was sitting and — paying no attention to the security guy — rushed headlong after the boy, heading towards the entrance himself. It was him! That little boy who'd clobbered almost all Andrei's fellow soldiers and a few officers in the ring! It was the kid who'd later turned out to be Ivan Morozov himself! The heir to a princely bloodline who'd been thought dead for a while! Andrei knew him! True, it had been in passing, but they'd been in contact, and more than once. This was his chance — his only chance!

Abandoning his doubts, Andrei rushed even more confidently ahead, ran through the main doors into the hall, and saw that the elevator the boy was on had closed.

Dwarf Saws! Andrei cursed. Now he'd have to wait for the elevator to stop to find out which floor he needed to go to. Security wasn't dozing off either. They'd try to throw him out again.

"Mr. Byshkovetz," said a man with a security badge whom he knew well. "I must ask you to leave the premises of the business center."

Eighth floor, thought Andrei, not responding — just following the numbers on the elevator's display. This wasn't a dream, was it?

What he hadn't even dared to think possible before was happening. It seemed like his heart had stopped for a second, because Ivan was going up to his office!

Could it be true? A slim ray of hope began to appear.

"Leave the premises of the business center!" Andrei heard a menace-filled voice behind him.

"And why should I do that?" he said angrily, turning around. "I'm the owner of the company IT 2.0, which is located on the eighth floor. Why can't I be here?"

"You stopped being that very recently," said the security guy, shrugging and taking his baton from his belt. "We're just doing our job. We've been ordered not to let you in here."

"Yes! Leave the premises!" said another one of the security guys threateningly. "Or else we'll have to use force."

"Well, then so be it! Do that!" Andrei laughed with unexpected anger, and — filling his body with spiritual energy — rushed towards the stairwell.

The security guy blocking his path to the elevator wasn't expecting that at all, so Andrei darted up the stairs as fast as he could.

If those swine would just let him get to the eighth floor! He'd easily show them there that he hadn't served in an elite special ops brigade for nothing! Not where he was now, though, because his future patron wasn't there.

Andrei was angrier than anything at the fact that the Spirit Shield he'd instinctively thrown up behind himself had managed to stop the blow of one of the quickest security workers' batons.

If it hadn't been for his reflexes, would he have had any chance at all? He ran up the stairs with all his strength.

* * *

When the elevator door opened on the eighth floor, I headed for the receptionist's desk just across from it.

So, Byshkovetz's company wasn't so small after all, I thought with respect, remembering the size of the business center. If this floor was being leased to only one company, then that wasn't bad at all.

"Good afternoon," I said to the young lady sitting behind the desk. Trying not to pay attention to the people scurrying around nearby, I said: "I'd like to speak to the director of the company — Andrei Valerievich Byshkovetz."

The employees froze for a moment.

"He doesn't work here anymore," said the receptionist, somehow hesitantly.

"Where did that come from all of a sudden?" I asked, surprised. "What, did he sell his share in the company?"

At that moment, the door leading to the stairwell opened with a crash, and Andrei Byshkovetz appeared in person.

He was dressed in stylish dark blue jeans, white sneakers, and a light jacket. In his outer appearance, he didn't look like an IT company director at all — he looked like a young man who wasn't in any way noteworthy.

"Hey, I was just looking for you," I said, signaling to my accompanying guard Nikolai that this was my guy. "They told me that Byshkovetz didn't work here anymore."

Andrei froze. His face lit up instantly in a timid smile, and in the next second a few more men flew out of the stairwell.

They immediately threw themselves on Andrei, who dodged a couple of well-coordinated blows and darted off in my direction.

Rushing forward, I stopped him from falling over, and in the next second I was already being attacked.

Judging by how the number of security guys had increased several times over, the receptionist had managed to hit the panic button.

However, to my surprise, the company's security wasn't trying to defend Andrei from strangers — on the contrary, they were attacking him, and us!

Dwarf Saws bash their heads in — what in the world is going on? I thought in bewilderment. Repelling them with another kick, I just snapped.

Filling my body with Shiki-Cho, I sped up and knocked out a couple of the nearby security guys with maximum efficiency, which Nikolai and Andrei actively helped me with.

I needed to put a stop to all this, I thought. Making my voice colder, I said harshly, "Freeze!"

Everyone around me seemed to stop in their tracks.

There was nearly perfect silence in the office — I could hear a fax machine running somewhere in the distance.

"What is happening here?" I said coldly, turning to Andrei. "Why are they trying to throw the director of the company out of his own office?"

Andrei didn't have a chance to respond.

The next moment, the door to the stairwell flew off its hinges. It was the Temnikov reinforcements that Nikolai had called.

Great job, my dear Nikolai, you had time to call them after all, I thought, glancing at the scared security guys who were watching what the new arrivals were doing.

Assessing the situation, the warriors immediately took their places behind me and got ready to fight.

"So, my question?" I turned to Andrei again.

"I'm not the director of the company anymore, and before long I may lose my share too," Andrei spat. "My business partner went behind my back while I was spilling blood in the Wastelands."

"Then you know what?" I looked around at everyone angrily. "Let's go chat with the current boss and find out how he sank so low."

* * *

The Assassins' League council of elders had gone on for about two hours already.

Sighing, Maria settled more comfortably into the leather couch and got to thinking again.

How long could this go on? There were only three jobs ongoing! Only three! Why was this taking so long? Huh?

To be fair, she had to note that she knew the reason for the hang-up full well. Maria, who'd been to the council many times, had had time to learn the habits and character of the people who gathered there well, and she could reproduce all the arguments of the council members who took part in the disputes almost verbatim.

However, the time was passing very slowly for her — not because of how long she'd been waiting (patience was one of the most important qualities for a good killer, after all), but for a slightly different reason.

This whole time, two of the league supervisors had been sitting across from Maria on another couch. Each of them had a few groups of killers assigned to them.

The sturdy, beastly man with coarse facial features and a spade beard, dressed in camo pants and a close-fitting vest, was an entirely tolerable and — despite his appearance — extremely smart person, and so he behaved quite prudently towards her.

His colleague, on the other hand — a short brunette named Xenia of about thirty years in a pretty, airy dress — was very, very irritating to Maria.

Bespalov — that was this specimen's last name — was someone Maria had never liked. She had many shortcomings: her overly chatty tongue, her inability to behave properly, her clumsy and elegance-lacking work, her excessively inflated ego, the achievements of others that she attributed to herself...

Not so long ago, such qualities hadn't bothered Maria too much. It may not have been entirely fair, but Xenia Bespalov fulfilled her role as a leader of league groups, and that was quite enough. In those days, Maria had been the one managing both Bespalov and her companion, as well as other supervisors. She'd been one of the council elders.

At present, Bespalov and the way she looked so haughtily at her former superior thoroughly infuriated her.

After her severe failure to eliminate George Temnikov, the council had made the decision to demote Maria to supervisor. As they said, nothing personal, just business. All in compliance with the rules of the organization. However, Maria could return to her position after recovering her reputation by eliminating one overly tenacious target.

At the moment, Maria had seven groups of killers working under her who fulfilled League missions throughout the country, while she herself was working in Morshansk on the best way of taking out George Temnikov.

Dwarf Saws take it! If only all this would end faster, Maria thought in irritation yet again. That Bespalov and her arrogant glare were simply infuriating her to the point of exhaustion. Maria wished she could beat her up. The beast! She didn't understand whom she could look at like that and whom she couldn't. Or did she think she could allow herself to do that? Truly... with her tiny brain, she'd only ever be a supervisor. She'd never climb any higher.

"They say you came to beg to get rid of Temnikov again," said Bespalov, not holding back and looking at Maria with her eyes full of superiority. "You used to be in a high position! Do you really not know that his assassination has been postponed for two years?"

Couldn't restrain herself, could she? Maria chuckled. She was curious to learn why she was so audacious.

"You know too much for someone with such low-level clearance," said Maria, glancing at her rival calmly. Narrowing her eyes dangerously, she repeated a piece of gossip she'd heard recently: "You haven't been sleeping your way into elder Dietrich's good graces again, have you?"

The arrogance in Bespalov's eyes quickly changed to hatred.

"Oh, you..." she said, trying to get a hold of herself and find words. Then she declared solemnly, "You scandalmonger! You've been listening to kitchen chatter like a peasant woman in the marketplace! How low you've sunk!"

"Well, only as low as you — as low as a marquis," Maria remarked, reminding Bespalov of a lie she'd told long ago that she belonged to an old-blood noble family. She added sharply, "I was on the council once. I can go back! See that you don't curse the day you dared to speak to me in that tone!"

"Oh, no, you won't get promoted!" exclaimed Bespalov with malicious solemnity. "While you're running after your Temnikov, the position could even disappear! There are contenders for it! Then you'll answer for everything!"

Is she really this much of a fool? thought Maria with a bit of pity. All she'd had to do was make a dig at her about the Dietrich thing and mention her childish affronts in passing, and she'd given everything away. Such pious naivety!

Seeing Maria's easy smile, Bespalov clenched her fists tightly.

"If they put you on the council after your antics in Dietrich's bed," said Maria with a passing glance at her perfect manicure, "I'll challenge you to a duel and kill you. Or maybe I won't challenge you — I'll just kill you. It seems to me you've forgotten who the head of the League is, and why that position doesn't go to silly little hens."

Bespalov grew pale and went silent, despite her obvious outrage.

That's right! You beast! thought Maria with satisfaction, cheered up a bit. Seeing her rival cower amused her.

The beastly-looking man, who'd been sitting there this whole time with an indifferent look, smiled with satisfaction, and at that moment the door to the council hall opened.

That man was smart, after all, Maria thought. Dangerous, too. If she had anyone to keep tabs on, it was clearly him. He and his scumbags could cause no shortage of problems.

"Maria, come forward." She heard a muffled voice. Paying no attention to anyone, she went into the hall.

"We've assessed your report," said an old man in a creaky voice once the door was tightly shut and the special runes had been activated. "And we've also verified the information. There really is a plan to add Morozov to Vitovt's class. The preliminary list has already been made, so your chances of approaching George Temnikov stealthily are lessening with each month." Pausing briefly, the man finished solemnly, "The council has decided to give you a license to kill. This job is yours."

Yes! Maria rejoiced after she'd bowed and silently left the room.

No words were necessary. She'd just been given a chance to correct her mistake, and she planned to use it.

Nothing personal, George, she thought contentedly. *Despite everything that came before this, you'll have to die.*

Chapter 19

THE IMPERIAL TOURNAMENT NATIONALS had a more ceremonial look than regionals. Before the contestants who'd made it to the finals were presented to the extensive crowd, there was a pretty lengthy and interesting theatrical performance in the arena portraying the olden days, the unexpected and treacherous arrival of demons in this world, and likewise the fact that without simple warriors and mages humanity wouldn't exist anymore. Then the performers sang a couple of songs that were popular with the kids these days. Next, the imperial minister of sports said a few words.

This elderly, muscular man clearly had significant experience working in a public leadership position — there was no other way I could explain his concise, intelligent, and laconic speech, which I could at least listen to without wanting to throw up. As far as I knew, functionaries vested with power loved to talk a whole lot at events like this.

After the minister's speech and the storm of applause that followed from the crowd that was tired of waiting for the fights, the first round finally began.

Nationals differed from regionals in the organization of the fights themselves, not just in the presentation that opened the event. At regionals, warriors had fought in both rings at first, and only after that had the mages fought, but here they'd decided to do things differently. Now one arena was shared between the mages and the warriors, and the two contests happened at the same time. I figured this way of doing things was very convenient for the audience, since they could watch two matches at once.

Also, just like at regionals, to ensure the audience's safety, the rings were fitted out with a special complex of defensive magical artifacts that warded off spells flying in their direction.

The fights, despite my apprehension, started off pretty interesting. The contestants wanted to show themselves off on TV for the whole Empire and laid it all out starting in the first few seconds.

They were totally bitter fights, but most of them didn't last long. A few warriors went in and out, and I was already mentally preparing for my upcoming fight. My name hadn't appeared on the scoreboard yet at all, however, so when the order of things finally got around to me, I was really struggling not to fall asleep.

* * *

The fairly tense days before the start of the competition, when I'd had to devote a lot of attention to my future projects and returning Andrei Byshkovetz's business to him, were taking their toll. To do that, I'd had to buy a share in the company from his former business partner in pretty short order.

That had seemed like a pretty difficult thing to do at first, since I was a child by appearance — I'd have to resolve a few sensitive matters. But I'd been offered help, and I hadn't dared refuse.

The person who'd made me such a generous offer turned out to be my older brother Theodore, who'd showed up at Andrei's office about an hour after I'd approached the business center.

"So ordinary kids get away to the capital city and immediately go to the Imperial Amusement Park, and you've apparently set your sights on the restoration of justice?" he said, barging into the office without knocking.

"I'm not like that, life is like that," I said, sitting in the company director's chair. "But this isn't about justice — it's about another, more vile human need like profit. Look, I just wanted to talk..."

Quickly bringing Theodore up to speed on what was happening, I proved my decent understanding of the local legislature and gave him a summary of the current issue, my goals in investigating this whole situation, and the possible paths to get to them.

"That is, you've decided to get hold of your own company?" Theodore chuckled, looking at me with surprise.

"I wasn't planning to do that at first," I admitted. "But when such an interesting venture rolls onto the road, why not take it? Besides, this is exactly the company I need. There's a reason I came here!"

Not giving him a chance to get a word in edgewise, I asked him an unexpected question.

"By the way, who exactly let slip to you about what was happening here?"

"No one. My very well developed intuition led me here today," Theodore chuckled. "I think the guy who explained everything to me wanted to give you some serious help. After all, I'm already here, and I'm going to help you with some sensitive matters out of the goodness of my heart."

"Why are you interested?" I asked, raising an eyebrow.

"Nothing crazy. Out of curiosity. I want to see what you've cooked up here. Not one of my brothers has yet decided to take on any kind of projects at such a young age, especially not such large-scale ones. Like Ignatius, he just drinks and runs from ball to ball."

Or Father ordered you to spy on me, I thought gloomily, but I still took the help he'd offered me — he'd find out about what I was doing sooner or later either way.

* * *

My first opponent at nationals was pretty good for his age. He dodged blows skillfully, used spiritual energy intelligently, and knew how to use a few techs pretty well. He was clearly saving his strength and attacking very cautiously — obviously, he'd already been brought up to speed on my effective counterattacks, so I decided not to torture him for too long. Taking the initiative into my own hands, I went on the offensive and finished the fight pretty quickly.

"Morozov wins! From the Gomel region, city of Morshansk!" said the ref, and I left the ring unhurriedly.

"You got him good!" Godimir congratulated me anxiously on my victory and sighed heavily.

"What? Is it almost your turn?" I immediately understood the reason for his mood.

"Yeah." He nodded, frowning. "Based on Mr. Viktorov's briefing, my opponent is one of the nasty ones."

"Hey, you're just as tough of an opponent to him," I said, giving him a hard clap on the shoulder. "So don't worry — on the contrary, stay calm and remember what I told you not long ago! The most important thing is not to get hot under the collar and not to try to finish the fight as quickly as possible. That's gotten you a few times already, and then you barely won. First study your opponent — learn his abilities, his strengths and weaknesses, how he can counter you, and only then attack."

"Okay!" said Godimir resolutely, hissing through clenched teeth. "I'll try."

While he gathered his thoughts and hyped himself up for the fight, I decided to devote a little bit of time to the mages' fight, after which I — not expecting it at all myself — passed a glance over the competing high school girls' interesting features.

Ew! They were still children! Disgusting! Not okay! What was I, a perv? I cursed at myself, but then I noticed something I had to be fair to myself about. My child body was most likely guilty of this state of mind — because of all the physical exercise and the corresponding growth, it was starting to become a teenager's body.

My guess that it was hormones was also confirmed by the fact that just a few months ago, I hadn't been so impressionable even in the presence of more well-endowed women like Ms. Dashkevich and Svetlana.

Meanwhile, the girls confidently exchanged spells, demonstrating a small but effective arsenal of tactics. At some point, one of them failed to put up her magical shield in time and got hit by a Fire Arrow, tossing her out of bounds.

There really could be a decent risk of injury in the magic tournament even at the beginner level, I thought.

After that, I got out my phone and decided to occupy myself by studying the information that the internet had about the national competition.

So! After a while, I tore myself away from my screen and tried to make sense of what I'd read. In my age category, there were one hundred and twenty people. After the first round, which was almost over already, there would be sixty left. Then thirty and fifteen, accordingly. Going by Mr. Viktorov's system, one of the contestants would go to the round after that by the will of chance and a computer program. So to get into the semifinals, I'd have to win five rounds...

Godimir returned and interrupted my musing.

He flopped heavily into the armchair next to me and said with relief:

"Share a healing potion with the winner like a good brother in arms, won't you?"

"You have your own!" I said, surprised, but I rifled through my bag anyway. "Or is something wrong with them?"

"Nothing's wrong with them," said Godimir, taking the flask I offered him. "Except the taste. It's completely disgusting, by the way. They're probably already expired. But yours are tasty and fresh. They're very pleasant to drink, and they kick in more gently somehow."

After sitting next to me and recovering a bit after his difficult fight, Godimir left for the changing room reserved for our team, and in the meantime I opened my bookie's webpage and started calculating the possible totals from my future winnings. By all estimates, the number would be simply enormous, and I thought with satisfaction that this had to be enough and then some for my first serious projects.

For good reason, the saying went that you like most of all to spend the money that you haven't earned yet. I remembered that folk wisdom from my past life with a laugh and turned off my phone.

Every member of our team finished the first day of nationals with two wins, after which — under the leadership of an incredibly pleased Mr. Viktorov — we went to go relax together at the hotel.

Mr. Viktorov was beaming like a shiny gold thaler. I could understand him. Not only had one of the biggest teams from Morshansk come here, we'd also managed not to lose anyone on the very first day. The Morshansk students had never gotten results like that before at the warrior tournament even once.

*   *   *

When I got back to my room, I cleaned up quickly and decided to call Andrei. I wanted to know what stage things were on now and get my finger on the pulse. I couldn't let him think that he could ignore me or put no stock in me just because I was a kid.

"Good evening. How are our plans going?" I asked. Hearing a distinctive noise, I added, "You're not still working, are you?"

"Yes, sir!" Andrei reported cheerfully despite the late hour. "Right now I'm doing an intensive audit of the company. This afternoon I dealt with our big clients and explained some of the nuances related to the changes in staff leadership and the active participation of a noble in that. Thank the Savior, everything went fine, no one walked out on us. Although, of course, a lot of people weren't happy about what happened."

"That's good," I said thoughtfully. "And how's the audit going? Have you discovered anything interesting?"

"Well, I can't call it an audit in the usual sense. It's more of an intensive once-over of the company by all metrics. I need to know what kind of specialists are working for me, what kinds of tasks they can do, and what stage the projects being worked on are at. In general, I'm concentrating on getting the company back under control. During my absence, it grew a lot, although a few good professionals were lost, too. I'll find their numbers while I'm at it so I can bring them back..."

Andrei talked on for a while and quite enthusiastically. I got the impression that he really liked what he was doing, and that was just splendid.

"What about the documents I gave you?" I asked after waiting for a short pause, breaking his stream of words.

"Everything looks great! They're currently being looked at by the department heads, and based on their first impressions, everything seems pretty promising. It seems like something that was lying in plain sight, but it's very unusual, fresh, and simple at the same time! There's clearly huge potential in these ideas!"

Of course there was! Even I knew that, I thought, pleased with myself. Lots of people from my world used apps like this. It would be a sin not to take advantage of that knowledge.

"Good. That means everything is going as well as it can. Good night," I said after a bit. Finished with the conversation, I sprawled out on my bed feeling satisfied.

How lucky I'd gotten with Andrei, I thought. Young, promising, educated — not to mention he was someone I knew! Although, what was even more important was that he would've been robbed and left with nothing if not for my timely help. So after I'd dragged him out of the depths, he just had to work like a dog! I couldn't imagine a better helper. It was truly incredibly good luck for me that he had such tough problems. Although... if not for that... then I would've needed to orchestrate something like that for him...

That last thought was like a bucket of cold water being poured on my warm bed.

What was I thinking? Could I really ever act like that? Or would my conscience still refuse to allow it?

After musing on questions like that for a while in my own mind, I tossed and turned a bit and fell into an uneasy, anxiety-filled sleep.

In the morning, I woke up completely overwhelmed and sleep-deprived. The day clearly promised not to be very pleasant. My fears were confirmed in the very first hour after the start of the next round was announced. Our team lost one of its contenders for the finals. To my great disappointment, that person was Godimir.

He got unlucky. He got put with a pretty strong opponent from a capital-city family that specialized in nothing but using spiritual energy. Even in this round, there were plenty of people Godimir could hypothetically have dealt with!

"That brute!" said Mr. Viktorov angrily, glaring inimically at the arrogant boy calmly walking past Godimir as he lay in the ring. Turning sharply, Mr. Viktorov said to me, "Remember that kid well, Ivan. I hope you'll have a chance to get even with him for your friend."

"But isn't that guy from a warrior family?" asked a frowning Oleg, who was sitting next to me. "As far as I remember, members of that family regularly get winning places in the tournament, and that guy was obviously not weak for his age."

"Winning places?" I asked, curious. "I hope we'll manage to break that tradition?"

After Godimir's defeat, the next bad development wasn't long in coming — to my surprise, my father showed up in our locker room with Ignatius and Theodore.

Weird, I thought he was at the family estate just this morning, I thought doubtfully.

Father didn't stay for long.

After asking me a few trite questions and verifying the state of my health several times, my begetter said some nice encouraging words to me and then just kinda disappeared in a hurry.

"What was that?" I asked Theodore, who was left in the locker room after Ignatius followed Father out of the room.

"I don't know," said Theodore with a pensive face, shrugging. "He got here not long ago by plane and headed straight from the airport to see you at the arena — he didn't even stop in at the house."

"And where did he rush off to just now?" I frowned.

"I think to see Ruslan. He's doing pretty well — he's even become one of the favorites in the magic tournament," said Theodore, smirking. "After that beat-down you gave him with Shiki-Cho, it was like a beast was unleashed in Ruslan. He trained every day, practiced his offensive spells to the point of exhaustion, and worked with Yamashita in the mornings. Clearly, our family altar appreciated that and generously shared its strength with him. Otherwise, it'd be hard to understand how the little guy managed to get so strong. I myself couldn't let off a dark aura at his age, but he's already got one!"

"Where did you hear about that fight?" I said, surprised, after thinking about it.

There hadn't been anyone else there, right? I didn't say that — let him cough up about his spies.

Theodore gave me a weird look, then fessed up regardless.

"Anna told me everything that very same day — I even watched the video and realized that you were holding back. I'd like to see your real strength."

"You should get away to Morshansk sometime and pop into the Wasteland with me and George. Believe me, that'll be extremely interesting and enlightening — you'll learn a lot of new things and see everything for yourself," I said.

"All right, I'll definitely do that." He nodded.

Here was yet another reason why Theodore had come to Andrei's office a few days ago and given me the help I needed, I thought. Or else he was using his curiosity as a cover, you see. Although there was no need to write off curiosity either.

"By the way, are you going to tell your brother what you were planning to do with that company?" Theodore unexpectedly changed the subject. "I've been doing nothing but help you these past few days, and I think I've been doing it pretty well."

I sighed heavily, then — choosing my words slowly — started giving him a brief crash course on a couple of my projects.

When I finished talking after a while, Theodore coughed with dissatisfaction and said:

"I know all that. I hope you'll be more open with me after some time."

Looking after him as he left, I felt grateful. Both that he hadn't tried to press me for all that info and that he'd truly done so much for me.

The thing was, after that momentous battle with the business center security guys, when Andrei and I had been in one office together with his business partner and I'd understood what I needed to do, one very important question had come up: how was I supposed to carry all this out?

I mean, an adult nobleman with a vocal family wouldn't have much trouble going to one of the local civil courthouses and asking for the information he needed. It was possible that he could pretty easily start the necessary processes for restoring justice and order by visiting a couple of offices and talking to their leaders...

But what was *I* supposed to do? Who was going to take a child seriously? He may have been a noble, he may have had a vocal family, but he was still a little boy.

Case in point — what happened with Andrei's (now former) business partner after my guards left the three of us alone in the office. He'd come to his senses pretty quickly. Yes, he'd realized that he was in serious trouble because of a few absurd coincidences, and that he wouldn't get any pats on the back from my family for what had happened. However, it had clearly seemed to him that he had a chance to work things out and settle the matter with Andrei, who'd been almost bled dry. Because the noble in the office was just a little boy who was asking uncomfortable questions in a businesslike manner.

"You've probably misunderstood the situation," I'd said, stroking my chin thoughtfully after his disrespectfully casual reply. Making my voice cold, I'd continued: "Before you sits not a little boy, but a member of a noble family. You've not only put his life in danger, but also tried to fraudulently seize his old friend's property. This might all seem like a game to you, you might think this can still be resolved so everything works out, but the unpleasantness will continue until you realize that even at my age I'm much stronger than you."

Running up to him abruptly, I'd grabbed him from below by his tie and punched him in the face a couple of times.

Waiting till blood spilled out of his broken lips, paying no attention to his weak resistance, I'd repeated the punishment. Then again, and again. And so on, until he'd gone still on the ground with no intention of lifting his head.

"I also want you to understand," I'd continued, as if nothing had happened, "that young nobles, unlike already accomplished men, strive to the full extent of their youthfulness, and with the desire to prove to everyone that they have the right to rule. And you're trying to question that right with your behavior."

After a brief pause, I'd grabbed him by the ear and said quietly:

"Give me one more condescending look or laugh, try to get at or mess with Byshkovetz, and there'll be a change in directors not because of a new deal, but because of the last one's sudden death. Understood?"

After waiting for an affirmative response, I'd calmly returned to my chair. After discipline had been restored, the conversation had immediately taken a constructive turn, and both partners had left the room under watch from my people.

It had turned out well, I'd thought, suppressing my conscience with an iron grip. The deal had gone fine right out of the gate, and I'd reminded Andrei what was what so that he wouldn't forget it.

*　*　*

After my conversation with Theodore, I returned to the stands, waited to be summoned for my next fight, and watched the mages' fights.

One way or another, I had to admit that magic was a more interesting and versatile discipline than martial arts. Also, that it was an important part of my future formation as a strong and independent head of a family.

So I solemnly resolved to concentrate on mastering magic after the tournament was over. My capabilities as a warrior were currently impressive, and if I did make Militant rank after the tournament was over, then that would be enough for now...

"Hooray!" Godimir yelled happily.

"Geez! You scared me!" I started. "Why are we celebrating?"

"What, did you miss the whole thing?" cried Godimir, grabbing his head.

Passing a glance over the ring, I saw Oleg from our team leaving the ring tottering, and his opponent — that same guy from Podlesk who'd beaten him in his first match at regionals — being carried away on a stretcher by healers.

"He did that?" I jumped to my feet and added enthusiastically: "Just beautiful!"

"It's just like you said," said Godimir, clapping me on the shoulder. "He managed to get it all back at nationals after all."

After that fight, all the members of our team ran around Oleg, helping him pull himself together and recover as quickly as possible. Still, the tournament was still continuing, and the next round could start very soon.

Oleg had a broken arm, two broken ribs, a couple of gashes, and ugly blood blisters all over his body. So, to speed up his recovery, I went into my stash of potions again without a moment's hesitation.

"Excellent! Just excellent!" Mr. Viktorov kept repeating, carefully wiping the blood off of Oleg's slashed forehead with a wet towel, then smearing the whole thing with a healing potion.

"How bad did I get him? Did you see?" Oleg grinned with his battered lips. "He thought he had me, and then I..."

After a while, when we'd finally gotten Oleg into an acceptable state and returned to the stands, we discovered that the emperor and his son had finally graced the tournament with their presence. They sat in a separate booth on the imperial balcony.

I didn't have much time to admire the royalty and was pretty quickly summoned to my next fight, which I of course won.

"You know your brother Ruslan hasn't lost yet either?" Godimir asked me quietly.

Despite his defeat this morning, Godimir was

fully content with life.

"You bet." I nodded to him. "I'm watching him, he's watching me. I hope we both get first place — that'll be just lovely."

"Yeah," Godimir agreed. "But if you hadn't changed your last name, it would be even better! Two Temnikov champions!"

"Well, it is what it is." I shrugged. "The magic decided, and my father is still alone."

Ruslan, incidentally, was really good. He'd started out at the tournament on the high end of mediocre, contending for tenth or eleventh place, but towards the end of day two he was already considered one of the crowd favorites for this tourney.

While we had some free time, I decided to count up the money I was supposed to get from my future victory, and I crossed myself mentally. I counted it up again and crossed myself again. Winning this tournament would really get me a lot, since the broker I'd chosen really did work under the government's patronage, and there wouldn't be any problems with the payout.

So I'd just have to not let my guard down and be extremely careful, I resolved solemnly. Apparently, the ones who'd made it to the finals were me and the capital-city boy from the warrior clan who'd beaten Godimir, and that meant I wouldn't be rid of him easily.

"Ivan," Father called to me, walking up to me and inviting me to step away into our locker room for a couple of minutes for a private conversation.

"I hope you thoroughly intend to win?" he asked in a serious tone after forming a Curtain of Silence around us with an amulet.

"Of course!" I said, a bit outraged. "What else?"

"Good." His face split into a satisfied smile. "I didn't doubt you."

Pausing briefly, he continued with the utmost seriousness:

"It's now very important to me, or rather to the whole family, that you win the warrior tournament."

Wonderful, I thought, mentally rubbing my hands.

"And what's in it for me?" I asked.

"What do you need?" Father answered my question with a question.

"I'd like to have the chance to turn to you with a few requests that you'll be obligated to fulfill. Just in case something bad happens to me that I can't deal with myself."

"I think five requests is enough in exchange for your victory," said Father, and without giving me a chance to object, he said: "I don't intend to bargain with you."

I wondered... had he made a sizable bet on me too, or what? What was the reason for all this commotion?

Epilogue

The next night, the night before the final fight, I also slept really badly for some reason.

I had a bad feeling. This wasn't the first time it had happened, so I didn't expect anything pleasant. Unfortunately, my fears were confirmed — a few minutes before my match, Vitovt himself came into our locker room.

"Your Highness." We immediately jumped off the locker room chairs.

"Good morning, gentlemen," Vitovt greeted us and addressed everyone else. "May I ask you to leave me alone with Ivan?"

The guys nodded and left the room.

"Ivan, we don't know each other well, but you've given me the impression that you're an extremely reasonable person," said Vitovt — I didn't like that sentence. After a bit, he continued, "Can

I ask you to fulfill my request?"

Oh, stick a Dwarf Saw up your butt! Something's not right here! I thought, straining my own intuition. I could hardly refuse — he was the heir to the emperor, after all. If I agreed, though, I was unlikely to be partial to his request. What should I do?

Vitovt stared at me solemnly, and when I realized that drawing out the silence any longer would be simply unseemly, I answered him.

"You may. If this request doesn't go against my code of honor and common sense, I'll fulfill it."

"You think I could ask you something like that?" Vitovt furrowed his brows.

What, had I guessed right? His request clearly wasn't a simple one. Vitovt hadn't been expecting that response either. I could see how tense he'd gotten. Now he was thinking about how to continue the dialogue.

"You asked, I answered," I said calmly.

After being silent for a bit, Vitovt directed a harsh gaze at me and spoke resolutely.

"I need you to lose your final match."

I knew it — I knew I wouldn't like his request one bit, I thought in dismay. Quickly assessing the situation, I spoke decisively.

"I cannot fulfill that request. I've already promised several people that I'll put all my strength into winning this tournament, and such deception is by its very essence against the Morozov family's code of honor!"

"That's why I called you a reasonable person.

You must understand whose requests are more important to you and your future." Vitovt frowned. "If necessary, I can order you to!"

Uh-huh — as if I didn't want to win myself. I had a ton of money at stake here! And I'd set up big plans for my future. And here was this guy with his incomprehensible requests. I'd try to resist.

"I'm not an employee of the state, and we're not in the armed forces or at war!" I replied to Vitovt.

"You're a noble! That means you're automatically in the reserves!" Vitovt flew into a rage.

Whoa! What had come over him? Was it really this serious? He was in over his head! Or was he just responsibly fulfilling an order from his father?

"I'm still a child, just like you, your Highness." I shook my head. "This isn't about my refusal to fulfill your order or request — you can call it what you like. It's about the fact that I can't allow myself to forget the honor of my family and betray the trust of those close to me."

"Well, you heard what I said," said Vitovt, calming down in an instant. "And you probably know that next school year, you're going to be studying in the same class as me. Think about that for a while. Perhaps you'll understand that it's not worth upsetting the future leader of your government?"

Having finished speaking, Vitovt turned sharply and left the room as I stood there and thought about what I should do next. *I wonder if this day could get any worse?*

Then the door to the locker room opened, letting in a pale Ignatius. "The helicopter that George was on crashed," he said quietly.

Apparently, it can, I thought as I slumped down on a chair.

End of Book Three

Want to be the first to know about our latest LitRPG, sci fi and fantasy titles from your favorite authors?

Subscribe to our **New Releases** newsletter:
http://eepurl.com/b7niIL

Thank you for reading *Living Ice!*

If you like what you've read, check out other sci-fi, fantasy and LitRPG novels published by Magic Dome Books:

NEW RELEASES!

The Selected
A LitRPG Action Adventure Series
by Vasily Mahanenko & Yuri Vinokuroff

The Afflicted
A LitRPG Apocalypse Adventure Series
by Konstantin Zubov

Law of the Jungle
A Wuxia Progression Fantasy Adventure Series
by Vasily Mahanenko

The Dark Summoner
A Portal Progression Fantasy Series
by Andrei Tkachev

The Banned
A LitRPG Adventure Series
by Michael Atamanov

How I Built a Magic Empire
A Portal Progression Fantasy Series
by Konstantin Zubov

The Order of Architects
A Portal Progression Fantasy Series
by Oleg Sapphire & Yuri Vinokuroff

The Hunter's Code
A Portal Progression Fantasy Series
by Oleg Sapphire & Yuri Vinokuroff

The One Who Changes the Future
A Dystopian Portal Progression Fantasy Series
by Boris Romanovsky

An Ideal World for a Sociopath
A LitRPG Apocalypse Adventure Series
by Oleg Sapphire

The Healer's Way
A Portal Progression Fantasy Series
by Oleg Sapphire & Alexey Kovtunov

The Last Portal Jumper
A LitRPG Progression Fantasy Series
by Konstantin Zubov

The Dark Healer
A Historical Progression Fantasy Series
by Alex Toxic & Nadya Lee

Lord of The System
A LitRPG Progression Fantasy Series
by Alex Toxic & Furious Miki

A Shelter in Spacetime
A LitRPG Apocalypse Series
by Dmitry Dornichev

The Coming of God of Death
A Portal Progression Fantasy Series
by Dmitry Dornichev

In order to have new books of the series translated faster, we need your help and support! Please consider leaving a review or spread the word by recommending *Living Ice* to your friends and posting the link on social media. The more people buy the book, the sooner we'll be able to make new translations available.

Thank you!

Till next time!